Meeting this man was destined to be the biggest thing that had ever happened to Lucy Hart...

Lucy waited on pins and needles for Theodore to make the first move.

But nothing happened.

He looked right past her.

Lucy was left with no choice. She screwed up her courage, waved until she finally caught his eye, and called out, "Here I am. Over here!"

"We agreed to meet at 8:30 sharp," she said accusingly, her nerves taut, voice almost shrill. "You are late."

"Am I? Then please say you'll accept my most humble apologies, Miss...Miss..."

"Don't you remember? You're to call me Lucy."

"All right, Lucy. And you can call me Blackie."

"*Blackie?*" she stopped abruptly, frowned at him. "Why on earth would I want to call you Blackie?"

He shrugged broad shoulders. "Most people do."

She made a face. "I shall call you Theodore, of course."

Even more nervous than she had anticipated being, Lucy found herself chattering up a storm, and likely sounding like a silly schoolgirl with her first beau. He suggested a walk.

Lucy considered declining. Giving her little opportunity to refuse, he guided her down the steep hotel steps.

At the bottom step he stumbled slightly, fell against her. His face was an inch from Lucy's for a split second and it was then she smelled the telltale scent of liquor on his breath. She was shocked and horrified.

"I knew it!" she said, pushing on his broad chest. "You have been imbibing alcoholic beverages! Have you not?"

He grinned. "I've been drinking whiskey if that's what you mean."

"Well, I never!" Her fair face flushed with high color.

"Then it's time you did."

"Theodore D. Mooney, you are inebriated!"

He laughed and said, "Him, too? Why, it's an epidemic."

Her brows knitted, Lucy scowled at him. "Mr. Mooney, I am afraid our agreeing to meet here in Atlantic City has been a big mistake on my part. In your letters you were not nearly so...so..."

"My letters?"

"Yes! All those wonderful letters you...you..." Lucy caught the amused glint of devilment flashing in his dark eyes and stopped speaking. Then her own eyes widened and a hand flew up to cover her mouth as it dawned on her. She had made an awful error. "Dear Lord above!" she exclaimed miserably, "You are not...you can't be..."

"Your Mr. Mooney? No, Lucy, I'm not."

Her delicate jaw hardened. "Well, just who are you?"

"Robert Jeffrey LaDuke, the third," he said. "Everybody calls me Blackie."

Other Books by Nan Ryan

Wanting You

The Countess Misbehaves

The Seduction of Ellen

The Scandalous Miss Howard

Naughty Marietta

Savage Heat

Silken Bondage

Written in the Stars

Love Me Tonight

The Last Dance

by
Nan Ryan

For
Dick Kleiner of United Media
Robin Kaigh
Richard Curtis
Aaron Priest
Perry Knowlton of Curtis Brown, Ltd.
Robert Barnett of Williams Connelly
Irene Goodman
Mel Berger of William Morris Agency, Inc.

Thanks millions

December 2003
Published by
Medallion Press, Inc.
225 Seabreeze Ave.
Palm Beach, FL 33480

The Last Dance

CHAPTER ONE

The 7:10 from Rochester was right on time, and so was Post Office Champ.

The big, silver furred husky waited alone on the train depot's deserted wooden platform. Panting rapidly in the August heat and pacing back and forth, Post Office Champ kept watchful eyes turned northward. With the first faint sound of the approaching train's whistle, Champ began to bark excitedly. Tail wagging furiously, he raced jubilantly forward to take up his designated post.

The early-morning freight train did not stop in Colonias, New York. It barely slowed. It whooshed through the station with the loud rhythmic clickity-clack of wheels turning on the tracks and sharp piercing blasts from its steam whistle.

In the open door of a rail car, four back from the engine, a short, muscular man in work clothes stood with his feet braced apart. In one canvas gloved hand he held a heavy leather mail pouch. His other hand was firmly locked around a steel stantion. As rail car and man reached the place where the barking dog waited, the man grinned, shouted a friendly greeting to the silver Siberian and tossed out the full mailbag.

Champ pounced on the heavy pouch as if it were a juicy bone. Snarling, he clamped the bag firmly in his teeth, yanked it up, and wheeled about. He leapt down off the platform, rounded the tiny depot, shot across the street, and raced the two blocks to the Colonias' white fronted post office.

Miss Lucy Hart had arrived at the post office at exactly seven a.m. She immediately brought the folded American flag outside, unfurled it, clipped it to the grommets, and raised the stars and stripes up the steel flagpole.

She went back inside, crossed the front lobby, and entered the small back room. She stepped up to the counter with its closed window, took a large stamp pad down from the shelf, and opened it. She pulled the cork stopper from a bottle of Parkers India Indelible, inked the pad, and restoppered the bottle. She picked up the cancellation stamp and rotated the tiny rotors until the present date was displayed on the wooden stamp's face.

A.M./Colonias, New York

August 11, 1899

A little shiver of excitement surged through her slender body.

Only nine more days.

The train's whistle pierced the morning quiet. Miss Lucy lifted the small face of the gold cased watch, which was pinned to the bodice of her crisp white summer blouse. She glanced at the watch, smiled, and began counting down the seconds.

Five. Six. Seven.

Before she reached eight, Post Office Champ bounded through the open door of the lobby.

"Good boy, Champ!" Miss Lucy praised enthusiastically, going to meet him and reaching out to give his big head a sound pat. "Such a good, reliable boy."

Miss Lucy followed Champ as he hauled the heavy mail pouch directly into the back room. Champ deposited his burden on the sorting table and then jumped up on Miss Lucy, putting his massive front paws on her full skirts, and barked a happy greeting to her. The postmistress laughed, leaned down, laid her cheek to the top of Champ's head and stroked the soft underside of his warm, throbbing throat.

Champ tolerated the demonstrative display for only a moment, then impatiently pulled free and marched pointedly to his empty food dish in the corner. There he sat down on his powerful haunches, turned his head, and fixed Miss Lucy with a baleful look. She knew what that look meant. She promptly gave him his treat.

Each day of the week--save Sunday--the mornings began pretty much this same way for Miss Lucy Hart, the town's postmistress, and Champ, the faithful mail dog. The big, beautiful husky, who belonged to the Western Union telegrapher's young son, met the 7:10 train every morning, picked up the mail, and delivered it to the waiting Colonias postmistress. Then, while Miss Lucy sorted and put up the mail, Champ eagerly ate the breakfast goodies she brought him, smacking and growling with bliss.

Turning her full attention to putting up the mail, Miss Lucy read the name on a long white envelope. Mrs. T. A. Rippcy. "Number Forty-Seven," Miss Lucy said aloud, inserting the letter in the box number forty-seven. "Milt Ledet," she mumbled and stuck the penny postal card into box number sixteen. Janis Wright. Number Twenty-Two. The Reverend Timothy Clarkson. Fifty-One.

Miss Lucy Hart had long ago memorized the number of each and every Colonias box holder. She identified half the people in town by their box numbers instead of their names. She'd look up and see a

3

particular lady approaching the post office and think to herself, 'Here comes Thirty-Two again; has she forgotten she's already been here twice?' Yesterday she'd seen a couple of men pass the office, laughing and talking together, and her first thought had been, 'Good grief, Nineteen and Sixty-Seven back on speaking terms after the bloody fist fight they'd had down at the lodge last week?'

Letters in hand, Miss Lucy cast a glance over her shoulder at the suddenly silent Post Office Champ. His plate clean, the contented Siberian husky was stretched out on the floor, yawning, settling down for a short, after-breakfast nap. Lucy turned back to the task at hand, humming softly as she worked.

She had finished sorting and putting up each letter, leaflet, circular and postal card by ten minutes of eight. People were beginning to congregate outside in the post office lobby. Lucy could hear them greeting each other, checking the time, opening their boxes and looking anxiously inside for their mail.

Lucy knew just how they felt.

For the past three years, she herself had anxiously awaited Champ's delivery of the mailbag with hope and expectation. How she had looked forward to those special letters...

Shaking herself out of her pleasant reverie, Miss Lucy Hart raised the window of her caged cubicle and began the workday in earnest.

It was after six p.m. when Miss Lucy lowered the flag, folded and boxed it, closed the grilled window, locked up, and left. Tired and hot, but in no great hurry to get to her empty house, she sauntered along the wooden sidewalk, stopping, as she had for the past several weeks, to admire a stunningly pretty dress in the front display window of Pauline's Apparel shop.

Lucy looked at the gorgeous gauzy white tulle gown with glazed eyes and watering mouth. She envisioned herself spinning about a spacious hotel ballroom in this one-of-a-kind summer white dress.

Lucy Hart drew a deep breath, swept into the shop, pointed to the dress in the window, and said decisively, "I've made up my mind. I'll take it, Pauline."

Pauline Simmons, the shop's owner and the town's most dedicated gossip, greeted Miss Lucy's command with undisguised surprise and wry amusement. Shaking her head in disbelief, she cut her eyes meaningfully at the pair of well-heeled, matronly customers to whom she had been showing a new shipment of kid gloves. The ladies returned Pauline's glance. They wondered, as Pauline did, just where the town's postmistress would go to wear such an exquisite dress.

Miss Lucy Hart knew exactly what they were thinking. Oddly, she derived a degree of pleasure from their puzzlement. It added to her steadily growing excitement. It had been a long time since anyone found her behavior worthy of speculation.

"If you'll just take the white tulle out of the window and box it for me, Pauline," Lucy again requested, smiling and nodding to the two watching matrons. "Mrs. Poyner, Mrs. Barnes."

"Miss Lucy," they responded in unison.

As Pauline removed the white dress from the store window, Lucy made small talk with Mrs. Poyner and Mrs. Barnes, politely inquiring about their health and their families, knowing they were hoping she might disclose the occasion for which she needed the expensive white dress.

She didn't.

She could hardly hide her glee at the fun of withholding the only information in which the ladies were truly interested

Miss Lucy was all smiles when she tucked the large box containing the new white tulle dress under her arm, bade them all good day, and left the store. Outside, she waved to them, positive they were watching and whispering.

They were.

"Whatever's gotten into Miss Lucy?" Fredda Barnes spoke in a stage whisper.

"I can't imagine," murmured Pauline, the shop owner. "She's been coming in every day for the past few weeks. She's tried on that white tulle dress a half dozen times, but I *never* thought about her actually buying it."

"A great waste of money if you ask me," said Myrtle Poyner. "Where does Miss Lucy go other than to the post office, church, a weekly card game at the Harrisons, those spring and fall piano recitals she gives, and the Fourth of July and Labor Day picnics." She shook her neatly coiffured head. "Mark my words, that fancy white tulle dress will yellow with age before it is ever worn."

There was a spring to her step and a smile on her lips as Miss Lucy Hart walked the four blocks to her home. On this warm August evening she felt uncharacteristically young, gay, and optimistic.

She was fully aware that the expensive white tulle dress was an extravagance she really couldn't afford to buy. By the same token, she couldn't afford not to. It was such a beautiful dress. A special dress for a special occasion.

The Last Dance

A dress she might well get to wear but once in her entire lifetime.

CHAPTER TWO

Miss Lucy reached the pristine white picket fence that bordered her small front yard. She pushed through the hinged gate, went up the flower-bordered walk to the porch and let herself inside the spotless, silent house, which was her home.

Miss Lucy Hart had lived all her life in this same white frame house on this same tree shaded street in this same small Genesee Valley farming community. For the past two of those years, she had lived in the white house alone.

The youngest of three children, Lucille had guessed long ago that she was neither planned nor expected. Her father, the big, gregarious, white-haired Steven Hart, had turned fifty before she was born. Her mother, Nell, was forty-four. It had been fifteen years since the birth of the younger of the two Hart sons. Paul was the firstborn, arriving in the spring of 1851. Louis came along in the summer of '54. The couple gave up on having a daughter.

Brothers Paul and Louis were gone from home before Lucille turned five years old. Her father assured her that she was the precious child of his heart, the pride of his life, the sweet comfort of his old age. A Civil War hero whose slight limp was a prized badge of honor, Steven Hart had been appointed by President Ulysses S. Grant to serve as the first postmaster of Colonias, New York.

Lucille always loved spending time at the post office with her patient, indulgent papa. She was helping him put up the mail when she was so small she had to stand on a chair to reach the boxes. By the time she was twelve, she knew everyone's box number and exactly how long it took for a letter to get from Albany to Colonias.

When Lucille turned sixteen, her mother fell suddenly, seriously ill. Doctor Spencer, the attending physician, sadly predicted that Nell Hart would never regain her health. Steven Hart took his young daughter aside, smiled reassuringly at her, and told her that she was not to miss out on any activities because she had a sick mother.

"Lucy gal, you're not to be turning down any invitations to parties and such because of your Momma," Steven Hart said to Lucy. "I don't want you worrying or feeling obligated in any way because it's not your responsibility. I'll take care of Nell."

And he would have.

But Steven Hart was killed instantly in a hunting accident less than a mile from home when Lucille was just eighteen. Her brothers lived in distant cities with families of their own. Paul was all the way out on the west coast of California running a land development company and raising four strapping young boys. Louis was down in Fort Worth working on a vast cattle ranch and struggling to support his wife and two baby girls. Neither brother could be counted on to share the burden. Their invalid mother, Nell, became Lucille's sole responsibility.

Young though she was, Lucille was appointed by President Benjamin Harrison to succeed her father at the Colonias post office. She became one of the United

9

States first and youngest postmistresses. The story of her appointment made the New York Tribune. She clipped and saved the article.

Stretched thin between her six day a week duties at the post office and the increasingly difficult task of caring for her ill mother, Lucille was left with precious little time for the fun and frivolous pursuits of her young, carefree friends.

Soon party invitations stopped coming. Friends of both sexes quit coming to call.

All but two.

The vivacious, dark haired Betty Thompson was Lucy's dearest friend. The two had met when both were just five years old and Lucy began taking piano lessons from Betty's mother. They played together on Lucy's very first visit to the Thompson home. By the time they started school, they were inseparable. They remained so ever after.

The blond, blue eyed Rob Grant had been Lucille's sweetheart since she was fourteen, he fifteen. He was patient for a long, long time. But finally, even he grew tired of waiting as the months turned into years. Rob Grant married Betty Thompson and the pair moved to St. Louis, Missouri.

And still Nell Hart had clung tenaciously to life, totally dependent.

Looking back on those lost years, Lucille felt no resentment toward Rob or Betty. Nor toward her mother. She loved her mother; she missed her still. But by the time Nell Hart finally gasped her last breath in the autumn of 1897, Lucille was twenty-seven years old and folks no longer called her Lucille or Lucy.

She was Miss Lucy. The unmarried postmistress. The single lady. The spinster. The old maid.

Of all the classmates with whom she had attended school, she was the only one who had never married. For the rest of her days she would be known as Miss Lucy. Aunt Lucy to her brothers' children. Never would she be some man's cherished wife. No sweet-faced child would ever call her mother.

Still Lucille Hart was not a bitter, unhappy woman. She was extremely proud of her position as the town's postmistress and took real satisfaction from her work. She had old and dear friends and acquaintances who liked and respected her. She had her strong faith in a merciful God, and numerous church activities. She had the piano recitals she presented for the young pupils to whom she gave lessons. She had a nice comfortable home, a nice comfortable life.

But her girlish dreams of love and adventure had all but died. Somewhere along the way she had changed. Lucy was painfully aware that she was no longer the lively, spirited girl she once was. She had grown slowly, steadily more settled and sedate. Had become more cautious and careful. More practical and pragmatic.

More of an old maid.

Yet deep down in her heart of hearts, she desperately yearned for something more--for romance.

The last summer of the century was also the last summer of Lucille Hart's fading youth. On the last day of August she would turn thirty. The years and the chances for happiness were rapidly slipping away, so Lucille had decided it was now or never.

She was planning--had been planning for months-- a two week holiday at that fabled oceanside resort, Atlantic City. The hotel reservations had been made.

The round trip train ticket to Port Hudson had been purchased. A cabin on the river steamer booked.

On Saturday morning, the 19th of August, Lucy Hart would leave for Atlantic City where she hoped to find a dash of romance if only for a few days. A few nights.

She hoped to fill these fleeting golden days with exciting escapades, the kind which would provide warming memories in her old age.

***

A slight smile touched Lucy's lips when, at bedtime that warm Friday night, she went to the tall mahogany highboy in her bedroom, opened the top drawer, and took out a neat stack of letters that were tied with a blue satin ribbon. The letters had accumulated over a three-year period. They were from a gentleman.

A Mister Theodore D. Mooney.

So far, Lucy's relationship with Mr. Theodore Mooney had gone no farther than exchanged letters and books and foolish little gifts. The two had never actually met.

Theodore D. Mooney was the postmaster in Cooperstown, Pennsylvania. Three years ago a letter, which should have gone to Cooperstown, had turned up in Colonias. Lucy had immediately forwarded the letter on to its rightful destination, along with a brief, personal note.

In return she had received a missive from one Theodore D. Mooney, Cooperstown postmaster. A regular correspondence began. From his letters, written in a neat, small hand, Lucy had learned that Theodore Mooney was a bachelor, thirty-seven years old, who lived with his older, widowed sister. He enjoyed music, literature, art, and the theater.

A long distance friendship had evolved and now at last--her post office to be left safely in the hands of a substitute from Rochester--the two were to quietly, secretly meet and spend the last two weeks of summer together in Atlantic City.

***

The big day finally arrived.

Saturday, August 19th, 1899.

Lucy was almost giddy with excitement. She was up and out of bed before the sun, although her train did not leave Colonias until 10 a.m.

Rushing about, Lucy mentally checked off the list of last minute things to be done. She inspected every room in the house, making sure nothing was out of place, that no clutter marred the general neatness, that no hint of dust coated the woodwork or furniture. She was a firm believer that a woman should never leave her home--even for a hour, much less two long weeks--in any condition other than absolutely spotless.

After all, life was uncertain. You never knew when you walked out the front door if you'd ever return. Accidents happened and she could think of nothing more horrifying than to have friends and neighbors find out that Miss Lucy Hart had been a slovenly housekeeper.

Inhaling the soft bouquet of lemon soap emanating from the sparkling white bathroom, Lucy walked on down the short hall and into the front parlor. She ran her hand along the slipcovered back of the sofa, rearranged a crocheted doily on a chair arm, and absently touched the fringed border of a cream linen window curtain. She turned toward the old upright piano, checked to be sure all sheet music had been put away.

Satisfied she was leaving everything exactly as it should be, Lucy hurried into her sunny bedroom to finish getting ready for her journey.

In minutes she was dressed in a freshly laundered, heavily starched traveling suit of pale yellow cotton and her naturally curly chestnut hair was meticulously swept atop her head and secured with an oyster shell comb.

The packing had been completed earlier, save for one particular item. The beautiful white tulle dress she'd bought at Pauline's still lay spread out on her neatly made bed. It would go into the big valise last.

Lucy took down from a shelf in the closet several sheets of white tissue paper saved from last Christmas. Her wide-set, green eyes sparkling, bottom lip caught behind her top row of straight white teeth, she carefully wrapped the white summer dress in the tissue paper and placed it in the large, open brown suitcase. She closed the case, patted the leather lid, then lifted and looked at her brooch watch.

Twenty minutes 'til nine.

"More than an hour to go," Lucy lamented aloud, frowning suddenly. Then she smiled immediately, snapped her slender fingers, and said to her silent, sunny bedroom, "I shall wait at the depot! Maybe the train will be early."

***

At straight up nine on that muggy August morning, a telegram for Miss Lucille Hart came over the wire. Nate Flatt, the Western Union telegrapher, not bothering to read anything other than the wire's addressee, placed the yellow message in a matching envelope, sealed it, went to the back door of the telegraph office, and called to his young son, Bobby. The boisterous eleven-year-old came running. Barking excitedly, Post Office Champ was close on Bobby's heels.

"What is it, Papa?" Bobby shoved a shock of dark hair out of his eyes with a dirty hand. "Me and Champ are pretty busy right now. We're tied up."

"Well you and Champ can get untied," said his skinny, sallow faced father. "I have a delivery for you to make." He handed Bobby the yellow envelope, put his hands atop his son's slender shoulders, and said, "This telegram just came for Miss Lucy. Get on your bike and take it over to her. Now."

"Yes, sir," said Bobby and Champ barked his agreement

The telegram tucked in his front shirt pocket, Bobby Flatt and Champ set out to Miss Lucy's house, Bobby pedaling furiously, Champ speeding ahead of his young master, the racing blood of his wild wolf ancestors coursing through his veins.

The pair had gone but a couple of blocks when they ran into a couple of Bobby's school chums. Sonny Davis and Mark McCalister had been to A. B. Cranford's Drug store. Sonny had a sack of colored jawbreakers. He offered one to Bobby. Champ got one too. The three friends sucked on their jawbreakers and made plans for a much needed visit to their favorite swimming hole late that afternoon.

By the time Bobby pedaled up to Miss Lucy's white house, his jawbreaker was gone and so was Miss Lucy.

Champ barked and Bobby knocked on the closed door again and again. But no one answered. No one was home.

Bobby looked about, made a face, and finally said to Champ, "Aw, heck, Miss Lucy'll be back any minute.

We'll just leave her telegram in the door so she'll be sure to find it."

Bobby stuck the sealed yellow envelope inside the screen door and left. When he got back to the telegraph office, Nate Flatt looked up, and asked, "You deliver that telegram to Miss Lucy?"

"Yes, Sir," said Bobby with round, innocent eyes, then raced out the front door and across the street to watch and wave to the crowded passenger train which was rolling out of the station

CHAPTER THREE

High up in a rooftop apartment overlooking Central Park west, Lilly Styvestant--the Park Avenue Goddess-- was wide-awake on that hot August morning.

The lovely, blond tressed Lilly was in bed, but she had not yet been to sleep. Nor had her male companion. The handsome, hedonistic pair had been out on the town all night, finally staggering home to Lilly's Park Avenue penthouse as the Saturday sun was coming up.

Intoxicated, as usual, and feeling amorous, as usual, they had begun stripping as soon as they entered the sky-high palace. Articles of clothing soon littered the lush drawing room carpet. Naked by the time they reached the bedroom, the eager, excited Lilly never made it to the bed.

She threw her arms around Blackie La Duke's neck and slid a bent knee up and around his thigh. She squealed with girlish delight when he lifted her from the floor, eased her down on his thrusting masculinity, and stood there flat footed in the middle of the bedroom, his dark hands manipulating the soft pale cheeks of her bottom, his own tanned buttocks flexing, his pelvis thrusting until she cried out in ecstasy.

"Darling, darling," Lilly sighed happily, knowing it was only the beginning.

An extremely passionate woman, constantly ravenous for prolonged sexual rapture, Lilly Styvestant had finally found the ideal lover. Handsome and hot

17

blooded, Blackie La Duke had been blessed with limitless stamina and amazing control of his lean, well honed body. None of Lilly's past lovers had been half so awesome as this dark sensual provider of incredible erotic pleasure. No other had ever given her the multiple orgasms she so desperately sought.

Other men had been intimidated by her fierce physical hunger, accusing her of being greedy and avaricious in bed, but nothing shocked the worldly Blackie La Duke. With him Lilly could be herself, admitting frankly that once was not nearly enough. Not for her. Not ever.

An experienced lover, Blackie had learned to gauge exactly how much it would take on a given occasion to fully satiate the glamorous, greedy Park Avenue Goddess--who made no bones about the fact that she was mad about him.

On this sticky, hot August Saturday morning, Lilly was unusually ravenous. Blackie had brought her to deep, shuddering climaxes several times and still she wanted more. After a couple of hours of performing, he was achingly aroused, but continued to hold back. He was so hot he was feverish, but if he climaxed he might not be able to pleasure her again.

There might be no quick duplication of the enormous erection he presently sported. Rather than risk it, Blackie called on all his powers of self control, determined to stay just as he was until he could be sure this beautiful, naked woman no longer wanted to touch it, or kiss it, or have it inside her.

At ten a.m. that had not yet occurred.

So as the high, hot August sun streamed through the uncurtained floor to ceiling glass of Lilly's penthouse bedroom, Blackie La Duke still sublimely exhibited that unique virility, that interminable readiness which made him such an exciting lover.

The black-haired, black-eyed Blackie lay spread eagled across Lilly's silk sheeted bed. His bare brown feet dangled over one side of the mattress, his dark head hung down backward over the other.

The pale-skinned, pale-haired Lilly was kneeling on the carpeted floor at Blackie's head, her hands kneading his muscular shoulders, her head bent over his face, her lips moving eagerly on his as she kissed him. Her loose, tangled hair falling into her eyes and onto his throat, Lilly kissed Blackie boldly, hotly until Blackie's arms came up off the mattress and his raised hands cupped the crown of her head and wrapped around the nape of her neck.

While blindingly bright sunlight washed over the naked, perspiring pair, they kissed like that until, breathless, her heart pounding in her full, naked breasts, Lilly tore her burning lips from Blackie's, whipped her head back, and pushed her wild blond hair off her face.

Blackie flipped fluidly onto his stomach, balanced his weight on an elbow, reached for her, and started kissing her all over again. For several minutes they kissed in that position--he lying on his stomach across the bed, she kneeling on the floor before him.

Abruptly Blackie released Lilly. He levered himself up, rose to his knees, and sat back on his bare heels. He crossed his muscular arms over his hair-covered chest, tilted his head to one side, and announced, "I need a drink. Join me?"

He smiled at the look of pure animal lust washing over her lovely face as she focused squarely on the throbbing tumescence rising and bobbing between his spread thighs.

"Noooo," she murmured petulantly, "I want you." She pointed a red nailed forefinger. "I want that!" she whined like a spoiled child demanding a favorite toy. "You give it to me, Blackie. I want it now."

Blackie grinned, but shook his head. He was tiring; he needed some rest. If he played his cards right, one more go around might satisfy even the lustful Lilly. But he couldn't be too quick about it. Unless he made her wait a while, drew out the titillation until she was really on fire, once more might not do her.

Blackie knew how to handle Lilly.

He yawned dramatically, turned about, and lithely rose from the bed. Without a word he padded out of the sunny bedroom, never looking back. Lilly, still on her knees on the far side of the bed, stared after him in disappointed astonishment. She made a face.

Blackie stood at the heavy liquor cabinet pouring scotch into a couple of shot glasses when Lilly walked up behind him. Her arms came around him and she pressed herself against his back while he downed a shot of scotch in one long swallow.

"Care for a drink?" he asked as her soft, searching hands slid down his hard belly and closed possessively around him.

Her lips brushing kisses to his clefted back, Lilly whispered, "In a minute."

Lilly's left hand cupped Blackie's tight testicles and her right began a slight sliding motion upward from the base of his swollen erection to the smooth tip. Blackie smiled to himself, shrugged, and drank down the scotch he'd poured for her.

This would be it. He'd called it correctly. One final earth shattering orgasm and she'd sleepily pass out.

First he'd let her play for a while. Let her get as hot as a pistol, then take her right here on floor, pump it to her until she cried uncle. Then hopefully he could go to his hotel and get some rest.

Blackie set the empty shot glass down and clung to the solid walnut cabinet while Lilly continued her skillful manipulation of his genitals.

She toyed. She stroked. She tickled. She squeezed.

And all the while she was licking and biting his broad shoulders, stabbing her hard nippled breasts into his back, and rubbing the moist blond curls of her gyrating pelvis against his bare, lean buttocks.

"God, Blackie, you excite me so," she murmured, nuzzling her flushed face into the deep cleft of his smooth warm back. "I wish I could just keep you locked up here with me forever and ever."

"Mmmmm," Blackie moaned, gripping the liquor cabinet, his lids lowering over passion-glazed, dark eyes and the muscles of his long legs becoming tense and weak.

"Every day could be just like Christmas," Lilly whispered provocatively. She sighed deeply thinking about it. Then laughed softly, huskily, and told him, "While other people decorate their Christmas tree, I could decorate this." Her forefinger moving in a circle around the jerking tip, she continued the fantasizing folly. "I could stand you naked before the tall windows overlooking Central Park and twine strings of sparkling diamonds and luminous pearls around the length of it. Then perhaps tuck tiny sprigs of fragrant mistletoe in the crisp black groin curls and...and...or...or...no...I know...it could be a fabulous Christmas present. I could sheath it in colorful wrapping paper of bright scarlet, tie a big

21

green satin bow around it, then eagerly unwrap you on Christmas morning...my most treasured gift of all. Wouldn't that be great fun, darling?"

"Sure," Blackie rasped, amenable, at that moment, to just about anything she might suggest, no matter how outlandish. "We'll try that come Christmas."

"Promise?"

"Promise."

"Oh, darling, darling. I believe I'd like that scotch now," Lilly told him breathlessly.

"Coming right up," Blackie's breath was short as well.

With shaking hands he poured a shot glass to the brim with scotch, and held it out beside him. He flinched and shuddered when Lilly gave him one last squeeze, released him, and reached for the scotch. She stepped back as Blackie turned to face her.

Lilly held the scotch in her hand, smiling wickedly up at him. She did not drink from the glass. She put out the pink tip of her tongue and made a slow, erotic circle of her ruby red lips. Then, puckering as if for a kiss, she dipped slender fingers into the scotch and spread the liquor slowly, seductively over Blackie's jerking, thrusting cock. When every inch was wet and glistening, Lilly handed him the glass, sank to her knees before him, and began licking the scotch away.

This was, she had confessed to him on more than one such occasion, her favorite way to drink. What sensual pleasure, she enthused, to consume her liquor and her lover at the same time. It never failed to make her deliciously tipsy and she was never quite certain which was responsible for the heady intoxication.

The scotch on her man or the man in her scotch.

The Last Dance

A few short moments of her mouth warmly enclosing him and both were at a fever pitch and in dire need of swift, deep release. His hands tangled in her wild blond hair, Blackie anxiously pulled her head up. A half dozen hot kisses and then they were going at it on the living room rug like school was out for good.

An hour later Blackie La Duke, bathed and dressed in his slightly rumpled evening clothes, the dark stubble of beard giving him a slightly satanic appearance, was saying good-bye to Lilly at her front door.

"I'll drop you a picture post card," he said, smiling, giving her bare bottom a playful squeeze.

"Don't go, Blackie. You'll be bored to tears down there," she argued. He just grinned, kissed her one last time, opened the door, and walked out.

Twenty-four hours later Blackie La Duke, rested, handsome, and impeccably dressed in a crisp beige linen summer suit, stood before the marble counter in the hotel lobby checking out of the Waldorf.

As Blackie turned to leave, the cashier called after him, "Mr. La Duke, where shall I forward your mail?"

Over his shoulder as he walked away. "The Atlantic Grand."

CHAPTER FOUR

Lucy Hart stood at the railing of the Hudson River steamer. Squinting against the early morning sunlight, she gazed at the tall timbered palisades rising on either side of the wide river. Any minute now she would see it. She was sure they must be getting close.

Moments later the steamer rounded a gentle bend in the Hudson River and, sure enough, there on the lofty cliffs above were the huge cannons and red brick buildings of West Point. Faintly, as if from far, far away, Lucy heard the sound of a lone bugle.

It gave her goose bumps.

She was reminded of another summer Sunday. She had been only a child--nine, maybe ten--but the memory of that day was as vivid as if it had been last week. She had come with her father and mother to the Military Academy for a reunion of the Grand Army of the Republic. Her father and the other proud Union veterans of the Civil War had worn their uniforms and medals for the stirring celebration.

There was a grand parade on the West Point plain. The Post band played, the Cadet Corps passed in review, and the old soldiers proudly stood at attention. Crowds cheered and women waved their handkerchiefs and tossed flowers at the aging heroes. It was patriotic and exciting and wonderful.

Lucy shivered in the warm August sunlight and for a fleeting second she missed her mother and father with such an intense yearning it was akin to physical pain. She clutched her throat, turned away from the railing, and shook her head as if to clear it.

This was no time for looking back.

She wanted only to look ahead. Two glorious weeks of adventure awaited her in Atlantic City and she meant to--had to-- make the most of it.

Lucy turned back to the railing. A gentle breeze loosened a lock of her chestnut hair. It whipped across her cheek and into her eyes. Impatiently she swept the wayward curl aside. Her green eyes sparkled once more and she smiled again with pleasure.

It was incredibly exhilarating to consider that *no one* in the whole wide world--save Mr. Theodore D. Mooney--knew where she was or would be for the next two weeks!

The Colonias post office could burn to the ground, her brothers could come for an unexpected visit, the house could blow away--and nobody would know how to get in touch with her.

Kitty Widner knew she was going on a two-week holiday. But nothing more. She'd had to let Kitty know she would be gone. Kitty and Bruce Widner were more than her next-door neighbors; they were her dearest friends. So she had told Kitty and naturally Kitty begged her to reveal her secret destination, but she had refused.

And she *sure* hadn't told Kitty that she was to meet a man. Kitty would never have believed it anyhow.

Lucy's face flushed with color. She could hardly believe it herself. She was on her way to a rendezvous with a stranger. The prospect of it was so exciting it made her heartbeat quicken, her mouth go dry. She felt quite daring and adventurous. And free. Free in a way she'd never been free before.

What the next two weeks might bring, Lucy had no idea, but she was ready and eager to find out. And she was certain of one thing if of nothing else, the two weeks she was to spend in Atlantic City would be a welcome change from the orderly life she led in Colonias.

Lucy gawked at the tall buildings when the steamer moved into and out of the wide, busy harbor of New York City. She had lived all her life in New York State and had never been to the city. Maybe next summer she would spend her holiday here. Lucy laughed, feeling almost giddy. Maybe she and Theodore D. Mooney would spend their holiday together in New York City next year.

The steamer picked up speed. The big city was left behind. The warm, lazy afternoon was a pleasant, restful one for Lucy. She watched the Jersey shore glide past as she lolled in a comfortable deck chair and spun lovely daydreams.

But when finally the steamer docked in the bustling port of Atlantic City late that Sunday afternoon, and Lucy Hart stood on the dock beside her valises waiting for transportation to the hotel, she found she had lost some of her earlier enthusiasm.

Suddenly, and without warning, she began to feel apprehensive. She had never taken a trip alone, never stayed overnight in a hotel, *never* agreed to a clandestine tryst with a total stranger.

But she quickly reminded herself that Theodore was no stranger. Once they were together, everything would be fine. Just fine. Lucy smiled again and drew a slow, steadying breath, feeling a little calmer.

An omnibus rolled up. People swarmed forward carrying heavy luggage, brushing rudely past her, quickly taking up all the seats before she could get on board. She would have to wait for another. Lucy made a face, looked about.

A carriage for hire was parked a few yards away. Lucy wondered how much he would charge, decided she didn't care. She was thrifty fifty weeks a year; for the next two she wouldn't be. She was spending five dollars a night for a room; she would ride to the hotel in style.

Lucy waved to the driver. He nodded, hopped down, and came running. He handed her up into the covered conveyance, scooped up her luggage, and said, "Where to, Miss?"

Calmly; "The Atlantic Grand."

***

Lucy was dazzled with the sights and sounds and scents of Atlantic City. The carriage moved slowly southward down traffic clogged Atlantic Avenue and Lucy found herself tingling with anticipation. Eyes shining, stomach tied in knots, she stared at the unending row of imposing, multi-storied hotels lining the shore and wondered which one was hers.

Lucy's heart beat in her throat when the carriage turned the corner at Indiana Avenue and headed straight toward the ocean. This was it! She was here at last. She could hardly wait to see everything there was to see, to do everything there was to do.

"My goodness gracious," Lucy murmured aloud when the carriage rolled to a stop before an enormous, white, ten-story hotel whose tall twin towers rose to meet the clear blue sky.

She stepped out in a daze of delight to admire the imposing white palace. Her gaze slowly climbed the huge structure, and she gaped at the huge letters mounted on the hotel's rooftop between the twin towers.

ATLANTIC GRAND

Ten foot tall letters spelling out the hotel's name were fashioned from hundreds of Edison's electric light bulbs. The carriage driver, noting where Lucy's attention was directed, told her, "Wait 'til nighttime, Miss. Those letters glow bright as day after dark."

Too overwhelmed to reply, Lucy paid the carriage driver and was immediately whisked by a smartly uniformed doorman up the stone steps to the hotel's main entrance. She swept eagerly through a massive set of revolving glass doors framed with burnished brass. When she stepped out of the heavy, whooshing doors, she was in a large, elegant, atrium-ceilinged lobby where oriental rugs graced floors of gleaming white marble.

Lucy attempted to act blasé. She didn't want to appear overly impressed and have the other guests thinking she was a country bumpkin who'd never been anywhere.

But she found it next to impossible not to stare in open-mouthed wonder at the huge, hanging crystal chandeliers and gleaming mounted mirrors and elegant, comfortable furniture.

The giant lobby was a beehive of activity and she was at once enveloped in the atmosphere of excitement. Porters and bellman hurried about. Two uniformed concierges sat at matching mahogany tables. Mail and key clerks were kept constantly busy.

Lucy was guided through the throngs of employees and guests toward the long, marble-topped front desk. On the way she noticed, directly across the vast lobby, a pair of tall French doors that opened onto a broad back veranda. She was tempted to rush out for a quick glimpse of the city's famed Boardwalk and sandy beaches beyond.

At the front desk, Lucy casually leaned on the marble topped counter and tried to affect aplomb. It wasn't working. Her hand shook as she signed the guest register and was given her room key. She was then promptly ushered to the elevator and accompanied to her third floor room by a courteous bellhop in a purple uniform trimmed in gold braid with gold buttons down his chest. On his blond head was a small, purple pillbox hat banded in gold braid.

Inside the large, comfortable room fronting onto the Atlantic, the bellman deposited Lucy's bags on the luggage rack at the foot of the four-poster bed. He followed an enchanted Lucy out onto the small private balcony and, making a grand, sweeping gesture with his arm, said proudly, "The Atlantic Ocean, Miss. Have you ever seen anything like it?"

"No. No, I haven't," Lucy replied truthfully.

"Lived here all my life," said the friendly bellman, "and I never tire of the splendid view." He started back inside. Lucy followed. He said, "You'll find ice water in the pitcher on the bureau." He pointed. "Bathroom is through that door, the wardrobe the other." Lucy nodded. "My name's Benny, Miss Hart. You need anything, you let me know, okay?"

"There is something, Benny," Lucy ventured hopefully. "A fresh white gardenia. Do you suppose you could find one for me by eight o'clock this evening?"

Benny snapped his gloved fingers. "A snap," said he, nodding confidently. "Look outside your door at eight. You'll find a florist box containing one fresh white gardenia."

"That will be wonderful. Thank you ever so much, Benny," Lucy handed him a coin.

Benny took the coin, pocketed it, and backed away, grinning. "I hope you have the time of your life in Atlantic City."

"So do I, Benny."

When the door closed behind Benny, Lucy lifted and looked at the face of her gold cased watch. Only two short hours to go until she was to meet Theodore.

Lucy reviewed their well-laid plan one last time.

The two had agreed to meet in the Atlantic Grand's lobby at exactly 8:30 p.m., Sunday evening the 20th of August. Today was the day. The hour was fast approaching.

From their exchange of letters Theodore Mooney knew he was to look for a 'tall, rather thin woman with unruly chestnut hair, a fair complexion, and wide set green eyes. Lucy, in turn, was to expect a tall, spare man with dark hair and dark eyes.

To ensure that they would recognize each other, Lucy had told Theodore that she would be wearing a beige linen dress with a square cut neckline, balloon sleeves that reached just below the elbow, and a gored skirt. She would be holding a white gardenia in her left hand.

Theodore was to be dressed in a summer suit of navy linen with a white dress shirt and a wine silk tie. A white gardenia matching the one Lucy carried would be tucked into the buttonhole of his lapel.

Foolproof.

Lucy again looked at her watch and decided there wasn't a moment to spare if she was to get everything done. First she had to unpack. Then she would take a nice, long, refreshing bath, shampoo and dry her curly chestnut hair, and be dressed and ready to meet Theodore at the appointed time.

And she sure didn't want to be late!

Lucy self-consciously stepped out of the elevator and into the hotel lobby at 8:25 that Sunday evening. A fresh white gardenia was clutched tightly in the stiff fingers of her left hand. Her searching green eyes made a long, slow sweep of the crowded Atlantic Grand's marble floored lobby.

She saw no gentleman fitting Theodore Mooney's description. She stood about feeling awkward and anxious, a false smile frozen on her tight face. Long minutes passed. Ten. Fifteen. Twenty.

No Theodore.

At three minutes of nine an uneasy and disappointed Lucy was ready to give up and return to her room.

And then she spotted him.

CHAPTER FIVE

A tall, spare man with blue-black hair who was dressed in a finely tailored, navy linen suit with a snowy white shirt and wine silk tie stepped out of the hotel's bar and into the spacious lobby. He paused, stood perfectly framed in the open arched doorway. A white gardenia blossomed from his lapel.

Theodore! Lucy breathed silently.

He looked nothing like the man she had pictured all this time. He was taller than she had imagined, and far, far more handsome with his deeply tanned skin and strong, classical features.

And, he seemed not the least bit ill at ease or shy. Quite the opposite. There was about him an inherent confidence. His relaxed stance suggested a cocksure manner, which she would never have associated with her gentle, artistic correspondent.

Lucy waited on pins and needles for Theodore to make the first move.

But nothing happened.

He looked right past her.

Lucy was left with no choice. She screwed up her courage, waved until she finally caught his eye, and called out, "Here I am. Over here!"

She thrust the ivory gardenia up into the air for him to see. His midnight dark eyes lighted and he grinned appealingly, nodded, and came directly to her.

"We agreed to meet at 8:30 sharp," she said accusingly, her nerves taut, voice almost shrill. "You are late."

"Am I?" Continuing to smile easily, he gently took her elbow and commandingly ushered her across the crowded atrium-ceilinged lobby toward the hotel's beachside double doors. "Then please say you'll accept my most humble apologies, Miss...Miss..."

"No. No. Not Miss. Don't you remember? You're to call me Lucy."

"All right, Lucy. And you can call me Blackie."

"Blackie?" she stopped abruptly, frowned at him. "Why on earth would I want to call you Blackie?"

He shrugged broad shoulders. "Most people do."

"Well, not I," Lucy said as if it were out of the question. "I would never consider calling you Blackie."

"Then call me anything but late for dinner," he teased, and brashly winked at her.

Lucy was surprised and totally taken aback. She would never have suspected Theodore of being the kind of gentleman who winked at ladies.

She made a face. "I shall call you Theodore, of course."

"Of course." He nodded agreeably. His long, lean fingers again encircled her upper arm and he guided her outside and onto the wide veranda.

Even more nervous than she had anticipated being, Lucy found herself chattering up a storm, and likely sounding like a silly schoolgirl with her first beau. She told him she arrived late this afternoon--explaining that she took the first passenger train from Colonias to Port Hudson where she boarded a steamer. Did he get in this afternoon, too, as planned? Yes, he replied, he sure did. Checked into the hotel around three.

33

"Three?" Lucy's eyebrows lifted. "You weren't supposed to arrive until well after five."

"So I was early," he said, cocking his dark head to one side and smiling as though she had just said something amusing.

Lucy was becoming increasingly uneasy. Theodore D. Mooney was certainly behaving strangely. The modest, intelligent gentleman with whom she had shared so many letters over the past three years seemed far removed from this forward, flirtatious man-about-town. His brazen manner was even more surprising than his striking good looks.

He suggested a walk.

Lucy considered declining, not totally comfortable she'd be safe alone with him. Giving her little opportunity to refuse, he guided her down the steep hotel steps.

At the bottom step he stumbled slightly, fell against her. His face was an inch from Lucy's for a split second and it was then she smelled the telltale scent of liquor on his breath. She was shocked and horrified.

"I knew it!" she said, pushing on his broad chest. "You have been imbibing alcoholic beverages! Have you not?"

He grinned. "I've been drinking whiskey if that's what you mean."

"This is unforgivable!" she said, bristling. She shook her head despairingly. "You have no idea how disappointed I am."

"Don't blame you. Shame on me," he said. "I certainly should have waited for you. Let's go have a drink together."

"Have a... well, I never!" Her fair face flushed with high color.

"Then it's time you did."

"Theodore D. Mooney, you are inebriated!"

He laughed and said, "Him, too? Why, it's an epidemic."

"What are you talking about? You must really be in your cups. You are making no sense."

"Ah, well now that's been said of me before." He stepped down off the bottom step, turned to face her. "Although I never understood why. I make perfectly good sense to myself."

Her brows knitted, Lucy scowled at him. "Mr. Mooney, I am afraid our agreeing to meet here in Atlantic City has been a big mistake on my part. In your letters you were not nearly so...so..."

"My letters?"

"Yes! All those wonderful letters you...you..." Lucy caught the amused glint of devilment flashing in his dark eyes and stopped speaking. Then her own eyes widened and a hand flew up to cover her mouth as it dawned on her. She had made an awful error. "Dear Lord above!" she exclaimed miserably, "You are not...you can't be..."

"Your Mr. Mooney? No, Lucy, I'm not."

Her delicate jaw hardened. "Well, just who are you?"

"Robert Jeffrey LaDuke, the third," he said. "Everybody calls me Blackie."

Anger mixed with embarrassment seized Lucy. "Mr. La Duke, I believe you owe me an apology! Pretending to be someone you're not! Luring me out of the hotel under false pretenses. Leading me to believe that you...that I...that we..."

"I did no such thing," he smoothly interrupted, smiling, totally unruffled. "Matter of fact, it was the other way round if you ask me."

"I didn't ask you and I don't care..."

"I was bothering no one," he again cut in. "Just standing in the hotel lobby, minding my own affairs when you brazenly summoned me over. Have you forgotten?" He chuckled at her look of dismay.

"But that was because I thought you were...I would never have..." She glared at him, feeling flustered and ridiculous. "Mr. LaDuke you are rude, impertinent, and unfeeling and I do not appreciate you allowing me to make a fool of myself!"

"You didn't, Lucy." Blackie looked straight into her snapping green eyes. "If you think you have, then you haven't lived much."

"I beg your pardon. I've lived plenty, thank you very much. I'll have you know that I own my own home, earn my own living and run my own life. I am the postmistress of Colonias, New York and highly efficient at what I do. I am nearly thir...I...I...am well into my twenties. For your information, I have seen a great deal of life."

"Really?"

"Really."

"Why is it I don't believe you?" He gave her a knowing look.

"Why is it I don't care what you believe," she said frostily and turned to leave.

He caught her arm, drew her back. "Perhaps you ought to care. Perhaps it's time someone made you care." He leaned a trifle closer and said in a low, resonant baritone, "Perhaps I'll make you care."

"Don't bank on it," she said with firm conviction, choosing to ignore the alarming chill of excitement that skipped up her spine at his arrogant suggestion. "If you'll kindly release me I shall go and..."

"Hunt for ole Theodore? Want me to help you look?"

"Certainly not!" She was almost shouting now, desperate to get away from this suave, insolent man who enjoyed making her uncomfortable.

She flatly refused to answer when Blackie asked how was it she didn't even know what her missing Mister Mooney looked like? He was a bit confused. Could she clear it up a little?

She had no intention of explaining anything to him. Shaking her head angrily, she attempted to free her hand from his.

Blackie stubbornly clung to it.

"Okay, Lucy from Colonias, I'll let you go. But if you don't find your Mr. Mooney, I'll be around the Atlantic Grand for the next couple of weeks. Won't be leaving until bright and early the morning after Labor Day." He rubbed his long thumb back and forth over her soft palm and teased, "If you decide you'd like to live--really live--ask at the front desk for Blackie LaDuke." He winked at her once more and made an evocative promise, "I'll show you the time of your life."

Lucy's face pinkened.

"You, Mr. LaDuke, could have done with some raising." She yanked her hand from his. "If you were any part of a gentleman, you could see that I am a lady!" She turned away with those parting words, "Kindly forget that we ever met because I certainly intend to."

"Good luck."

CHAPTER SIX

Blackie LaDuke's low, annoying laughter followed Lucy up the hotel steps where she anxiously disappeared inside.

Blackie stayed as he was for a moment, then shook his dark head, turned away, and hurried off down the Boardwalk toward Delaware Avenue and Dutchy's Club in search of a card game or a cutie or both.

Robert 'Blackie' LaDuke the third was the devil-may-care black sheep scion of an old and illustrious family. His childhood had not been a particularly happy one. Displays of affection between his parents and their children were rare.

The raising of Blackie and his two older brothers was left mostly to the domestic staff. Sent away to a very proper school for young gentlemen when he was only seven years old, the precocious Blackie showed little interest in intellectual pursuits; a pattern that never changed.

Placed on scholastic probation his first year at Princeton, he was asked to leave the university in his second term. Blackie was reluctantly taken into the prosperous real estate firm jointly owned by his father and an old family friend, the powerful Judge Harry O'Connor. For a few short months Blackie worked hard, learned rapidly, and it appeared that he was going be an asset to the company.

But trouble had a way of following Blackie.

Just when his future seemed bright, bad luck intervened.

The widowed Judge Harry O'Connor had, only months before, married a gorgeous stage actress who was young enough to be his daughter. The new Mrs. O'Connor liked Blackie's looks and let him know it.

And so it happened that on an afternoon when Blackie was supposedly with a prospective client, he was caught in a compromising situation with the new Mrs. O'Connor.

The good looking Blackie was used to receiving overtures from lonely, lovely women, but Mrs. O'Connor was persistent. He finally succumbed to her charms and he was the one who failed to escape retribution.

Mrs. O'Connor cried and swore it was all Blackie's fault, she had wanted no part of him, but he wouldn't leave her alone. He had heartlessly seduced her. Mrs. O'Connor was coddled and comforted by her powerful, white haired husband. Blackie was tossed out of the family firm.

Blackie's parents were and always had been some of the wealthiest on Park Avenue, but they didn't speak to their wayward youngest son. He was no longer welcome in the drawing rooms of Long Island cottages, though it was whispered he was still more than welcome in the some of the boudoirs of those cottages.

An extremely handsome, debonair young man, the jaded Blackie had for years provided the tabloids with meaty headlines because of his numerous lady friends.

From time to time his name had been linked with the young Princess Wilhelmina of the Netherlands, the lauded actress Ginny Lind, and Lady Randolph

Churchill, twelve years his senior. Lovely Lilly Styvestant, known at home and abroad as the Park Avenue Goddess, had hardly allowed Blackie out of her sight since she spotted him buying French cigarettes in the lobby of the Waldorf Hotel one cold winter evening.

Now Blackie LaDuke had come down to Atlantic City to escape the heat of the city and the matrimonial heat being put on him by the willful Park Avenue Goddess. A resourceful man who generally managed to live almost as good as he did when he was actually rich, Blackie LaDuke would, for the next two weeks, occupy the lavish pent house suite of the Atlantic Grand's North Tower, thanks to the last of a small inheritance from his maternal grandmother.

His afternoon arrival at the seaside resort had already generated gossip, but Blackie was one guest who didn't give a damn what people thought.

***

Lucy Hart did.

Mortified to find herself alone in such an awkward, awful position, and worried sick over the whereabouts of Theodore D. Mooney, she didn't know what to do.

After freeing herself from the rude rounder, Lucy milled about in the opulent hotel lobby, searching in vain for yet another dark haired, dark eyed gentlemen dressed in a navy suit with a white gardenia in his lapel.

There were none.

Lucy finally went to the front desk. A short, slim man, neatly attired, his thin graying hair brushed carefully in place, looked up and smiled politely. His face, heavily lined, had no strong features save a pair of intelligent hazel eyes. "Yes? May I be of assistance, Miss?"

Lucy nodded. "I hope so." She looked about, then quietly asked, hoping not to attract attention, if there had been any messages left for her. "Lucy Hart," she told the clerk, "room 313."

The slender man with the thinning gray hair looked at the empty box under which her room number was written, again faced her, and folded his hands on the marble counter.

"Not a thing, Miss. Were you expecting...?"

"Oh, no, no. I just...no." She hurried away.

Sighing with frustration, Lucy sat down in one of the many wine upholstered chairs that were strategically arranged in clusters throughout the spacious hotel lobby. She purposely chose a chair that would give her an unobstructed view of both the hotel's revolving doors and the beachside entrance. No one could get into or out of the lobby without her seeing him or her.

Lucy sat uneasily in the easy chair, nervously twisting the leaves of a nearby potted palm until she thought she'd scream. Dozens of people went in and out but none fit the description of Theodore D. Mooney.

After an interminably long hour, Lucy rose, squared her shoulders, marched back to the front desk, and asked again if she had received any messages. The frail, graying desk clerk's answer was the same.

A disappointing no.

She nodded, smiled weakly, and moved away. She lifted the gold watch pinned to the bosom of her beige linen dress. Eleven o'clock. No use staying downstairs any longer. If Mr. Mooney should finally show up, he would surely have a hotel employee inform her immediately of his arrival.

Lucy went to the elevator. Eager to flee to the privacy of her room, she stepped into the box-like conveyance and started to give the uniformed operator her floor number.

Before she could speak, he said proudly, "Third floor, isn't it?"

Lucy stared at him. The man was young--just a boy really-- and he was huge. He stood well over six foot, had hair the color of sand, and a neck that required a size eighteen shirt. His face was well scrubbed and he had a mouth full of teeth, all of them presently showing in a broad, open smile.

"Yes, that's correct," Lucy said, turning about and leaning her shoulders against the rear wall of the elevator.

"I've only missed a couple all afternoon," the young man said, pleased.

"I beg your pardon."

"Floor numbers," he told her. "I pride myself on memorizing every guest's floor." He grinned at her. "My name's Davey, Miss Hart. I took you up to three when you checked in this afternoon. Then I brought you back down around eight o'clock."

"Why, yes, you did," she nodded, recalling him now that she was no longer as excited as before. "We have something in common, Davey. I'm the postmistress of Colonias, New York and I pride myself on memorizing postal box numbers."

"Hey, I bet you're good at it," Davey's grin was ear to ear now. "You're a postmistress?" He whistled under his breath. "I didn't know there was such a thing as lady postmaster...ah...a...mistress."

"There are very few," Lucy told him. Then; "Now, if you'll kindly take me back up to the..."

"Please hold that car, Davey, my boy," came a low, rich masculine voice.

An imposing gentleman stepped into the elevator. Immaculately attired in a silver gray summer suit that matched his fine, full head of gleaming silver hair, he was tall, dignified, massive and magnificent. In his lapel was a red carnation and in his hand an ivory-handled walking cane.

"Miss," the silver haired gentleman smiled warmly and nodded to Lucy.

"Sir," she acknowledged softly, studying his strong-featured face. He could have been any age between forty and sixty, a handsome, dignified individual who immediately put her in mind of her beloved father. She liked him on sight.

"Evening, Colonel." Davey's ham-like white-gloved hand slid the elevator's folding inner door across the opening in preparation for the car's ascent. "You two know each other yet?" Davey asked before putting the elevator in motion.

"I've not had the pleasure," said the tall, silver haired gentleman and Lucy could tell by his slow, courteous speech that he was a southerner.

Beaming, Davey made the introductions.

Colonel Cort Mitchell, the neatly clipped mustache above his smiling pink lips a stark silver white against his sun darkened skin, took her hand in his, said, "Pleased to meet you, Miss Hart," and then said no more.

"My pleasure, Colonel Mitchell."

His keen gray eyes quickly discerning a touch of misery in her clear green gaze, he immediately wished he could fix whatever had gone wrong for her.

He said in a slow, gentle drawl, "May you enjoy every moment of your stay in Atlantic City, child."

"You're most kind, Colonel," Lucy replied, concealing from this gracious southern gentleman that there was little chance of that.

"Guess what Miss Hart is back in Colonias, Colonel," said Davey.

"Ah, that's too easy," said the Colonel diplomatically. His eyes and his manner warm, he smiled at Lucy and said, "One of the prettiest young ladies in town."

"Naw," Davey shook his sandy head, thought how that sounded, and quickly corrected himself. "I mean, yes, she's that, but that's not all. She's the postmistress!"

The car began to rise.

"And a most competent one, I'm sure," Colonel Mitchell said.

Both Davey and the silver haired Colonel wished Lucy a pleasant good evening when the elevator door opened at the third floor and she stepped out into the deserted corridor.

. And then Lucy was alone in her silent room.

She sighed wearily and kicked off the newly purchased kid slippers, which were pinching her toes. She wandered restlessly out onto the small balcony and inhaled deeply of the heavy, sea-scented night air.

She stood gripping the smooth white railing, leaning out, and looking down at the hotel's broad veranda with its empty wicker rockers moving slowly back and forth in the rising night winds. Her gaze slid over to the steep center steps where she had stood earlier with the incorrigible Blackie LaDuke.

A handsome couple stood there now in the exact same spot, in the same exact way. The young man below turned facing the girl who stood on bottom step. The skirts of her blue summer dress were billowing in

44

the breeze, wrapping around her companion's white trousered legs. The pair whispered and laughed as though they shared delightful secrets.

Lucy sighed again and looked away from the happy couple. She focused on the dark, restless ocean stretching to infinity in the pale moonlight. Foamy, white-capped breakers rolled in and splashed loudly on the Jersey shore. Voices and laughter carried on the night air as lively, lighthearted people strolled up and down the wooden Boardwalk and trod the sandy beaches below it.

Lucy felt an acute stab of loneliness.

She had so hoped that she and Mr. Mooney would be among their carefree number on this, her first night at the splendid seaside resort.

Now she wondered if it was to be her unfortunate fate to come and go from this romantic place without having done any of the exciting things the others took for granted.

Lucy's disappointment abruptly gave way to concern. What if something terrible had happened to Mr. Mooney? Suppose he had been in a disastrous train accident and even now as she stood here feeling sorry for herself they were freeing his limp, lifeless body from the twisted steel wreckage. Or what if he...

Oh, for heaven sake, now she was being downright irrational! Nothing bad had happened to Theodore D. Mooney. Had there been a train wreck, the news would have already reached Atlantic City. He probably missed his train and would be on a later one.

There was every possibility that he was speeding across Pennsylvania toward the Jersey Shore this very moment.

He would come.

She knew he would.

And then the long planned holiday could really begin.

CHAPTER SEVEN

Lucy slept fitfully.

She was glad when morning finally came and a bright new sun spilled into room 313 of the Atlantic Grand and across her face.

Her eyes opened and she lay totally still for a long moment examining the unfamiliar surroundings.

Hers was, even at the astronomical sum of five dollars per night, one of the more modestly priced of the Atlantic Grand's three hundred rooms. But it was a handsome, high ceilinged room nonetheless. The bed in which she lay was a large, sturdy four-poster canopied in yards and yards of gauzy white muslin.

Overhead, the thirteen-foot high ceiling sported artful fretwork embellishments--scrolls and cherubs and angels with harps. On the floor a hand loomed carpet of lush aqua wool was bordered with intricate patterns of ivory flowers abloom and white sea gulls in flight. Accenting the striped wallpaper of pale aqua and cream, a long, comfortable aqua sofa sat directly across from the bed. Two wicker-backed chairs with aqua cushions were on either side of the sofa.

A chest of drawers, which was taller than she, stood against the wall. At the room's center was a round drum table of gleaming cherry wood. A white porcelain vase sat atop the table, delicate, lovely, empty, crying out to be filled with a fragrant bouquet.

Lucy abruptly threw back the bed covers and rose. A degree of her former optimism returning, she hurriedly dressed, telling herself it was highly probable that Mr. Theodore D. Mooney was now a registered hotel guest. She'd be meeting him within the hour and he would explain what had happened and she would assure him no harm had been done and together they would laugh over the mix up.

Half an hour later Lucy, wearing a daffodil yellow cotton dress, her curly chestnut hair wound into a neat bun atop her head, left her sun-filled, third floor room. She moved hurriedly down the long hallway at a brisk, determined pace, her mood light once more, her hopes high.

At the elevator bank, she waited impatiently for the car. Toe tapping, she fidgeted nervously. She could hardly wait to get downstairs. What was keeping the elevator?

Finally a loud creaking of machinery and the heavy elevator door slid open. The muscular Davey was not on duty. She nodded almost imperceptibly to the short, bald, uniformed operator and stepped past him.

And found herself standing face to face with a disheveled, darkly whiskered Blackie LaDuke.

There was LaDuke leaning against the elevator's rear wall with his eyes shut, his hands in his trouser pockets, his dark head sagging forward onto his chest. He wore the same clothes as when she'd stood outside with him last night on the Atlantic Grand's rear steps.

Only now the hand tailored navy linen suit jacket had been removed and was tossed carelessly over his wide left shoulder. The wine silk tie was loosened and askew; the white shirt rumpled and unbuttoned half way down his dark chest.

There was a smudge of something that looked suspiciously like lip rouge on his unshaven jaw, a three corner tear in the knee of his fine, navy linen trousers, gritty grains of sand spilled from one turned down trouser cuff onto the floor of the elevator.

"Disgusting!" Lucy murmured to herself.

"I heard that," said Blackie and long sweeping lashes lifted over bloodshot dark eyes. He grinned. "Morning, Lucy. I trust you'll excuse me if I don't get up."

"You silly goose, you are up," she snapped, cutting her eyes at the elevator operator, hoping he didn't think she and Blackie LaDuke were actually acquainted.

"I am?" Blackie lifted his dark head with effort, looked curiously at her, and added, "Well, of course I am. I always rise for a lady."

Lucy rolled her eyes heavenward. The car lurched into movement. Lucy very nearly lost her balance. Blackie's slightly unfocused dark eyes widened. He reached out, grabbed her, pulled her flush against him, and declared, "Jesus God, hold on tight, Lucy. It's an earthquake!"

The balding elevator operator laughed.

Lucy did not.

Her jaw rigid, face flaming, she promptly pulled away, put her hands on her hips, and said acidly, "Mr. LaDuke, you obviously need a keeper, but you'll have to look elsewhere." She dramatically brushed herself off as if being next to him had contaminated her. "I have better things to do than suffer drunken fools."

"I am not drunk," he defended himself, taking no offense at being called a fool. "I'm just sleepy. May I lay my weary head on your shoulder?"

49

"Oh!" She whirled around, stood facing the front of the car. Over her shoulder she said, "Do me a favor, Mr. LaDuke."

"If I can," said Blackie and, grinning wickedly, puckered his wide full lips and blew ever so gently on the exposed nape of Lucy's delicate neck.

Lucy immediately lifted a hand to rub the back of her neck, unsure if she'd actually felt anything or if it was her imagination. She brushed at the sensitive flesh, lowered her hand, and continued to stare straight ahead. Behind her, Blackie's bloodshot black eyes twinkled.

He leaned a fraction closer, puckered, and blew a little more forcefully. A shudder ran through Lucy's slender frame. Her hand flew up, wrapped protectively around the back of her neck while her green eyes narrowed with growing suspicion.

Seconds passed.

Nothing happened.

Warily, she lowered her hand and spun about catching him just as Blackie was puckering again.

Her spread fingers smacked roughly over his puckered lips, surprising him, and, no longer concerning herself with what the elevator operator thought, Lucy said, "Back home in Colonias a four year old child lives next door to me and she is more mature than you." She withdrew her hand, rubbed her fingers on her skirt. "Isn't it time you gave some consideration to growing up and behaving like an adult?"

Before he could reply the car stopped at the ground floor and the operator threw the door open. Lucy marched grandly out into the crowded lobby, leaving Blackie calling after her, "The favor? What's the favor, Lucy? You forgot to ask me."

Ignoring him, Lucy headed directly to the front desk. A beak nosed man with bushy eyebrows and large prominent ears was on duty this morning. He looked up, smiled pleasantly.

"Are there any messages for Miss Lucy Hart of Colonias, New York. Room 313."

The desk clerk checked. "No, Miss. Nothing."

She gave him a weak smile. "Thank you."

Lucy swallowed hard. She mustn't panic. There was a simple explanation. Theodore would surely arrive before the day was over.

Lucy realized suddenly that she was famished. In the anxiety of last evening, she'd totally forgotten about dinner. She hadn't eaten a bite since arriving here yesterday afternoon. Lucy inquired where she would find the dining room and was directed down a wide hallway to the left of the reception desk, at the end of which she was to turn right and she would be there.

Lucy paused at the arched entrance to the immense dining hall, filled now with hungry guests enjoying sumptuous breakfasts. She was led to a table meant for two, which, to her dismay, was situated squarely in the center of the crowded room. Seated there alone, Lucy felt as if she was in a fishbowl, as though everyone was staring. Her appetite departed. After only a few forced bites of toast and jam and a half-cup of coffee, Lucy anxiously fled.

She again took up her station in the lobby, choosing a chair with a clear view of the hotel's front entrance. Pretending to be nonchalant and relaxed, Lucy sat waiting, hoping Theodore D. Mooney would walk through the revolving doors and make everything all right.

The long anxious hours of a day-long vigil had begun.

From her lookout post there in the elegant lobby, Lucy watched a steady stream of hotel guests come and go, but paid little attention to any of them.

There was only one guest for whom she diligently searched; only one person she hoped would walk into view. But an hour passed, then two, with no sign of Mr. Theodore D. Mooney.

Lucy was relieved and delighted to see a friendly face when, at shortly before twelve noon, the silver haired Colonel Cort Mitchell stepped off the elevator. The tall, distinguished southerner immediately spotted Lucy, smiled warmly, and came directly to her.

The Colonel, immaculate in a powder blue linen suit and sporting his ivory-headed cane, greeted her as if they were old friends. He sat down in the chair beside her, took the hand she offered, shook it gently, and asked why she wasn't outdoors enjoying the sun and the sea with rest of the young people. Lucy explained that she was waiting for someone. The Colonel smiled and nodded knowingly.

"And you, Sir?" Lucy politely inquired, "going out for a stroll on the Boardwalk?"

Colonel Mitchell shook his silver head. "No, not this morning, Lucy. May I call you Lucy, my dear?"

"I insist you do," she said. "To tell you the truth, I hate being called Miss Hart."

"Then Lucy it is," he said, releasing her hand. His fingertips idly tapping on the cane's ivory head, he told her, "I was just leaving for the train depot. I'm on my way into the city to spend a couple of days at a series of business meetings." Nodding, Lucy felt like begging him not to go. His authoritative bearing coupled with his natural southern friendliness drew her to him like a magnet. In his strong fatherly presence, she didn't feel so alone, so out of place and anxious. He was the kind of man you instinctively felt safe with. She was sorry he was leaving.

Lucy wondered if her thoughts showed on her face when, after a few brief minutes of polite small talk, the Colonel, looking earnestly at her, said in that slow, southern drawl, "My dear, I wish I didn't have to go. I hope you'll do me the honor of being my guest for dinner upon my return."

Lucy smiled at the handsome gentleman who bore such a striking resemblance to her dear, deceased father.

"I should be delighted to have dinner with you, Colonel Mitchell," she told him.

"Good, good," said the Colonel. "Now you take care of yourself, you hear?"

"I will," she promised.

Too soon he was gone and Lucy was again left very much alone in a crowd of strangers. Hunger drove her once more to the great dining hall at shortly after two that afternoon. She requested a less conspicuous table and was taken to one at the very back near the kitchen. It suited her fine.

On returning to the lobby she caught sight of a tall, black haired man in a cream colored suit. His back to her, he stood at the cigar counter. Lucy's heart slammed against her ribs. Adrenalin flooded her system. Her hopeful gaze fastened on him, she held her breath as he slowly turned, spotted her, and smiled.

Blackie LaDuke!

Lucy didn't bother acknowledging him. She turned her head quickly and hurried away, darting into the hotel's shelf-lined library where she chose a book at random, sat down, and stared at the pages.

Lucy checked the reception desk at least a dozen times during that endlessly long Monday afternoon. There were no messages for her. By nightfall she had finally given up.

She couldn't bear another hour of sitting alone in the lobby. Not with swarms of pretty women and successful looking men constantly exiting the elevator. Their laughter rang in her ears as they breezed through the lobby and out of the hotel. They seemed to be having such fun. Their excited chatter filled the lobby along with the pleasing scent of soap and perfume.

The night was young. The glamorous guests were obviously looking forward to an enchanting evening of dining and dancing and romance.

Lucy blushed when the doors of the busy elevator opened just as a tall man inside leaned down and kissed his female companion squarely on the lips. Embarrassed, Lucy quickly looked away, but couldn't resist stealing a glance as the couple passed her. The same pair she'd seen last night on the hotel steps.

The man was slim and handsome, a well-scrubbed, suntanned blond in a tailored white dinner jacket. The dark haired young woman was fresh and pretty in a shimmering evening gown of sky blue chiffon. They made such an extraordinarily attractive pair it was hard not to stare. A truly golden couple, they served as the perfect living advertisement of the place.

They didn't notice Lucy or anyone else.

Conspicuously in love, they had eyes only for each other. Hand in hand they floated across the spacious lobby and disappeared into the sultry summer night.

Lucy rose.

She went one last time to the front desk.

The beak nosed man with prominent ears was still on duty behind the marble counter. He looked up, smiled pleasantly, just as he had on each prior occasion.

Before she could ask, he said, not unkindly, "No, Miss Hart. No messages. I'm sorry."

"Thank you." She started to walk away, stopped, turned back. "Can you tell me if a guest has checked into the hotel?"

His eyebrows lifted. "It is against hotel policy to give out room number information."

"Yes, I understand that. I'm not asking for a room number. I only want to find out if a certain party has checked into the hotel." She smiled weakly.

"Very well," said the clerk. "What is her name and where is she from?"

"He," Lucy corrected. "The guest is a gentleman. He's Mr. Theodore D. Mooney from Cooperstown, Pennsylvania. Mr. Mooney was supposed to arrive around five o'clock yesterday afternoon, but I haven't seen him and I thought perhaps... Has he registered? Is he in the hotel?"

"I'll see." The clerk left her, carefully investigated his room reservation and occupancy records. He returned to the desk to tell Lucy that Mr. Theodore D. Mooney had sent a telegram canceling his reservations.

"No," Lucy murmured aloud, stunned. "Why would he...when? When did he cancel the reservation?"

"I believe the wire arrived late Saturday informing us to release his hold on the room."

"He isn't coming? He won't be arriving later? Perhaps someday this week? He made no other reservations?"

"No, Miss. Apparently Mr. Mooney won't be staying at the Atlantic Grand this season."

Her face pale, hands icy, Lucy nodded and turned numbly away. In a daze she wandered aimlessly across the lobby, forced to face the awful truth.

Theodore was not coming.

He had changed his mind. Gotten cold feet. He didn't want to meet her. He was *not* going to meet her.

And here she was stuck in this enchanting seaside resort. Alone. All by herself in a warm, sunny playground where everyone else was enjoying themselves. Everywhere she turned were carefree, laughing people. Men and women. Couples falling in love, holding hands, finding romance.

Everyone but her.

CHAPTER EIGHT

In the beautiful *City by the Sea*, a title that was greatly favored by Atlantic City, there was a vast wooden Boardwalk. It was the fifth and latest of its kind to be built at the popular oceanside resort.

The first Boardwalk was dedicated in the summer of 1870. Ten feet wide and a mile long, the promenade stretched from Congress Hall to the Excursion House. At season's end, the Boardwalk was taken apart and stored for the winter.

A new wooden path was laid down in 1880, a little longer, a little wider than the original. Four years later, a storm took the Boardwalk and everything on it.

A third was set on pilings five feet above the beach. The sea couldn't get this one. The tides could wash safely beneath it.

Wind, unfortunately, was a different story. A forceful hurricane completely wrecked the Boardwalk in September of 1889.

But by the following spring, a new improved Boardwalk appeared. Twenty-four feet wide, ten feet high, and nearly four miles long. A sturdy, permanent structure with railings on both sides, the Boardwalk became Atlantic City's main attraction.

The famed wooden walkway was so popular, an expanded fifth and final version appeared in 1896. The proud city fathers predicted the Boardwalk would last for 'at least a hundred years'.

Perhaps longer.

Along that forty foot wide, four-mile long Boardwalk were fifty-seven commercial bathhouses, ten amusement ride centers, eight sellers of saltwater taffy-- and no less than five hundred hotels.

But the finest of all, the undisputed glittering jewel in the crown of the seaside resort hotels, was the majestic, twin-towered Atlantic Grand. The Grand's treasured guest registry read like a Who's Who of noted Americans and Europeans. Presidents, potentates, millionaires and royalty had found comfort and luxury beneath its steep roof.

Rarely were there empty rooms in the Atlantic Grand. Even in the cold of winter when the sea was dark and the sky was gray, the big stately inn sheltered many illustrious guests.

Some came for a day.

Some came for a week.

Some came for the Season.

Some came for the rest of their lives.

Residing year round in the Atlantic Grand's south tower penthouse suite was a sixtyish, once beautiful woman known as Lady Strange. Divorced decades ago from Great Britain's powerful Lord William Strange, the woman was, on her wedding day, a tiny, five-foot doll-like creature weighing barely ninety pounds.

Now Lady Strange tipped the scales at one hundred ninety five pounds sans clothing. While her round face was as unlined and as pretty as ever, she was a mountain of quivering flesh that rippled with every struggling breath she drew.

Lady Strange spent most of her time in an oversized chair in her lavish penthouse parlor, gorging on goodies. She denied herself nothing. Rich chocolates and tempting pastries were always within reach of her small, pudgy, bejeweled hands.

She spoiled herself and she spoiled the huge, overweight black Persian cat whom she called Precious. When Lady Strange was not holding Precious or a bonbon, or both, she was studying tea leaves. Satisfied customers and fellow mystics swore Lady Strange could see into the future.

In a slightly smaller suite one floor below Lady Strange resided another permanent guest. The silver-haired, dignified, sixty-six year old Colonel Cort Mitchell was a native son of the Old South. Brevetted to Colonel for outstanding bravery in the War Between the States, the tall, dapper southerner was still addressed as Colonel out of respect.

Widowed twice, he lost both a son and two daughters in the New Orleans yellow fever outbreak of '75. Colonel Mitchell--now a successful broker representing Southern cotton interests on both sides of the Atlantic--was a charming, mannerly, much sought after escort for the hotel's middle-aged ladies. But he had no interest in romance.

At least not for himself.

Two floors below, on five, forty-two-year old Lochlin MacDonald was quietly living out his last days with as much dignity as he could muster. A former seaman, once vigorous and strapping, who had sailed all over the world, the painfully thin, wheel chair bound MacDonald never allowed his infirmity to slow him down. A warm, friendly man who loved to laugh, his mind was razor sharp, but his wasted body no longer heeded the commands sent by his brain to his withered extremities.

Lochlin MacDonald suffered from an incurable degeneration of the nerve cells that control most muscles. A team of physicians had told him that he would likely die of respiratory failure within two to four years.

And that bit of bad news had been given to him four years and three months ago.

In the face of his fatal illness, Lochlin MacDonald had vowed to live every minute of the time he had left. He did just that. A ready smile masking the pain that was his constant companion, Lochlin MacDonald never missed a single social event at the Atlantic Grand and a day never passed--winter, summer, spring, and fall--that the laughing Lochlin MacDonald couldn't been seen down on the Boardwalk.

An ever-changing roster of temporary guests included, on these last days of the season, a pair of starry-eyed young newlyweds from Pittsburgh. A prominent New York City physician and his sour, complaining wife. A loud, boisterous family of eight-- the mother and all six children had flaming red hair-- were crowded into two connecting rooms. A wealthy railroader. A hypochondriac banker on three. A fading stage actor on six. A petty thief. A circus clown. A recluse writer.

The Atlantic Grand Hotel was completely sold out and full at the height of this waning summer season.

But one guest room remained empty.

The room which had been reserved months in advance by Mr. Theodore D. Mooney of Cooperstown, Pennsylvania.

CHAPTER NINE

So Lucy Hart was alone.

Alone at mealtime in the huge paneled dining room. Alone at a table meant for two. Alone on a visit to the souvenir shop next door. Alone on the crowded Boardwalk while laughing lovers passed by in the wicker rolling chairs. Alone in her third floor room after dark.

Lucy was alone and that was nothing new. But here in this sun drenched resort, which existed solely for play and for pleasure, it was somehow much worse to be alone than it was back home in Colonias. Being alone here made her feel lost and lonelier than she had ever been in her entire life.

Lucy was not just lonely; she was humiliated as well. She just knew that she stuck out like a sore thumb, as if the words *old maid* were stamped on her forehead in bright red letters for the entire world to see. Was it her imagination, or had she detected something like sympathy in the passing glances of some hotel guests? If there was one thing she couldn't stand it was the thought of people feeling sorry for her.

On Tuesday afternoon, after two incredibly long wretched days--and even longer, more wretched nights-- Lucy began to seriously consider cutting her failed holiday short and returning home at once. It made no sense to stay on here and be unhappy.

She was deliberating on the very real possibility of leaving on the Wednesday afternoon train when she went down for dinner that Tuesday evening.

***

Since his Sunday afternoon arrival in Atlantic City, Blackie LaDuke had diligently cast an eye about for suitable female companionship and had found no one that struck his fancy.

Sauntering through the lobby of the elegant hotel a half dozen times each day, the handsome thirty-three year old Blackie turned heads, attracted attention.

Including Lucy's.

There was a roguish aura about him, an air of adventure, which made him impossible to ignore. But Lucy held herself aloof, was pointedly chilly, did not return his friendly waves and warm smiles.

Blackie was mildly amused by her haughty scorn. He was not amused to see that she was still very much alone. She was, he could tell, attempting to appear at ease and in charge, but she failed miserably. Bless her heart, she looked frightened, forlorn, and woefully out of place.

Despite all her best efforts to appear poised, her manner was almost diffident. When she walked through the lobby she seemed almost to apologize for herself.

Wondering what had happened to her Mr. Mooney, Blackie hated to think that she had been stood up. Left out in the cold in this warm summer place. The sight of her looking lost and alone evoked long buried memories of his first frightening days at boarding school.

Lucy Hart was very much on his mind when, at shortly after eight that Tuesday evening, Blackie realized he was hungry and went down for dinner. He paused in the open arched doorway of the filled dining hall, looked about impatiently. The captain came up to him; Blackie smiled and waved him away.

Strains from a string quartet mingled with subdued laughter and the clink of crystal. Waiters dressed in starched white jackets and dark trousers moved with silence and grace, huge silver, serving platters balanced on their raised hands. Families sat at large, round tables. Couples at small square ones.

Squinting his darkly lashed eyes, Blackie spotted, across the crowded hall, Lucy Hart. She was seated at a table for two.

Alone.

From where he stood he could see that she was as stiff as a poker. So uncomfortable, so utterly miserable it was a wonder she could digest her dinner. It was a painful to witness her distress. His mood immediately became somber. He needed a drink. A stiff drink. He exhaled, frowned, and shook his dark head.

Then all at once a smile came to his lips.

Blackie walked into the dinning room and made his way directly to Lucy Hart's table, fully aware that everyone was watching. He reached the small, square, white-clothed table, smiled warmly, leaned down, and kissed the startled Lucy's cheek.

He said, loudly enough for half the room to hear, "Sorry I'm late, dear. Forgive me?"

He pulled out a chair, sat down opposite the surprised Lucy, shook out a white dinner napkin, and draped it across his knee while flabbergasted guests stared and whispered and Lucy Hart turned crimson.

Blackie leaned up close to the table, grasped Lucy's icy hand, and favored her with a smile, which was full of confident charm.

A raffish glint in his night-black eyes, he said in a low, warm whisper, "What do you say we do the town after dinner?"

Aware that many of the diners, especially the ladies, were staring at the two of them, Lucy disengaged her hand from his as unobtrusively as possible, forced herself to smile for the benefit of their audience, and said so softly only he could hear, "Is there no end to your brashness and bad manners? It's obvious that you are not aware of even the most rudimentary arts of social intercourse."

Blackie shrugged wide shoulders and grinned. "Is that anything like sexual intercourse?"

Lucy's breath came out in a rush as if someone at socked her in the stomach. Her green eyes widened with shock, then narrowed with anger. She longed to shout her outrage at him, but knew she couldn't without making a spectacle of herself.

She said through clenched teeth, "I do *not* have to tolerate the company of a man whose primary characteristic is coarseness."

"No, you don't," he said, leaning back in his chair in an attitude of total relaxation, "leave if you like. I'm staying." He raised a long arm in the air, motioned a waiter over while saying to Lucy, "You don't really dislike me, do you, Lucy?"

"If I gave you any thought I'm sure I would."

He laughed. "Well, now that the unpleasantries have been exchanged, tell me what's good this evening. The roast beef? The halibut? I'm famished."

Lucy didn't know quite what to do. She had never dealt with a man like Blackie LaDuke. She had made it clear she did not want his company, but he refused to behave the gentleman and leave. If she got up and stalked out, she would draw even more attention to herself and that was the last thing she wanted.

As if he had read her thoughts, the devilish Blackie winked at her and said, "Face it, you're trapped. Might as well relax and enjoy yourself."

Glancing furtively about, Lucy leaned across the table, and whispered, "What is it with you, Mr. LaDuke? What do you want with me?"

"I don't know yet, Lucy," Blackie replied, his black eyes twinkling, "what have you got?"

Lucy expelled an exasperated breath. "What I *don't* have is the time or the patience to endure any more of your vulgar nonsense!" She tossed her napkin down on the table.

"Stay right where you are or I'll make an awful scene," he warned, all the while wearing a wide, charming smile.

Lucy sighed and her slender shoulders slumped. "Why are you doing this to me, Mr. LaDuke?"

"Because, Lucy," Blackie leaned back up to the table, again reached for her hand, "you need a little fun in your life whether you want it or not."

Innate pride made her instantly defensive. "I'll have you know that I don't need you to teach me how to have fun. I have plenty of fun."

Blackie arrogantly predicted, "You're going to have even more with me."

Lucy shook her head and gave him a withering look. "Forgive me for saying this, but you, LaDuke, are a conceited ass."

"You're forgiven."

CHAPTER TEN

Lucy Hart had scrimped and saved and treated herself to this trip and to an extended stay at the Atlantic Grand, one of the most regal hotels in country. It was out of character, but she deserved it.

Or so she had told herself.

Now she was here and Theodore D. Mooney wasn't and there seemed to be no point in her staying. She would have to pack up and go right back home where she belonged. Where she should have stayed in the first place.

Tomorrow morning, soon as she got up, she would go down to the depot and see about purchasing a rail ticket. Hopefully she could get booked on an afternoon or evening train and get out of here.

Lucy inwardly cringed.

It was going to be terribly embarrassing to return to Colonias early. While no one knew *where* she was, quite a number knew that she was gone and was supposed to stay gone for two whole weeks. She wasn't due back until after Labor Day. What would they think, what would they say when she showed up at home after only a few days. Well, nothing could be as bad as staying on here alone.

She would go home.

"The only sensible thing to do," Lucy assured herself as she crawled into bed that Tuesday night.

It *was* the sensible thing to do. She knew that, but she sighed wistfully.

She hadn't slipped off to Atlantic City to behave sensibly. She hadn't saved and planned and dreamed for months, only to come here and be her old sensible self. She had spent a lifetime being sensible. Surely she deserved a couple of weeks of being frivolous.

Lucy lay awake in the patterned moonlight spilling into her third floor hotel room weighing the pros and cons of leaving Atlantic City immediately. Still undecided as midnight came and went, her thoughts drifted from the train and home and the absent Mr. Mooney to her unexpected, uninvited dinner companion, the cocky Blackie LaDuke.

Lucy made a face.

Blackie LaDuke was as opposite from her as night was from day. He had probably never done anything sensible in his entire life. His kind never had to. The Blackies of this world never bothered to concern themselves with mundane little matters like earning an honest living or making a home or contributing to the good of the community.

Everything was a nonsensical game to Blackie La Duke, including his decision to join her at dinner tonight. It did no good to point out that no invitation had been extended, that she did not wish to have him seated at her table. He just grinned and refused to leave. And he wouldn't allow her to leave.

She was forced to sit there and smile and nod and act civil throughout the lengthy, five-course meal he ordered. LaDuke--the cruel devil--had teased her unmercifully, making her squirm and blush and threaten him under her breath.

If that was not enough, when finally the agonizingly long dinner was over, he invited her to take a stroll on the Boardwalk. She gave him quick, resounding no and hoped that would be the end of it.

"Good night, Mr. LaDuke," she said, none too sweetly, as they exited the near empty dining hall well after ten o'clock.

"I'll see you to your room, Lucy," he told her and placed a proprietorial hand at the small of her back.

"That will not be necessary," she informed him, attempting to shrug from his amazingly warm touch.

But Blackie grinned and curled his fingers around the wide, lace-trimmed belt of her green, dotted swiss dress. He pulled her close against his side and said softly into her ear, "Lucy, Lucy...isn't it time you try something is that isn't necessarily necessary?"

Momentarily flustered, Lucy felt a hint of a chill skip up her spine from his overwhelming nearness.

She quickly regained her equilibrium and replied in low, level tones, "Mr. LaDuke, I'm sure scores of ladies are charmed by your adolescent conduct, otherwise you surely wouldn't continue to behave like a mentally underdeveloped delinquent." She shook her head piteously and gave him a patronizing look. "I, however, am not one of that number. The truth is I find you and your crude childish conduct totally intolerable."

The devilish twinkle never dimmed in Blackie's dark eyes. "So...do you want to go for a walk or not?"

"Oh, for heaven sake!" Lucy frowned at him. "No! The answer is no. Do you understand plain English? No, definitely not!"

"Hey, I can take a hint," Blackie said, still wearing an easy grin. "Maybe tomorrow night." He began gently propelling her across the main lobby toward the elevator.

Lucy balked. Stopping stubbornly in the center of the lobby, she again said, "Goodnight, Mr. LaDuke."

"I'll see you up to your room," Blackie replied. Lucy opened her mouth, but before she could speak he said, "I know, I know. It isn't necessary. But I'm doing it just the same."

She knew it was no use to argue.

They moved to the elevator, waited. Momentarily the elevator door opened and Davey, the young, muscular operator, greeted them with a wide grin and wider eyes. His surprise at seeing the two of them together was written all over his open, boyish face.

Lucy saw it.

So did Blackie.

And what did demonic Blackie LaDuke do? As soon as they were inside the elevator he grabbed Lucy up, drew her intimately close, and purposely said in a whisper loud enough for Davey to hear, "Sweetheart, where do want to spend tonight? Your room or my suite?"

Horrified, Lucy quickly looked from Blackie to Davey. The burly youth had turned to stare straight ahead, but his ears were a bright pink. He was, Lucy supposed, almost as embarrassed as she.

"You lunatic!" she said, furiously shoving the smiling Blackie away.

Anxiously she stepped up beside the burly Davey, touched his massive shoulder, and said, "Davey, I hope you don't actually believe that..."

"Why, Lucy," Davey interrupted, glancing at her, "I didn't hear a thing, not a thing, so help me I didn't." His Adam's apple moved up and down as he swallowed nervously. "And anyway, it's none of my business how you and Blackie spend your evening."

"See what you've done!" Lucy whirled about to glare at Blackie. "You can just explain to Davey that you were making one of your futile attempts at being amusing!"

Blackie, leaning nonchalantly against the back of the car with his arms folded over his chest, nodded his dark head. "If you say so, dearest."

"I say so!" Lucy hissed and hastily turned back to face the closed elevator door.

Blackie's arms came unfolded. He leisurely pushed away from the elevator wall, stepped quietly forward and, catching Lucy totally off guard, slipped his long arms around her slender waist, clasped his wrists in front of her, and drew her back against his tall frame.

He said to Davey as the car came to a jerking stop at floor three, "You won't tell anybody about us, will you, Davey, my man?"

"No, sir, Blackie," Davey promised and threw the heavy door open wide.

"There's nothing to tell!" Lucy's voice was shrill and her hands were plucking savagely at Blackie's enfolding arms. "You tell him the truth, Blackie LaDuke!"

Blackie grinned, winked at Davey, and quickly urged the angry, mortified Lucy out into the empty third floor corridor. The elevator door closed on the smiling Davey.

"Let me go this minute!" Lucy ordered frantically. Blackie immediately released her. Furious, she spun about to face him. "Why did you do that?"

"Do what?" Blackie turned innocent dark eyes on her.

"You purposely lead Davey to believe that you and I are...are...that we..." She couldn't finish. Her face was red, her cheeks burning hot.

"I was just having a little fun." He shrugged. "No harm done."

"No harm done? No harm done! You ruin my reputation and then you tell me..."

"Lucy, calm down. Please." Blackie's voice was almost tender when he added, "Davey knows I was joking."

"How could he know? He couldn't! He doesn't and I'll never be able to look him in the eye again or..."

"He knows because he knows me. He knows better than to pay any attention my foolishness." Blackie's smile changed, became the reassuring kind. "Honest, he didn't believe me. I never meant for him to believe me."

Still skeptical, but calming a little, hoping it was true, Lucy said, "You're sure?"

"Absolutely positive."

She exhaled loudly with relief and her tensed shoulders lowered. She turned away from Blackie, started down the silent corridor toward her room. Blackie looked after her, smiled, shook his dark head, then easily caught up with her.

At her door, he said casually, "You going to ask me in?"

Lucy stared at him, incredulous. "Mr. LaDuke, your refusal to take anything seriously is really tiresome. As matter of fact, *you* are tiresome." She put her key in the lock, turned it, and opened the door. "And I am tired. Now goodnight!"

"You have," he said, grinning, "managed to hurt my feelings."

"That's surely a first," she replied bitingly, swept inside, and started to close the door.

Blackie's hand shot out, flattened on the solid oak of the heavy door, and held it ajar. "So...what do you want to do tomorrow?"

Lucy glared at him for a long moment, then finally she laughed. Shaking her head, she said, "To stay as far away from you as possible."

Then she shut the door in his face.

* * *

Thinking back on it now, as she lay sleepless in the silvery summer moonlight, Lucy smiled foolishly and felt her face suddenly grow warm.

What, she wondered idly, might have happened had she allowed the devilish Blackie LaDuke to come inside?

Lucy immediately laughed at herself, knowing the answer to her question. Nothing would have happened. Not a thing.

Blackie LaDuke had known all along that she wouldn't allow him to come inside; therefore he was perfectly safe in suggesting she invite him in. It was presumptuous and silly of her to suppose that he would actually want to come into her room.

She had taken leave of her senses if she for one moment imagined that such an impressively handsome man as Blackie LaDuke, sophisticated in the ways of the world and sought after by scores of eligible women, could be the least bit interested in a stuffy, straight-laced, less-than-beautiful old maid postmistress.

Thank the good Lord.

CHAPTER ELEVEN

In her lavish South tower penthouse suite on that warm Tuesday evening, the one hundred ninety-five pound Lady Strange waited impatiently for a late night visitor.

Lady Strange was dressed for the occasion in a lush, loose fitting robe of vivid, ruby red velvet. On her small feet were satin bedroom slippers trimmed with ostrich feathers. In her carefully coiffured dark hair a wide ruby velvet band was decorated with luminous pearls and on both plump wrists pearl and diamond bracelets flashed. Diamond rings graced her short fingers.

At exactly five feet in height, Lady Strange was as broad as she was tall. Her unfettered breasts were enormous; her short arms like small hams. Belly like a dome, thighs that quivered and danced and were continuously chapped from rubbing together when she walked.

Her face, as round and unlined as a baby's, was freshly powdered and painted; the small mouth stained a ruby red to match her velvet dressing gown. Her hair was a dark, lustrous mahogany with not one single strand of gray. Her crowning glory, the thick luxuriant locks fell to her waist when unrestrained.

The obese Lady Strange sat sprawled in her favorite easy chair in the antique- and art-filled penthouse parlor. With legs far to short and fat to cross, she sat with her dimpled knees wide apart while her plump, velvet, covered buttocks--like fattening shoats--overflowed the chair.

On her ample lap, watching every move she made, lay the corpulent, black, long-haired cat she had named Precious. Sensually the cat arched its back and its sharp claws appeared on the ruby velvet of Lady Strange's robe. Lady Strange cooed and giggled and caressed the cat, but the cat was having none of it. He turned cold, slitted golden eyes on her and made low demanding moans in the back of his throat.

"You lazy boy," scolded Lady Strange. "You just get it yourself."

The black cat fixed her with a chilly stare.

She giggled.

"Oh, very well, Precious. If you insist. Mama will feed her bad boy."

Lady Strange reached short, diamond-bedecked fingers out to the small silver platter. With thumb and forefinger she picked up a chunk of fresh salmon and presented it to the cat. The greedy cat snatched the dripping salmon from her, choked it hurriedly down, licked her fat fingers clean, and promptly made the same demanding sound in his throat.

Precious wanted more.

Lady Strange smiled and wagged her painted face back and forth and shook her short, fat finger at the cat. "You'll just have to wait your turn. Mama's hungry too."

And ignoring the snarls of the impatient Persian, Lady Strange reached the same fingers with which she had fed him into a nearly empty box of clotted cream candies, chose a piece, picked it up, and popped it into her red mouth while the cat watched.

Rolling her blue eyes with relish, she immediately reached for another chunk of salmon, fed the fussy feline who was so impossibly spoiled he refused to eat if his fat mistress did not hand-feed him.

She always did.

Eccentric and almost as spoiled as the jewel-collared cat, Lady Strange led a secure, pampered existence. A nocturnal creature by nature, she spent most of her waking hours in this elegant penthouse parlor with its priceless paintings and antique furniture and cherished photos and mementoes of her glorious youth.

Lady Strange was not unhappy, nor was she lonely. An interesting conversationalist and an attentive listener who was always ready to hear a good story, she welcomed a steady stream of visitors into her parlor.

A celebrated reader of tea leaves, she vowed she could look into the future and many an eager believer sought her fortune telling services.

Besides the many patrons and a wide circle of casual acquaintances from around the globe, Lady Strange had a handful of very dear friends of whom she was especially fond.

One of those was the quintessential southern gentleman, Colonel Cort Mitchell, who lived, as she did, in the Atlantic Grand. The two of them had been close since the first week the Colonel had moved into the Atlantic Grand some eight years ago. A gentle, intelligent man, Cort Mitchell rarely allowed a day to go by without calling on her.

Another treasured friend was the wheel chair bound Lochlin MacDonald. Then there were the Langfords, an aging, devoted couple who lived on the second floor. And her patient, caring physician, Doctor

Haney. A couple of widow ladies from the small inn next door. The Atlantic Grand's middle-aged assistant manager, Timothy Stone.

And her favorite of all, a lovable, bad boy whom she didn't get to see nearly enough, the handsome New Yorker, Blackie LaDuke.

Lady Strange had known Blackie since the days when he was a shy, adorable little boy and she was the tiny, doll-like wife of the British aristocrat, Lord William Strange. The two of them had remained friends after Blackie was ostracized by his influential family and she divorced by the restless, roving-eyed Lord Billy.

Lady Strange had gotten wind of Blackie's arrival within hours of his checking into the hotel. She had sent word that he had better not wait too long to come up if he knew what was good for him. His reply had been delivered along with the large, satin covered box of clotted creams, which she had just polished off. The card said she was to expect him 'Tuesday at the stroke of midnight'.

Lady Strange had spent the evening primping and preparing herself for Blackie's anticipated visit. And now the appointed hour was at hand.

Lady Strange glanced at the ornate gold clock on the marble fireplace mantle. She immediately snapped her short plump fingers and ordered the startled Precious to get down off her lap. The over-weight black Persian gave her a ferocious look, hissed meanly, but leapt down and strolled regally from the room without looking back.

Groaning and struggling, Lady Strange managed--with effort--to get up out of her easy chair. Puffing as she waddled about, she anxiously tidied the parlor, clearing away Precious's empty silver dish and the empty candy box.

Then she tidied herself.

She plucked long black cat hairs off the ruby velvet dressing gown as she went into her silk walled boudoir. There she washed her soiled hands thoroughly, dusted her shiny nose with a new coat of powder, checked her carefully dressed dark hair, and then spritzed herself generously with the scandalously expensive perfume Colonel Mitchell had brought her from his last trip abroad.

Lady Strange was back in the spacious parlor and seated in her chair when she heard the knock. Her fat, baby face immediately breaking into a wide grin of pleasure, she stayed where she was, carefully arranging her ruby velvet dressing gown and folding her hands atop her dome-like belly in an attempt to appear regal.

She called out, "If it's Blackie, come on in. If it's somebody else, come back in the morning."

Blackie came through the door laughing.

"Blackie, my sweet Blackie," Lady Strange greeted him warmly; her short arms lifted and outstretched, beckoning to him. "Come here to me!"

Blackie crossed to her, put a hand on each arm of her easy chair, leaned down, kissed her fleshy cheek, and said against her small pink ear, "You look like a million dollars unspent."

"Oh, you shameless flatterer," she said, fondly pressing her powdered cheek to his.

"Tell me this, sweetheart," said Blackie, "is it my imagination, or is there more here to love than the last time I saw you?"

Lady Strange giggled good-naturedly, pushed him away, and said, "If I've gained a pound or two, it's your fault!" Blackie straightened and smiled down at her as she accused, "Sending me that enormous box of delicious clotted creams! Blackie, honey, you know I can't resist clotted creams."

"And why in the world should you?" said Blackie, backing away, dropping agilely down onto the comfortable white sofa across from her. "Good god, can't a girl have a piece of candy?" Smiling broadly, he leaned back and made himself comfortable.

"This girl sure can," Lady Strange said, patting her fat belly. "Now, what can I get you, Blackie? Bourbon? Scotch? A glass of Rosé?"

Blackie stopped smiling. He screwed up his face as if thinking, finally said, "Mmmmm, I believe I'll just have a couple of pieces of that clotted cream candy." He grinned then, his black eyes twinkling with devilment.

Lady Strange made a mean face at him. "You know very well there is none."

"What? No candy left?" Blackie's heavy black eyebrows shot up as if he was shocked. "You've already devoured that entire five pound box of..."

"And what of it?" she cut in. "I had a light dinner. I needed a little nourishment if I was to stay up this late."

Blackie chuckled at her lame excuse. Lady Strange stayed up late every night, had for as long as he'd known her.

"Want me to hop down to the kitchen and see about a roast beef sandwich to tide you over until breakfast?"

Blue-white diamonds flashed as Lady Strange waved a dismissive hand. "Don't be getting smart with me as soon as you're back in town!" She pointed toward the liquor cabinet and inclined her head. "Pour me a glass of apricot brandy and let's talk."

Lady Strange sipped her sweet brandy and accepted a cigarette from the silver case Blackie withdrew from the inside breast pocket of his dark suit jacket. He struck a match with his thumbnail, held the tiny flame to her cigarette as she puffed it anxiously to life.

Blowing out a great cloud of smoke, then plucking the lighted cigarette from her ruby red lips, Lady Strange quickly warned, "You're not to tell a soul about this. It wouldn't do for people to know I smoke cigarettes like some common strumpet."

"And cigars," Blackie blithely reminded her, lifting the still burning match to his own cigarette.

"Oh, hush up," she said, waving the cigarette at him. She leaned back in her chair, attempted to press her dimpled knees together beneath the flowing velvet robe, and said, "Sit down and tell me about yourself. Where's that haughty, blond, Park Avenue socialite? What's her name? Tillie? Millie? I can't seem to remember."

"Lilly. You know very well that her name is Lilly Styvestant. She's not with me. I'm very much alone."

A well-arched eyebrow lifted. Lady Strange said, "Why, you must be losing your touch, Blackie, my boy." She clicked her tongue against the roof of her mouth. "In Atlantic City for more than forty eight hours and still without a lover?" Smiling naughtily, she puffed on her cigarette, blinking as the smoke drifted up into her eyes.

"Feel sorry for me?"

She laughed and so did he.

They continued to laugh and talk for the next couple of hours. Catching each other up on all the news, they interrupted one another often, talking at once, firing questions and supplying answers.

Inquiring about everyone, Blackie said, "I saw Lochlin down on the Boardwalk yesterday afternoon.

He looked awfully pale to me, but said he was feeling good. He alright?"

The smile never left Lady Strange's round face as she nodded. She and Colonel Mitchell--nobody else-- knew that the cheerful, wheel chair imprisoned Lochlin MacDonald would not live to see another summer, likely wouldn't last until Christmas. Both had promised Lochlin, who abhorred being pitied, that they wouldn't tell anyone.

"Ah, Lochlin's fine," she said now. "He needs to get more sun."

Finally Blackie, yawning sleepily, glanced at the ornate gold clock on the mantle. Half past two. He rose from the sofa, stretched lazily, and refused to listen when Lady Strange protested his leaving.

"You're not going! You just got here. Please, stay a while, Blackie."

Blackie stifled a yawn, crossed to her, put out a hand and--with effort--drew the mountainous little woman to her feet.

"Can't. Walk me to the door," he said. "I need some sleep. I'm awfully tired."

Lady Strange immediately let him know she knew everything that went on in the big hotel. "I would imagine you are a little tired," she said pointedly. "Staying out all night both Sunday and Monday."

They had reached the door. Blackie turned to face her. He plucked a long ebony cat hair from the shoulder of her ruby red dressing gown. "I see you still have that spoiled tom." He frowned.

"Don't change the subject. You stayed out all night..."

"You're a busybody, Lady Strange."

"Clairvoyant," she corrected. "For instance, I know that you had dinner this evening with a reasonably attractive, but rather retiring postmistress from Colonias, New York." She laid a plump spread hand on Blackie's white shirtfront, looked up at him with questioning blue eyes. "I wouldn't suppose that a woman like Miss Hart would by your type." She waited for him to speak. Blackie said nothing, just smiled easily at her and remained maddeningly silent. "So...?" she prompted.

"So...what?"

Exasperated, she said, "So, what's the story, Blackie? What's going on?"

"You're the fortune teller," he said with a teasing grin. "Read your tea leaves."

CHAPTER TWELVE

Wednesday morning.

Lucy had decided.

She would return home as soon as she could. This afternoon if possible. There was no earthly reason for her to stay on in Atlantic City and squander away even more of her hard earned money.

Lucy's green eyes narrowed as she considered the cost of her failed adventure. The round trip train fare, the steamboat charges, the expensive hotel room, the clothes she had purchased specifically to wear at the oceanside resort.

In particular, the exorbitantly priced, white tulle evening gown, which would have no place back in Colonias.

Her initial disappointment at Theodore D. Mooney's puzzling failure to keep their long planned engagement had turned to resentment and anger. If she could just get her hands around Theodore's throat, she would...

A knock on the door startled Lucy.

She dropped a carefully folded, lawn nightgown into an open valise and frowned, puzzled. She moved dubiously toward the closed door.

Reaching it, she said, "Yes? Who is it?"

"Benny the bellhop, Miss Hart. I have something for you."

Curious, Lucy opened the door. The smartly uniformed Benny smiled broadly at her.

"Good morning to you," he said brightly and presented her with a long white box tied with a wide blue ribbon.

"For me? What's this?" she said, staring at the box, then at the beaming Benny. "I don't understand."

"Looks like flowers to me," he said, bowed, and began backing away.

"But I...wait, Benny, I have some coins in my..."

"Keep your money," he said, waving a gloved hand as he hurried away.

Lucy closed the door. She untied the blue ribbon, took the lid of the long white box, and pushed aside the green tissue paper. Her emerald eyes grew round and she stared unbelieving at a dozen freshly cut ivory gardenias.

Her heartbeat quickened.

Who but Theodore D. Mooney would be sending her gardenias?

Lucy anxiously placed the open box on the cherry wood drum table, searched for an enclosed card, and found it tucked inside. She tore the small envelope open with shaking hands and read the brief message.

I enjoyed last night's dinner. So did you.

Admit it.

Blackie

Lucy couldn't keep from smiling.

She shook her head, laid the card aside, and lifted the fragrant bouquet of velvety petaled gardenias from the tissue-lined box. She placed the flowers in the delicate porcelain vase on the table and arranged the blossoms with an artist's eye, then stood back to admire them.

She was carefully pouring water into the vase to keep the gardenias fresh when the thought struck her that this was the first time in her entire life a gentleman had sent her flowers. Lucy smilingly corrected herself.

Blackie La Duke was no gentleman.

All the same it was flattering and pleasurable to receive a bouquet of fresh cut flowers from a member of the opposite sex and it seemed a terrible shame that she wouldn't be staying to enjoy them. She would check out of the Atlantic Grand early this afternoon and the maid who came to clean the room would dispose of the beautiful gardenias.

Well, it couldn't be helped.

There was no time for sentimentality; she had things to do. First on the agenda was a dash down to the Boardwalk stalls to hunt for an Atlantic City souvenir for sweet little Annie Widner.

Annie was an adorable child and Lucy cherished the four-year old almost most as much as Annie's parents. Lucy was grateful to Bruce and Kitty for sharing their loveable daughter with her. The happy, golden-curled little girl had brought a world of sunshine into Lucy's well-ordered life.

The gardenias momentarily forgotten as she considered what might be the ideal trinket to take home to Annie, Lucy decided she'd finish her packing later. She glanced toward the doors standing open to her tiny balcony. A strong, bright sun was shining down from a cloudless summer blue sky.

Lucy put a floppy brimmed straw hat on her head, tilted it slightly down over her face, took up her reticule, and left the gardenia scented room.

Downstairs in the lobby she looked anxiously around to make sure Blackie LaDuke wasn't lurking about, ready to tease and torment her. Actually there was little danger of running into the charming rascal. After all, this hour of the morning was Blackie LaDuke's bedtime.

Lucy automatically went to the registration desk and checked for messages. Wondering why she had bothered, she headed for the double doors at the back of the main lobby. She stepped out onto the wide veranda, paused, drew a deep breath of the fresh sea air, and looked out at the awesome Atlantic.

She suppressed a sigh and started down the steep steps to the Boardwalk. And stopped short midway down. Her lips fell open in astonishment.

At the base of the steps Blackie LaDuke stood leaning against the banister, smoking a cigarette. He looked wide awake and as fresh as a daisy in starched white duck trousers and a close fitting summer shirt of pale blue cotton. A coconut straw boater sat atop his head, the stiff brim pulled low over his dark dancing eyes.

"Well, look what the tide's brought in," Blackie said, grinning as he pushed the boater's brim back, releasing a shock of thick raven hair. "If it's not Lucy with the light brown hair."

He began to sing Foster's ballad, *Jeannie With the Light Brown Hair*, substituting Lucy's name.

Passersby slowed and stared.

"Will you stop it!" Lucy said, glancing around, embarrassed. She hurried down to him, "Shhhh!"

Blackie stopped in mid-lyric. He pushed away from the banister, dropped his cigarette, and crushed it out beneath his left shoe.

He said cheerily, "Where we going this morning?"

"In opposite directions!" Lucy told him frostily, stepping past him, and marching off down the Boardwalk.

Blackie easily caught up and fell into step with her. "Lucy, I hate to have to say this, but I'm a little disappointed in you."

"If you're expecting me to ask why," she told him with a dismissive glance, "you'll again be disappointed."

Blackie laughed. "I like you, Lucy Hart, damned if I don't. So I've decided to forgive your rudeness at not acknowledging the gardenias I sent and go on as though you properly thanked me for my thoughtfulness."

They were out on the busy, four-mile long Boardwalk now, passing musicians, jugglers, and street entertainers.

"You may go on any way you please, Mr. LaDuke," Lucy's tone was biting, "so long as it isn't with me."

And so saying, Lucy hurried ahead and ducked into the open door of a small souvenir shop. She stayed in the shop for several minutes, looking over the myriad variety of merchandise, hunting a memento for Annie Widner.

She finally chose a large beautiful pink seashell with Atlantic City, New Jersey painted on it in bright blue enamel letters. Lucy walked out of the store with her treasure and was half surprised to see that Blackie LaDuke was not waiting there for her.

She shrugged slender shoulders and was ready to start back to the Atlantic Grand when she caught sight of Blackie several yards on down the Boardwalk. He must have felt her eyes on him because he looked up and motioned for her to join him.

He stood in a small gathering of people before a man seated in a hospital chair directly beside a large standing scale. As Lucy watched, a brawny sailor stepped up before the man in the chair, slowly turned about in a circle.

The wheelchair bound man looked keenly at the big sailor, sizing him up, then said loudly, "Two hundred thirty-two pounds."

The sailor stepped up onto the tall Toledo scales. The black needle on the large white face of the standing scale zipped over to two hundred thirty-two pounds. And stopped.

Laughter and applause erupted as Lucy, intrigued, ventured closer. His coconut straw boater gone, black hair ruffling in the breeze, Blackie hurried to her, took her elbow, and said, "I want to introduce you to an old friend." Blackie waited a moment or two until the crowd thinned and cleared out, then steered Lucy forward. "Lochlin, may I present Lucy Hart. Lucy, say hello my old pal, Lochlin MacDonald."

"Mr. MacDonald," Lucy said, reaching out to shake his hand.

"A real pleasure, Lucy," he said and she could tell he attempted to firmly grip her hand, but failed.

His smile was as warm as the August sunshine but he was delicately built and his skin had a gray, wax like pallor. A long sleeved shirt concealed his arms and a lightweight lap robe covered his legs and feet.

"Lochlin can guess your age right on the money," Blackie boasted.

Lucy smiled. "Oh, Really? Just how old am I, Mr. MacDonald," she asked, taking off her floppy brimmed bonnet so he could he get a good look at her face.

"That's too easy," Lochlin MacDonald was graciously flattering, "you can't be a day over twenty four."

"Why it's uncanny," Lucy exclaimed, as if believing he meant it. Then she laughed and said, "that's close enough. No second guesses allowed!"

"Let him guess your weight," Blackie prodded. "He can come within two pounds, I promise."

"No kidding?" Lucy said, continuing to smile at the infirm man in the chair. "I don't know, I'm heavier than I look, Mr. MacDonald."

"Call me Lochlin," he said and she nodded.

"Turn around, let him get a good look at you," Blackie instructed, gesturing.

Feeling foolish, Lucy slowly pirouetted before the seated Lochlin MacDonald. When she was again facing him, she said, "How much? What's your guess?"

Lochlin MacDonald rubbed his chin thoughtfully. "Well, let's see, you're about five foot five inches tall so I figure you weigh around, oh...I'd say one hundred eight pounds."

"Here, I'll hold your sea shell while you get on the scale." Blackie reached for her package.

"How do you know it's a seashell?" She handed him her reticule and bonnet too.

"Step on the scales," he said.

She did and the needle moved quickly, zoomed right past one hundred eight, and kept moving. Jumped up to one fifteen and continued. One twenty five and still it didn't stop.

Her green eyes riveted to the damning black needle, Lucy said, "Good grief, I don't understand this...I've never weighed more than one ten in my..."

Deep masculine laughter alerted her to the joke. She looked down, saw Blackie's leather shot foot planted firmly on the scale. She whirled about and shoved on his chest.

"Very funny!" she said, hitting at him as he bobbed and weaved and dodged the harmless blows.

Lochlin MacDonald's loud belly laugh was infectious. Lucy and Blackie laughed with him. And they lingered on the sunny Boardwalk, enjoying their visit with the likeable Lochlin. He was full of vim and interesting stories and the morning whizzed by.

Lucy had no idea so much time had passed until she noticed that many of people on the crowded Boardwalk and beach beyond were stopping their various activities to have lunch. She lifted the watch pinned to her bodice, looked at its face, and frowned.

She put on her big-brimmed straw hat and, addressing the seated Locklin, said, "My stars above, it's noontime. I really must be getting back to the hotel." She laid her hand atop his for a moment in a gesture of friendliness.

He smiled and said, "Lucy, it's been a genuine pleasure. You're the best listener I've had in ages. I look forward to seeing you again real soon."

"Ah...well, no, I...actually...I'm afraid we won't meet again," she said, absently patting the back of his hand. "I'm leaving this afternoon."

"Leaving?" he said and looked disappointed. "So soon? Blackie tells me you just got here Sunday. I thought you were staying through Labor Day."

"I've changed my plans," she said.

"Aw, that's too bad," he said, shaking his head. "You'll miss the Atlantic Grand's End-of-Summer dance. The Last Dance is the biggest social event of the entire season." His gaze shifted to Blackie. "Can't you make her change her mind, Blackie?"

Blackie smiled and picked up his coconut straw boater "Leave it to me," he said.

Lucy would have corrected him, but she didn't want to start bickering in front of Lochlin MacDonald.

When they left the agreeable man who supported himself by guessing people's age and weight on the Boardwalk, Lucy said quietly, "What happened? Was Lochlin in an accident?"

"No. No accident," Blackie replied evenly.

"What is it?"

Blackie shook his dark head. "A disease, a strange, terrible disease. Four years ago Lochlin MacDonald was a two-hundred pound, able-bodied seaman and as strong as an ox. He could have easily lifted you and me at the same time without breaking a sweat. Then his muscles began to mysteriously atrophy."

"That's so terrible," Lucy said, her eyes riveted to Blackie's dark, somber face.

"He baffled the doctors down at Johns Hopkins in Baltimore. They have no idea of the cause or the cure. His weight fell off and he lost muscle tone. Within a few months he couldn't work, couldn't walk. Since it happened, he's grown steadily worse." Blackie stopped speaking.

"Is there any chance he'll walk again one day or..."

"He'll never get out that chair," Blackie said. "The damned disease has left him permanently crippled. But it hasn't changed his disposition. It's amazing, the guy's unfailingly cheerful and optimistic, has never lost his zest for living. He's always ready for a laugh and a good time."

Lucy said, "That is truly remarkable."

"It is," Blackie agreed. "And what about you, Lucy? You ready to laugh and have a good time?"

They had reached the Grand.

"The only thing I'm ready for is home. And since I know you're rude enough to ask the reason why I'm leaving early, I'll tell you before you get the chance." Lucy drew a deep, slow breath. "The gentleman I embarrassingly mistook you for on that first evening that I arrived..."

"Ole Mooney?" Blackie interrupted.

"Mr. Theodore D. Mooney," she corrected, glaring at him. "Theodore Mooney was to meet me here in Atlantic City and..."

"Why did you think I was him? Do we look alike?"

Lucy exhaled irritably. "If you must know I have never seen Mr. Mooney so I..."

"Jesus, you came down here to spend two weeks with a total stranger?" Blackie again interrupted, placing a hand on his heart. "Why, Lucy Hart, I'm so shocked I just don't know if I'll ever..."

"Oh, shut up! I didn't come down here to spend two weeks *with* him or anyone else." She exhaled loudly. "You won't understand this, but I'll try to explain. Mr. Mooney is the postmaster in Cooperstown, Pennsylvania and I'm the postmistress in Colonias. A letter that should have gone to his post office showed up at mine. I sent it on to him and he...to make a long story short we began corresponding. That was three years ago. We discovered--through our letters--that we have a great deal in common. So several months back we agreed to meet in Atlantic City and get acquainted in person. But...Theodore never came."

She waited for Blackie to smirk and make a caustic remark. He did neither.

Lucy tried to smile, failed, hurried on to admit, "I have been stood up, LaDuke, and there you have it. Left here alone without so much as an explanatory telegram. Forsaken. Deserted. Dropped. Choose any term you like, they all add up to the same dreadful truth." She smiled then, squared her shoulders, and looked him straight in the eye, silently daring him to make a smart comment. He didn't, so she announced, "And now I am going to the train depot to see about purchasing a ticket so that I may go back home where I belong." She put out her hand, "It's been a real experience knowing you, LaDuke."

Blackie took her hand. "You don't know me."

"I know enough to know that I don't want to know you better," she said none too sweetly, freeing her hand from his. "Everything is a big joke to you and I don't particularly like being constantly derided. Nor do I like..."

"You're scared, aren't you?" Blackie cut in smoothly. "That's it. You're afraid."

"Afraid?" She knitted her brows as if bewildered. "Afraid of what?"

"Of life. Of me."

Lucy rolled her eyes heavenward. "Your self delusion is extraordinary," she said. "Me afraid of you? Don't make me laugh! If you had enough sense to get in out of the rain you'd know what a ridiculous statement that is."

"Is it?" Blackie grinned, shoved his hands deep down into the pockets of his white duck trousers. His blue summer shirt strained at the shoulders, the fabric taut. His dark eyes were getting that merry gleam. "You don't find me," his voice dropped an octave, "fascinating?"

Lucy emitted a scornful huff and said tartly, "Yes, but then the Wild Man of Borneo down at Hammerstein's sideshow is fascinating, LaDuke. You're a rude upstart with abominable manners and an inflated opinion of yourself. While you're not without a degree of flashy charm, your come-what-may attitude and inability to take anything seriously smacks of hopeless immaturity and childishness. Furthermore you..."

Warming to the subject, Lucy bluntly and bitingly pointed out all the glaring faults and unacceptable character traits he possessed.

Blackie listened silently throughout the speech, giving no indication of his feelings. When finally she wound down and fell silent, he laughed.

Then he repeated, "You're scared of life. I know you are. Don't be. Stay. Stay, Lucy." His hands came out of his pockets and he moved closer. He ran a thumb and forefinger along the edge of her floppy hat brim and his obsidian gaze focused on her lips. "Stay and show me you're not afraid of life. Prove me wrong."

CHAPTER THIRTEEN

Blackie LaDuke's accusation kept ringing in Lucy's ears as she finished packing. 'You're afraid of me. You're afraid of life. I know you are.'

Well, perhaps he was right. Maybe she was afraid of life.

And maybe she was afraid of him. Who in her right mind wouldn't be?

Bad boys were charmers. She knew that. Everyone knew that. Blackie La Duke was unquestionably a bad boy, and much as she hated to admit it, he was definitely a charmer. Half the time his behavior was aberrant, yet she caught herself smiling foolishly at the outrageous things he said and did. Blackie made her squirm and blush and have a good time in spite of herself.

LaDuke was dangerous.

He was dangerous to all women and doubly dangerous to a woman like herself. She was, she knew, woefully unsophisticated and totally unschooled in the tricky arts of frivolous flirtations and transitory romances.

The man was undoubtedly trouble with a capital T, but he was also fascinating. Tremendously entertaining. And good-looking. Oh, lord, Blackie LaDuke was a handsome devil.

Tall, trim, and muscular. His custom clothes fitted him perfectly. The white silk shirt he'd worn at dinner last evening with the collar open appealingly accentuated his dark throat, the width of his shoulders. A full head of rich, luxuriant hair was so black it produced blue highlights and tumbled in careless curls over his high forehead. A piratical grin flashed frequently and there were sexy little crinkles around his eyes. Night-black eyes that were penetrating, arresting, absolutely beautiful.

Blackie LaDuke was a physically attractive man who exuded such healthy masculine energy it was easy to understand how women of all ages would be prone to fall under his spell. Pity the woman foolish enough to give her heart to the handsome, insensitive, happy-go-lucky Blackie.

Lucy finished packing.

"There," she said aloud, closing the last of the three valises. She lifted and looked at the gold cased watch pinned to the bodice of her blue and white seersucker shirtwaist.

1:30 p.m.

She had told Benny the bellhop to come up for her luggage at two. Lucy preferred waiting in the privacy of her room rather than downstairs in the always-crowded lobby. She crossed to the open French doors, stepped out onto the tiny balcony, and blinked in the bright August sunlight.

Her eyes narrowing against the glare on the water, she looked out at the endless Atlantic Ocean. Bathers, hundreds of them, laughing and shrieking with joy splashed about in surf. Pretty young girls were taking their daily swimming lessons from big athletic clubmen. Alert lifeguards from the Atlantic City Beach Patrol prowled the water's edge, keeping watchful eyes on the scores of bathers.

On the sandy beach happy children with colorful tin pails and miniature shovels built castles while their parents napped in the warm sun. High above the beach, wicker rolling chairs and pedestrians jockeyed for position on the long Boardwalk. Hawkers moved up and down the wooden walkway, shouting in sing-song voices, peddling their wares.

The concession stands were doing a landslide business. Stalls selling candy, popcorn, ice cream, cold drinks, and hot dogs were surrounded with hungry customers. Closely curtained cubicles of a half dozen Gypsy fortune-tellers were powerful drawing cards for the gullible. Sweethearts holding hands and laughing hurried into the photo galleries to have their memories preserved forever on film.

To the north, between New York and Kentucky Avenues, the awesome Observations Roundabout rose high above the busy Boardwalk. A thrilling diversion favored by the truly courageous, the Roundabout's tall, twin Ferris wheels sat side-by-side, turning in opposite directions. Just the sight of those giant rotating wheels made Lucy's heart throb. She couldn't imagine anyone having the nerve to actually climb aboard one. Yet a steady stream of loud, carefree young people eagerly lined up to take a turn on the frightening ride.

On the newly built steel pier at Virginia Avenue and the beach, a uniformed band was setting up their instruments in preparation for the daily afternoon concert. Music lovers strolled out onto the pier to claim the limited number of seats that were always filled for the rousing recitals.

Lucy stood unmoving on her private hotel balcony.

Watching.

Watching from the sidelines.

She was not a part the bustle and activity going on below. She was only an observer. She had done almost nothing out of the ordinary since her arrival in Atlantic City. Nothing she couldn't have done back home in Colonias.

Her fashionable new bathing costume had never been wet. She hadn't been to the Heintz pier or the Sea View Excursion House or to either of the two Revolving Observation Towers. She hadn't sampled the famous Salt Water taffy or enjoyed a picnic on the beach or ridden a bicycle down south to the Turkish Pavilion. She hadn't had her photo taken or her fortune told or been to a dance in the Atlantic Grand's opulent Blue Room.

She was going home without doing any of the things she had read about in the pamphlets and newspaper advertisements proclaiming the many wonders of the popular seaside resort.

Lucy solemnly reflected on the disappointing turn of events. It struck her that she had once again been cast into the role of the observer. For too many wasted years that's all she had been. She felt as if she had spent her entire life watching others do the things she longed to do.

They lived while she only observed.

Circumstances had made it so. She'd had obligations, responsibilities others didn't. But those obligations and responsibilities no longer existed. She now enjoyed the freedom others knew, was totally liberated. Nobody was thrusting the mantle of the observer on her now. If she again assumed the role, she had no one to blame but herself.

There were ten full days of her long planned holiday remaining and all kinds of adventures to be enjoyed in exciting Atlantic City. Why should she be in such a big hurry to go home? She would be a coward and a fool not to stay and take advantage of the resort's many possibilities and pleasures.

If Mr. Theodore D. Mooney from Cooperstown, Pennsylvania had chosen not to come here and meet her, well, it was his loss not hers. And no cause for her to go running home. So she wouldn't. She would stay.

The decision made, Lucy immediately began to relax and feel wonderfully lighthearted. From the moment she had arrived in this magical place she had felt years younger than she did back home. That alone was reason enough to stay. How long had it been since anyone had called her simply Lucy?

Years. Too many.

Here it was different.

The devilish Blackie LaDuke called her Lucy. The crippled Lochlin MacDonald called her Lucy. Even the dignified Colonel Cort Mitchell called her Lucy. And she liked it. She liked it a lot. Especially when Blackie spoke her name. The way he said *Lucy* made her feel like a saucy young woman, not some dried up old maid.

She was sick to death of being Miss Lucy, the spinster postmistress. Here she was Lucy and she could go on being Lucy through Labor Day.

She would be an observer no longer.

She would live.

Laughing merrily now, Lucy whirled about and went inside. She hurried downstairs to inform both Benny the bellhop and the dark suited clerk behind the reception desk that she had changed her mind. She wasn't leaving after all.

Benny grinned, nodded, and told her she wouldn't regret it. The thin desk clerk with the bushy eyebrows and big ears smiled politely and said, "Speaking for the entire staff of the Atlantic Grand, may I say we're pleased you have changed your mind, Miss Hart?"

"Lucy," she corrected cheerily, "and you certainly may!" She turned to leave.

He called her back "One moment, please, Lucy. I almost forgot. I've been asked to deliver a message to you. Colonel Cort Mitchell is to arrive back at the Atlantic Grand around six this evening. He has requested the pleasure of your company at dinner tonight."

Lucy was pleased. "Kindly inform Colonel Mitchell I shall be delighted to have dinner with him."

"Very good, then. The Colonel will meet you here in the lobby at eight o'clock sharp."

"I won't keep him waiting," Lucy said and left.

She returned to her room in high spirits and her good mood persisted throughout the long, lazy August afternoon. She leisurely unpacked and considered taking a short spin on the Boardwalk, decided against it. There was no longer any urgency. She was staying through Labor Day. She could stroll on the Boardwalk tomorrow and the next day and the next. She felt wonderfully lazy and relaxed.

Lucy ordered a late lunch sent up from room service. She found it delightfully decadent to enjoy a sumptuous meal while seated cross-legged atop the bed in nothing but her lacy underwear. She sighed with satisfaction when she finished the last bite of rich chocolate pudding. Full and content, Lucy read for a while. Soon she laid the book aside, stretched out fully across the soft feather mattress, sighed, and cat napped.

She could and would have a high old time in Atlantic City on her own. She didn't need Theodore D.

Mooney to make her holiday complete. And she wasn't-
-as Blackie LaDuke so arrogantly accused--afraid of life.
Or of him. Besides, Blackie's teasing attention
undoubtedly resulted from restlessness and boredom.
The minute a really pretty woman crossed his path, he'd
pay her no more mind.

And that was okay, too.

***

Colonel Cort Mitchell smiled from across the
spacious lobby when Lucy stepped off the elevator at
eight o'clock sharp.

Lucy felt her heart squeeze painfully in her chest as
she looked admiringly at him. He was so much like her
adored papa she was tempted to give him a big hug.

The Colonel's countenance, like his fine figure,
bespoke proud masculine power. His shoulders hunched
ever so slightly; other than that his stance was majestic
and his six-foot three-inch frame was that of a vital,
much younger man.

He was nattily attired in signature pearl gray, his
suit's fashionably cut trousers sharply creased, tailored
jacket unbuttoned, the snugly fitting vest double
breasted. A red carnation in his lapel was matched by
the healthy rosy hue of his ruddy cheeks. His flowing
silver hair was brushed straight back and his mustache
was neatly trimmed.

He was a handsome, self-assured gentleman and it
was easy to envision him the valiant southern knight on
horseback, masterfully commanding divisions of loyal
confederate troops.

Lucy lifted the skirts of her yellow poplin dress and
started toward the tall, compelling man. The long
legged Colonel Mitchell was to her in seconds, beaming,
greeting her warmly, offering her his arm.

"My dear, I'm flattered you've agreed to join me," he said in that pleasing southern accent. "Thank you so much for brightening my evening."

"My pleasure, Colonel," she said and meant it.

The Colonel tucked Lucy's hand around his bent arm, then frowned down at her, his gray eyes questioning. "I understand you considered leaving us today."

Lucy nodded. "I did, sir. Yes."

"You must tell me the reason."

Lucy smiled, but made no reply. She had no intention of telling him about Theodore D. Mooney and of her humiliation at being stood up by the Cooperstown bachelor.

But Lucy was hardly seated across from him in the paneled dining hall before she began to feel totally comfortable in the company of the easy going Southerner. In no time she was confiding in him as if she had known him all her life.

She was, she told him, proud of her position as Colonias' postmistress. She explained why she had been offered the coveted post. She told of her father's tragic accident and talked about her mother's lingering illness. She told him her two older brothers lived so far away she rarely saw them or her six nieces and nephews.

By the time coffee and desert arrived the Colonel knew a great deal more about Lucy Hart than she had intended to reveal. Lucy, in turn, had candidly questioned the friendly southerner. She learned that he was a cotton broker who looked after the interests of several southern cotton producers. He lived permanently at the Atlantic Grand, but traveled to England two or three times each year to deal with his London cotton buyers.

Lucy kept waiting for him to mention a wife, a family. He didn't, so finally she said, "You live here alone here at the Atlantic Grand and sail to England several times a year." She smiled at him and stated, "You are obviously a bachelor, Colonel Mitchell."

The Colonel smiled back at her. He lifted his half-full cup of coffee and took a drink. He lowered the cup.

"I suppose I am." He placed the fragile coffee cup in its matching saucer. "Now."

"Now?" Lucy's arched eyebrows raised. "You're getting married soon?"

He chuckled good naturedly. "No, no, child. I like my life just as it is."

"Then you were married once?"

"I've been married twice," he said and the smile never left his lips, the expression in his gray eyes never changed. Lucy waited expectantly, but he said no more.

"Colonel, please," she prompted, realizing it was rude to continue questioning him, but unable to stop herself. "Surely you know you can't tell a curious woman that you were married twice and leave it at that. I must know what happened."

Nodding almost imperceptibly, the Colonel told her, but in the briefest terms possible. Offering few details he said that, unfortunately, both his wives had predeceased him. What about children, Lucy asked. Were there any? Three, he said calmly. Lucy gazed unblinkingly at him.

"Where are they now? Do you see them often?"

His face devoid of emotion Colonel Mitchell softly stated that all three of his children--two boys, ages nineteen and twenty, and a girl sixteen--had perished in the deadly New Orleans yellow fever epidemic of '75.

"Oh...Colonel," Lucy said, horrified, wishing now she hadn't pressed him so intensely. "I'm sorry. Such a terrible tragedy." She bowed her head. "Please forgive me for so stupidly..."

"Now, there's no need for that," the Colonel interrupted. "Look at me, Lucy." Lucy lifted her head; her eyes met his. He said, "One day you'll learn an invaluable lesson, as I have. The human memory is an amazing and a marvelous thing. We remember that which we wish to remember and we forget the bad, the unbearable. I have more than my share of beautiful memories; no sad ones whatsoever." He reached over, gently patted her hand. He smiled then and said, "Now you came down to Atlantic City for a two week holiday and I'll wager you're hoping take home some nice memories. Am I right?"

Lucy smiled, nodded. "Yes, you are."

"Then why did you consider leaving today before you've had an opportunity to gather any?"

Lucy's shoulders lifted, lowered. "I'm afraid there's little chance of collecting many memories and if you really want to know why I say that, I will tell you."

Lucy related to the Colonel exactly what had happened. He listened attentively, a look of concern and understanding on his face. She told him about Theodore D. Mooney and the exchanged letters and their agreement to meet in Atlantic City to share their two-week holiday. She concluded with Theodore's being a no show.

"And there you have it," she spoke softly so fellow diners wouldn't overhear. "Theodore never came nor did he bother to send a message of explanation. Naturally, I was both disappointed and embarrassed, so I thought it would be best if I returned home at once."

Colonel Cort Mitchell said exactly what Lucy needed to hear, what a father might say to a daughter whose tender feelings had been bruised.

"Forget about Theodore Mooney." His gray eyes twinkled with warmth when he added, "You're a bright, sweet, and pretty young woman, Lucy Hart. Something better surely awaits you."

Lucy's response was immediate. So spontaneous, so unguarded, the Colonel felt his heart kick against his ribs in quick alarm.

Her wide set, green eyes suddenly glowing with an inner light, Lucy asked, "Colonel, do you know Blackie LaDuke?"

CHAPTER FOURTEEN

"Sure, I know Blackie," said the Colonel evenly. A short pause, then, "So you've already met the infamous Blackie LaDuke from New York City?"

"Yes. Yes, I have. We met quite by accident Sunday afternoon shortly after I arrived." Lucy smiled, shrugged, glanced down at the table, and toyed with a silver spoon, "Blackie's...that is, Mr. LaDuke is...well he's a wicked tease, isn't he, Colonel?"

"That he is, my dear. He certainly is."

"Is he always like that? Does nothing upset or worry him?"

The Colonel smiled. "If life is ever serious for Blackie, he has the good grace never to let us know it."

Lucy nodded. "He seems always to...I'm not sure...I wonder..." She looked up. "What do you think of him, Colonel?"

"I like Blackie," he said without hesitation. "He's an incredibly charming young man, always entertaining and easy to be around."

"He is, I agree. But that isn't what I mean," Lucy said, hoping to learn more about the handsome, dark-haired New Yorker. "What's your opinion of him? As a man."

"Blackie's all right," the Colonel said. "Or he will be one day." Smiling easily, he shook his silver head. "Blackie has a great penchant for getting into scrapes. He's been coming down to Atlantic City every summer for as long as I've been here and I've never known him to make it through an entire week without getting into a fist fight."

"I can't say that I'm surprised." Lucy frowned, recalling Monday morning when she'd stepped onto elevator to see the disheveled, unshaven Blackie with a tear in the knee of his trousers. "Likely he's the instigator in such fisticuffs. His behavior is outrageous."

"Sometimes it is, yes," the Colonel agreed. "Blackie's trouble is that he's brilliant and restless. He has no real purpose, no objective. Nothing to sap the boundless energy he possesses. He's never found the proper channel for all that excess power."

Left unsaid was that unless he did, it would burn him up. Blackie LaDuke was as yet unmarked by the dissipations in which he relieved his constant restlessness, but neither his brilliance nor his beauty would last if he continued to live his life the way he now did. Blackie LaDuke was slowly, surely destroying himself, liquor and women being his favored agents of annihilation.

"Perhaps you're right," Lucy said. "But I sincerely doubt that Blackie LaDuke will ever aspire to any greater goal than the endless pursuit of his own personal pleasure."

"A distinct possibility," said the Colonel, nodding, heartened to find she was so astute.

Lucy Hart, he decided, had a good head on her shoulders. She was an unsophisticated young lady, but a wise, well-brought-up one. Then, too, while she was, in his view, quite attractive with her slender girlish figure, arresting emerald eyes, slightly tilted nose, and determined chin, she was hardly the type Blackie

LaDuke or the other hot-blooded young swells down for the season would eagerly pursue.

"Colonel, do you know what I'd like to do?" Lucy said, curbing her desire to ask more about Blackie LaDuke.

"What's that, child?"

"I would love to take a short stroll down the Boardwalk this evening." Lucy picked up her crystal water goblet and took a sip. "Could I impose on you to chaperon me?"

The Colonel smiled broadly. He needn't waste time worrying about Lucy Hart. She wouldn't, like many an unsuspecting young lady visiting Atlantic City for the first time, get herself into trouble.

Trouble walked through the door at precisely that minute.

Neither Lucy nor the Colonel noticed Blackie LaDuke, handsome and immaculate in a beige summer suit of cotton poplin, step into the dining hall's open archway.

Other diners did.

Heads immediately turned and low whispers began and unattached females blatantly smiled his way as Blackie walked through the crowded dining hall. The buzz of excitement that accompanied him momentarily attracted the attention of Lucy and the Colonel.

They simultaneously glanced up and saw Blackie coming toward them. Once Lucy caught sight of him, she didn't look away. Her wide-eyed gaze remained fastened squarely on the approaching Blackie.

After spotting Blackie, the Colonel turned his attention back on Lucy. Caught unawares, nothing was hidden. It was all there in her emerald eyes. A warm glow of excitement flashed and her face was flushed as though some potent drug had suddenly been released inside her.

Blackie reached their table.

"Evening, Blackie," greeted the Colonel and started to rise.

"Don't get up," Blackie said, placing a hand on the Colonel's shoulder.

"Mr. LaDuke," Lucy quietly acknowledged.

"Miss me?" he said, and as he spoke he looked directly at Lucy.

"Terribly," she replied sarcastically, but her emerald eyes continued to glow.

Blackie smiled at her, drew up a chair, and sat down. Only then did he ask, "Mind if I sit down?"

The Colonel said, "If we twist your arm, Blackie, can we persuade you to join us?"

"Why, thanks, Colonel. Be happy to," Blackie replied, grinning, and winked at Lucy. He took from his lapel a fragrant ivory gardenia. He held it out to Lucy. Lucy automatically took the gardenia and the Colonel noticed, as her fingers brushed Blackie's, her hand trembled slightly. "You stayed," Blackie stated the obvious, looking at her as if they shared a secret. "Good for you, Lucy Hart." He leaned closer. "And good for me?"

"My decision to stay had nothing to do with you, Mr. LaDuke."

"Then why did you stay?" His dark dancing eyes said he didn't believe her.

Lucy didn't answer. She glanced at the Colonel. "I'm ready if you are, sir."

The Colonel nodded, laid his white dinner napkin on the table. "Sorry you didn't get here sooner, Blackie.

You'll have to dine alone, I'm afraid. Lucy and I were just leaving."

The Colonel pushed back his chair, stood up. Blackie sprang to his feet. He easily beat the older man to Lucy's chair, pulled it out for her.

"Fortunately I've already had dinner," Blackie said. "I dined with Lady Strange an hour ago." Helping Lucy to her feet, he addressed the Colonel. "That's why I'm here. Her Ladyship sent me to find you and give you a message."

Skeptical, Colonel Mitchell arched a silver eyebrow. "Oh? And what's on her mind?"

Blackie shrugged wide shoulders. "Beats me. All I know is she needs to see you right away. Pronto. Immediately."

The trio started from the room, the two men flanking Lucy. Over Lucy's head, the Colonel said to Blackie, "Kindly tell Lady Strange I will be up in an hour." He put a hand to the small of Lucy's back. "I promised Lucy a stroll down the Boardwalk."

They exited the dining room, moved down the carpeted corridor toward the lobby.

"Oh, never mind that, Colonel." Lucy was understanding. "Some other evening will do just as nicely."

"No need to wait," Blackie quickly put in. "Luckily I'm free this evening. I'd be honored to stand in for you, Colonel." He gently drew Lucy away from the Colonel, adroitly maneuvered her to his other side.

They had reached the lobby.

"You can go on up to Lady Strange," Blackie coolly instructed the Colonel. "I'll take Lucy for that walk."

Colonel Mitchell had been smoothly finessed and knew it. But there was little he could do but stand helplessly by while Blackie skillfully guided Lucy across the spacious lobby, through the beachside double doors, and out into the summer night.

As soon as they were on the hotel veranda Lucy stopped short, turned to the tall, dark man she considered too handsome for his own good or hers and said, "Tell me something, LaDuke."

"Sure. Anything. Ask me and I'll answer."

"Did this lady with whom you supposedly dined..."

"Lady Strange," Blackie interrupted. "A dear friend to both the Colonel and to me. You must meet her."

"Did Lady Strange really tell you to send the Colonel up?"

"You're questioning my word?"

"That's exactly what I'm doing. Now answer me."

Blackie grinned, said nothing.

"I knew it," she accused. "You made the whole thing up! Didn't you?"

Blackie's grin grew broader. "*Nolo contendere*."

"I think that's deplorable."

"How else was I to get you alone?"

Shaking her head, Lucy said, "I just don't how to take you, LaDuke."

"Swiftly," he told her, moving nearer. "Right now, tonight, before it's too late."

Lucy felt her face grow warm. "I mean I..."

"I know what you mean." He clutched her wrist, drew her closer, and looked into her eyes. "Let me tell you what I mean."

"No. I don't want to hear it."

"Yes you do." He guided her toward the steps. "If you didn't, you'd have gone home this afternoon."

"I told you, my staying on in Atlantic City has nothing to do with you."

Blackie ushered her down the steps, stopped at the bottom, and turned her to face him. "Who said it did? Did I?"

"No. Not exactly."

"Whatever your reason, you stayed." He took back the ivory gardenia he had given her, tucked it into her hair at the side of her head, leaned close, and inhaled its sweet fragrance. "Are we going for that walk?"

"Well..."

"You got something else to do?"

"Not exactly."

"Then you're coming with me."

"But..."

"Why not?"

"Well...I..."

"What, Lucy? Let's have it."

"To tell the truth I can't understand your interest in me."

The simple, honest statement touched Blackie. Lucy Hart was not yet thirty, yet she was so spinsterish, so self conscious and unaware, she couldn't imagine a man being physically attracted to her. She had no idea of her own passionate nature; it was hidden deeply within her.

"Want me to show you?" he said, and before she could answer Blackie clasped her upper arms, drew her up onto her toes, and kissed her fully on the lips.

Caught totally by surprise, Lucy was stunned into helplessness. His lips, hot and smooth, smothered hers and she felt as if all the breath was being sucked from

111

her lungs. The unexpected kiss sent a meteor shower rocketing through her brain and Lucy felt weak in the knees. She anxiously clutched at his lapels for support.

Blackie pressed her against him, holding her gently within the protective arch of his tall, lean body. He felt her tremble. His lips left hers. He released her.

Instantly Lucy's hand reached out and slapped him hard across the cheek. The mark of her five fingers outlined on his tanned face, Blackie stood stock still, a dangerous sparkle flashing for a second in his dark, expressive eyes. It faded fast and was replaced with a satiric grin.

"Next time I start to kiss you," he said, rubbing his stinging jaw, "I'll tell you first."

Green fire flashing from her angry eyes, Lucy said, "There will be no next time, LaDuke!"

"You're wrong, Lucy. There'll be lots of next times."

CHAPTER FIFTEEN

Eight a.m. Thursday. August 24th.

The morning after Blackie kissed Lucy and Lucy slapped Blackie.

Blackie was downstairs waiting when Lucy stepped off the elevator. He gave her no chance to evade him. He was up out of his chair and to her, blocking her path, before she had time to advance or retreat.

Smiling down at her, he said, "Good morning at last. I was beginning to think you meant to stay in bed all day."

"Will you kindly keep your voice down," she said, glancing anxiously about the lobby.

"Sure," he whispered, leaning closer. "Let's go have breakfast. I'm famished."

"I was not going to the dining room," she frostily informed him.

"No? Well, okay. We'll go down to the Boardwalk. Lots of places serve good food."

"I'm not hungry," she lied. "I...I was on my way to the ladies' parlor." She'd be safe there; he couldn't follow.

"Liar."

"I beg your pardon."

"You were not going to the Ladies' parlor. You're hungry and so am I." He grinned and added, "Besides, we have to plan our day."

113

"*Our* day?" Lucy laughed in his face. "You may do anything you choose with *your* day, LaDuke. Let me assure you, it has nothing to do with *my* day." She started to step around him.

He caught her arm, stopped her. "You still mad because I kissed you last night?"

"Shhhh!" she hissed, her face immediately coloring, "will you be quiet!"

"Only if you'll agree to have breakfast with me." His long fingers slid slowly down her arm to her wrist. He gently clasped her hand in his. "Give me a chance to compensate for my ungentlemanly behavior of last night." He favored her with his most disarming smile. "Please."

Lucy hesitated. "You'll behave yourself if I agree?"

"You can count on it," he promised, placing a spread hand over his heart, looking as earnest as possible.

Lucy wrenched her hand free of his. "Very well then. Let's go on to the dining..."

"No. Let's don't," he interrupted, taking her elbow. "I'm told the Waldorf-Astoria fixes the best omelettes on the East coast."

"I don't like omelettes."

"Don't be disagreeable, Lucy," he said. "Order anything you can think of and the chef will fix it for you."

"You'll bring me right straight back here after breakfast?"

"If you want to come right straight back here," he said, the impish twinkle in his dark eyes predicting she wouldn't. "Now let's go before I pass out from hunger."

Secretly Lucy wanted to go. She was, in fact, dying to see the Waldorf-Astoria. Opened just weeks before, the six-story Waldorf was the first brick hotel to be built on the Boardwalk. The prospect of having breakfast at the brand new showplace greatly appealed to her.

Understated opulence and an uninhibited festive spirit reigned in the Waldorf's plush restaurant. The hum of gossip filled the vast, marble-columned room where well-heeled patrons were gathered for their first hearty meal of the day.

Blackie's promise that she could order anything and the Waldorf's chef would fix it had been no idle boast. Everything imaginable was listed in the leather bound menu a white-jacketed waiter handed her. A long, linen-draped buffet table at the room's center held huge silver serving dishes stacked high with pyramids of exotic fruits and fluffy French pastries and golden-crusted breads.

"What sounds good?" Blackie asked as they studied their menus.

"I believe I'll just have a glass of freshly squeezed orange juice and a hot cinnamon bun," she said, lowering the red leather menu.

"That's all?" Blackie's dark eyebrows lifted. "We've got a big day ahead of us, Lucy. You'll need energy."

"Nothing more, thanks," she said, too excited to be really hungry.

Blackie nodded and ordered for them both. A waiter poured steaming hot coffee into their porcelain cups. Blackie passed Lucy the small silver pitcher of cream. She poured freely, then offered it to him.

"No. Just sugar for me." He took a long swallow, sighed. "Ahhh. Perfection."

"It looks a little strong," Lucy remarked, stirring.

"There's an old Arabic saying that coffee should be black as night, sweet as love, and hot as Hell."

"You made that up."

"I did not."

Their breakfasts arrived. Lucy had never seen anybody order as much food at one time as Blackie. Fresh strawberries and cream. Half a honeydew melon. A glass of pineapple juice. A plate of hot cakes swimming in maple syrup. A fluffy cheese omelette. A rasher of crisp bacon. A side order of ham. A half dozen Buttermilk biscuits and peach jam. A tumbler of cold milk.

Lucy shook her head, certain half the food would go to waste. Nobody had that big an appetite. Certainly not a well-built man without an ounce of fat on his tall, lean body.

She teased him. "Now, Blackie, you know that thousands are starving in Ireland. You won't be allowed to go out and play if you don't clean your plate." Chewing, he gave her a half puzzled look. She said, "Didn't your mother ever say that to you?"

He swallowed, then smiled. "Nope."

"No? She never once..."

"My mother never had a meal at the same time or the same table with me."

Lucy stared at him, dumbfounded. "Your family didn't eat dinner together?"

Blackie shook his head. "Not that I can remember." He said it as if it was perfectly normal. "Don't worry, I'm a growing boy. You'll see all this food

116

disappear so quickly you'll think you're across the table from a magician."

Lucy smiled and asked casually, "Why didn't your family dine together?"

Blackie cut up his syrup-smothered pancakes. He said, "Do most families in Colonias, New York actually break bread together?"

"Yes. Yes, of course."

"Well, mine didn't." He offered no more information. Quickly changing the subject, he said, "Your cinnamon bun's getting cold."

"Mmmm. Smells good, doesn't it?" Inhaling the pleasing scent of cinnamon, Lucy picked up a heavy Georgian sterling fork and cut into the large bun. She took a bite, chewed, and immediately declared it to be the best pastry she had ever tasted.

"Did you know," she asked, suddenly feeling gay and in a good mood, "the divine recipe for the holy oil of anointment that Moses recorded in Exodus included cinnamon?"

Blackie swallowed a mouthful of food, took a drink of black coffee. "No! Well, I'll be damned," he murmured. Then, as if pondering it thoughtfully, he mused, "I did not know that. Boy, am I glad you set me straight."

Lucy made a mean face at him. "You think you're so smart, Blackie LaDuke."

He grinned, unruffled. "Did *you* know that Nero bought every stick of cinnamon in Rome to burn on his wife's funeral pyre? Is that romantic enough for you?"

"Romantic? For your information," Lucy said, shaking her head, "Nero stomped his wife to death in a tantrum."

"Oh." Blackie shrugged. "Well maybe she wouldn't let him play his fiddle."

Lucy smiled at him. Blackie smiled back.

It was a long, leisurely breakfast and Lucy enjoyed every minute of it. They lingered over fresh cups of coffee and discussed what they would do with the rest of their day. After convincing her that she didn't really want to go 'right straight back' to the Atlantic Grand, Blackie did most of the talking.

"We'll ride up and down the Boardwalk in a rolling chair," he told her enthusiastically. "No. No, we'll rent a couple of bicycles and pedal out to the old light house at...I've got it, we'll go down to the Heintz pier and..."

"Blackie..." She attempted to get a word in edge wise.

"...we'll go to the Constitution Pavilion," he continued as if she hadn't spoken. "Or, we'll grab some bathing costumes and take a swim in the ocean..." He shook his head. "Nah, too soon after breakfast. We'll visit Hubin's and buy every picture post card in the place. Or maybe we'll take off our shoes, go down to the beach and watch the sand sculptors work. Or spend the afternoon at a beer garden or..."

"Blackie, Blackie," Lucy finally threw both hands up, palms out, to silence him.

"Hmmm?"

Tilting her head to one side, she said, "Do you have trouble making up your mind?"

"Well, yes," he said, "and no."

Lucy laughed.

***

"Lucy."

"Yes?"

"I'm going to kiss you."

"No. No, Blackie, don't."

It was the end of the day. The sun had set. Darkness was not far off.

A late summer dusk was slowly settling over the East Coast. It was that brief daily interlude when the usually crowded Boardwalk was, for the moment, nearly deserted. Tired, sunburned people had gone in for the day. The young fast set had not come out for the night. Electric lights lining the Boardwalk had not yet blazed to life to illuminate the long wooden promenade.

Lucy and Blackie stood at the railing of the near empty Boardwalk, so far down the four-mile walkway they were almost at its end. The enveloping smell of the ocean was strong in the heavy air. The water had turned a deep, gun metal gray, the breakers rolling in to crash in lacy foam on the sandy shore.

Somewhere in the distance a man was whistling the popular melody, *You Tell Me Your Dream, I'll Tell You Mine*.

Neither of them had spoken a word for several long minutes. Both leaned on the heavy steel balustrade and stared at the endless ocean. After an active and eventful day, there was now a gentle languor, an ethereal peace that had settled over them.

At last Blackie had slowly turned about, leaned back against the railing. He studied Lucy's serene face as she gazed at the dark Atlantic. He trailed the back of his hand down her bare forearm. She shivered and looked up at him.

"It's getting late," she said, turning to face him.

"Or it's very early," he replied, his teeth flashing white in the darkness of his face. "According to how you look at it."

Lucy smiled. "It's been a very pleasant day, Blackie, but it's time I went back to the Grand."

"I know you're tired." He took her hand in his, drew it up and folded it against his chest.

"A little," she said, so exhausted she felt as if she couldn't make it back to the hotel.

"We're a long way from the Atlantic Grand," he said. "Let's ride back."

So saying, Blackie promptly put two fingers in his mouth and gave a long, loud whistle. From out of nowhere a white wicker chair rolled swiftly up. Blackie handed Lucy inside. He took a roll of bills from his white trousers pocket, peeled off a couple, handed them to the chair's pedaler, and said, "The Atlantic Grand." He lowered his voice, added softly, "We're in no hurry, pal."

There wasn't as much space in the graceful white wicker chair with its sloping swanlike neck as Lucy had supposed. Blackie was seated very close to her in the cozy conveyance; so close his long arm was around her and her head was on his shoulder. He allowed his knees to spread apart so that one of them was touching hers. The intimacy was both disturbing and delightful.

The slow ride back to the Grand in the rolling chair was every bit as bewitching as Lucy had dreamed. And more. The smooth seductive motion of the chair stirred wisps in her curly chestnut hair, pressed cooling ocean breezes to her warm cheeks, and gently swayed her against her compelling companion.

Lucy listened, entranced by the deep, level timbre of Blackie's voice as he pointed out the famous hotels lining the Boardwalk. The Dennis. The Traymore. The Brighten. The Chelsea. The Ambassador. The Claridge.

"We'll go to the dance at the Ritz-Carlton Saturday night," he said matter-of-factly. "Tomorrow night we'll go to the grand opening of the Auditorium Pier."

Lucy smiled, said nothing, more content than she could ever remember being. She felt wonderfully safe and secure. As if she were in a splendid dream from which she never wanted to awaken. The lovely lassitude claiming her, the breathless beauty of the coastal resort in the summer dusk, the comfort and intimacy of the rolling chair, all these things conspired to make it seem natural and right to snuggle up trustingly to Blackie.

Lucy sighed and her lashes lowered when Blackie's free arm came around her to press her closer. He held her so close she could feel the slow, regular cadence of his heart beating against her breasts. It was the sweetest of sensations. Her eyes closed completely and she swallowed convulsively.

Then Lucy held her breath.

Any second Blackie would whisper, as he had earlier, 'Lucy, I'm going to kiss you.' She could hardly wait. This time she just might not say no.

It never happened.

The unpredictable Blackie LaDuke made no attempt to kiss Lucy, either in the rolling chair or at the door of her third floor hotel room when he said goodnight. Lucy was frankly puzzled.

And more attracted than ever.

CHAPTER SIXTEEN

From that day forward, Lucy was never by herself again. The playful, devilish Blackie wouldn't leave her alone. Even though Lucy avoided him like the plague.

Or tried to.

Instinctively, she recognized him as trouble. Blackie LaDuke was not only wickedly good looking, he was wild and worldly, a handsome heartbreaker if ever there was one. There was an aura of attractive danger about him and Lucy knew better than to associate with such a man.

To allow one's self ever to care for a happy-go-lucky rounder like LaDuke was absolutely out of the question. Colonel Cort Mitchell--whose opinion she valued highly--had stated flatly that while Blackie was charming and likeable, he had neither deep convictions nor high ambition. Lucy congratulated herself on being far too clever to fall victim to the shallow charms of the hedonistic hellion.

She hadn't been around much, but she was nobody's fool. She would continue--no matter how strongly she was tempted to do otherwise--to hold the teasing, tormenting Blackie at arm's length for the duration of her brief holiday.

Then, of course, she would return home.

And never see Blackie LaDuke again.

***

Blackie, for his part, found Lucy's firm indifference rather refreshing. He was not accustomed to such standoffish behavior from a female. The beautiful Park Avenue Goddess had fallen into bed with him only hours after they met. And she wasn't the only one. Women usually threw themselves at him.

Not Lucy Hart.

From their chance meeting on Sunday, she had actually wanted nothing to do with him and hadn't hesitated to let him know it. Which amazed him. And amused him no end. It made her a bit of a challenge. So, he doggedly pursued her to the total exclusion of anyone else, leaving dozens of disappointed women puzzled and incensed by his strange behavior.

Blackie liked being with Lucy.

He was delighted to learn that Lucy Hart was not only wholesomely pretty; she was also extremely bright. She had a caustic wit, which was totally at odds with her spinsterish propriety. She was wonderfully simplistic and at the same time mysteriously complicated. Most of all, there was about Lucy an appealing vulnerability.

Surprisingly, he found he was more than a trifle intrigued by the well bred, straight laced, small town postmistress.

Nonetheless, Blackie's main concern was that Lucy Hart had an exciting, enjoyable time on her brief seaside holiday.

He hadn't forgotten the circumstances surrounding their unlikely meeting. Lucy had been let down by her Mr. Mooney, the bumbling bachelor Pennsylvania postmaster who had promised to meet her and then had never showed up. And hadn't even had the common decency to send her a wire of apology or explanation.

The thought of it rankled Blackie. Made him mad as hell. Made his hands ball into tight fists. Made him itch to get mitts on Mooney so the could throw a couple of well-aimed punches at the callous bastard's ugly mug.

On Lucy Hart's behalf, of course.

Blackie laughed at himself for feeling so passionate about the situation. He'd be the first to admit that it was out of character to concern himself with anyone's feelings but his own, so he wondered at himself. What was it to him? Why did he feel inclined to champion the prim postmistress?

He honestly didn't know.

All he knew was Lucy Hart had touched something in him he hadn't known was there. Lucy had suffered an undeserved, hurtful disappointment and he hated it that she had.

Blackie didn't fully understand why, but he felt strongly compelled to make it up to her. As if he should personally see to it she got to do all the things she hadn't done, to see all the sights.

Blackie appointed himself the guardian of Lucy's good times. He wanted her to have the vacation of her life in Atlantic City. And who better qualified to show her a few fleeting days of fun?

*****

"What's he up to?"

"Up to? My dear Colonel, what do you mean, up to?'

"What's his motive?"

"Motive? Why, Cort Mitchell, you should be ashamed of yourself," scolded Lady Strange. "What makes you think there is a motive?"

"Because he knows Blackie as well as we do," Lochlin MacDonald told her with a cheerful laugh.

The Last Dance

The three old friends were on the sunny balcony just outside Lochlin's fifth-floor suite. Hanging in the corner window was ship's bell with a rope on the clapper, a memento of the days when Lochlin had been a mate aboard the S. S. Lisbon. At the balcony railing was a powerful swivel telescope mounted on a tripod. The expensive telescope was Lochlin MacDonald's pride and joy. The former seaman whiled away many an hour with his eye pressed to the powerful lens, watching the great ships navigate the seas he used to sail.

It was early Friday afternoon. They had just finished having lunch. Lady Strange, in a broad brimmed straw hat shading her round face and wearing a yoked shapeless dress of bright pink cotton sat sprawled in a padded love seat meant for two. There was only room enough for her and her spoiled, fat black Persian, Precious.

Lochlin MacDonald, in his wheel chair, was seated underneath the enormous black-and-white striped umbrella that rose from the center of the round table. A tray, attached to his wheelchair's arms, was across his knees. As he talked and laughed, he played a game of solitaire in an attempt to keep his weak, withering hands and fingers nimble. Usable.

The lanky Cort Mitchell stood at the balcony railing peering through the telescope.

Colonel Mitchell was not looking at the ocean. He had the telescope turned on the Boardwalk. He caught sight, far down the wooden promenade, of a bareheaded, smiling Lucy Hart. She was not alone. Blackie LaDuke was with her. As the Colonel watched, Blackie leaned close and said something against Lucy's left ear. She immediately burst into fits of laughter and playfully hit at Blackie. Blackie caught her hand and, walking backward, drew her, laughing gaily and shaking her head, toward a Boardwalk photo gallery.

The Colonel, frowning, watched until the laughing, battling pair disappeared within. He pushed the telescope away. He gritted his teeth. He drew a thin brown cigar from inside his linen suit jacket, came over and sat down in a chair near Lady Strange.

He struck a match, puffed his smoke to life, and said, "Tell me I'm worrying needlessly, if you will, but..."

"I will," Lady Strange interrupted, "you are worrying needlessly and I do wish you would stop it." She stroked the purring Precious and irritably told the Colonel, "Unless this young woman is a raving beauty, I doubt that Blackie's interest in her will last another twenty four hours."

"I know," mused the Colonel, puffing on his cigar. "And I hate to see that happen because..."

"Well, make up your mind! Isn't that what you want?" Lady Strange's many chins quivered as she spoke. She pursed her lips and added, "If the danger of seduction is your concern, then surely the sooner he tires of her the better."

Struggling to place a red jack on a black queen, Lochlin MacDonald spoke up. "Has it occurred to either of you that what may or may not take place between Lucy Hart and Blackie LaDuke is strictly between the two of them?" He glanced at the Colonel. "Lucy is not a child, my friend. Nor is she a feather-headed fool. I met her. The young lady possesses a natural dignity and reticence that should keep even our brash Blackie in his place." Lochlin tussled with a red nine, managed to push it onto a black ten. He laughed then and added

"Unless, of course, she doesn't want to keep him in his place." He chuckled happily.

Lady Strange nodded her hearty agreement. Shaking a short, plump finger at the Colonel, she said, "He's right, Cort. Men like to think that they seduce women, but actually it's the other way around." She giggled like a girl. "Why I remember when I first met Lord William. He didn't stand a chance, poor thing. I decided then and there that I was going to have him. It took me less than a week to make him fall helplessly in love." She smiled, remembering, and her fair, round face colored. "I shall never forget how I..."

Both men had heard the story of her royal romance many times before. But they never stopped her when she felt like telling it once again. They listened now as she boasted of her easy triumph, talked wistfully of how she had been a beautiful seventeen-year-old commoner who took the thirty year old, titled British nobleman away from the stuffy Dutch princess to whom he was betrothed. She related with glee how Lord Strange had fallen head over heels in love with her after spending but a few stolen hours in the moonlight with her.

They had married within a few weeks and the lord had pampered and petted her, spoiling her outrageously. Lord William Strange was so mad about her he was absolutely dotty!

That was as much of the tale as Lady Strange ever told.

She kept to herself how her besotted bridegroom showered her with presents when seeking sexual pleasures. Gifts of sparkling diamonds and peek-a-boo French lingerie and rich Belgian chocolates literally filled her private pink boudoir where she eagerly entertained her amorous husband.

To please the lusty lord she went about in the privacy of their suite wearing only gobs of precious jewels and naughty lingerie. She eagerly devoured the exquisite chocolates and just as eagerly made love with her handsome royal husband.

Theirs was life of privilege and pleasure. They divided their time between London and New York, moving easily among the varied levels of society. From the glittering Court of St. James to the opulent drawing rooms of Manhattan, they caused a sensation. What a striking couple they were; the handsome blond lord and his petite brunette lady. He of the towering frame and majestic bearing and she of the tiny form and sensual manner.

Neither he nor she noticed--for several years at least--that she was becoming more and more voluptuous. Her flashing diamond rings grew tight and uncomfortable on her fingers. Her lush womanly curves, both top and bottom, spilled out of the wispy lingerie until the lord was forced to purchase the gauzy goodies meant to display the lovely female form in increasingly larger sizes. The big boxes of chocolates evaporated with alarming speed.

She did notice that the lord spent more and more time at London's exclusive clubs, White's and Boodle's and the St. James Club. It was the same in New York. He began to spend his afternoons and evenings at the Jockey Club.

Until that fateful day when Lord Strange visited their boudoir for the final time. She had awaited him in their Fifth Avenue mansion throughout the long summer afternoon. After lingering in a bath filled with exotic perfumed oils she donned a daring black lace negligee and brushed her dark hair out about her naked white shoulders.

She was posed prettily amongst the many pink satin pillows pushed up against the headboard of their gold leaf bed when at last the lord arrived. He walked through the door, glanced at her, and frowned. He strode across the room and there was an unforgettable look of disgust on his aristocratic face when he told her he was through with her.

It was not until he had gone, leaving her to weep out her misery alone, that she fully realized she was no longer the ninety pound sugar dumpling he had married fifteen years earlier. She had more than doubled in size. She weighed a hundred and ninety-five pounds. She was so large there was no longer room in the lord's life for her.

Within a week she was stepping off the train in Atlantic City in that summer of '73. Banished from the lord's life like a discarded mistress. She was thirty-two years old.

She had been in Atlantic City ever since.

"...don't you think so?"

"What? I...I'm sorry, Lochlin," Lady Strange sighed and returned to the present. "Did you say something?"

"I said, your Ladyship, 'Lucy Hart is neither as young nor as pretty as you when you so easily seduced Lord William'."

Lady Strange nodded, pleased. Preening a little, she said, "No, no, of course not." She stroked the underside of Precious' throat with a forefinger. The black Persian made low rattling sounds of pleasure and his slitted golden eyes closed completely. "How old is this small town postmistress?" Lady Strange asked, looking from one man to the other. Neither knew.

"Maybe you can tell us," said Lochlin. "Blackie's coming up around one o'clock to wheel me back down to the Boardwalk. If they're becoming close friends, he'll likely bring Lucy along."

"Oh, I hope so," said the smiling Lady Strange. "Don't you, Cort?" No answer. "Cort?"

"Blackie ought to leave her alone," said the Colonel, unsmiling.

CHAPTER SEVENTEEN

"Hey, anybody home?"

The deep masculine voice came from just inside Lochlin MacDonald's parlor.

"Where is everyone?"

"On the balcony, Blackie," Lochlin called to him. "Come on out here."

Lucy stepped out first. Blackie was right behind her. Both were smiling and blinking in the bright August sunlight. Both looked younger than their years.

Lucy's fair face was flushed from the sun, the added color giving her a healthy, youthful radiance. Tendrils of her chestnut hair, having escaped the neatly dressed bun at the back of her head, curled appealingly around her flushed cheeks and trailed in coiled ringlets down her graceful neck. Her freshly laundered dress of lilac and white-checked gingham had a tightly belted waist, fashionably full, puffed, elbow-length sleeves, and a gored skirt fitted closely over her hips.

She was, on this August afternoon, prettier than usual.

Blackie, in turn, was tall and striking, with flashing black eyes and curly black hair. As dark as Lucy was fair, he was dressed in a cool summer shirt of sky blue Egyptian cotton with a pair of white duck yachting trousers. Always one to break barriers, stretch rules, and ignore conventions, he wore no socks or stockings of any kind. His brown feet were bare inside the soft, well-worn moccasins he'd owned for years. Whether casual or in white tie and tails, Blackie was good-looking.

He was, incredibly, even handsomer than usual on this sunny Friday in August.

Greetings were exchanged all around. The Colonel rose to his feet, smiling and nodding. Lochlin invited the pair to have a seat. Blackie introduced the two women.

Lucy extended a hand. "I'm honored to meet you, Lady Strange," she said graciously. "Black...er...Mr. LaDuke tells me you're a reader of tea leaves."

"A royal reader of tea leaves," Blackie corrected, leaned down, and kissed Lady Strange's fleshy cheek.

"You must come up to visit me, Lucy," Lady Strange said, gripping Lucy's hand. "And allow me to look into your future."

"I'll do that," said Lucy, politely.

"Lucy, you and Blackie pour yourselves some iced tea," Lochlin MacDonald said. "And sit down, sit down!"

Blackie shook his head no to the iced tea. Lucy passed as well. She sat down at the end of a long white settee, close to the Colonel's chair. Blackie purposely waited until she was seated, then he plucked at the creases in white trousers and dropped down directly beside her. Ignoring the quick frown that appeared on the Colonel's face, Blackie raised a long arm and draped it over the settee's high back behind Lucy's shoulders.

"So you are actually a postmistress?" Lady Strange said, smiling at Lucy.

"I am," Lucy said, nodding, "In Colonias, my hometown in upstate New York."

"This world is changing rapidly," Lady Strange commented. "In my day a young lady would not have been considered for such an important position."

"I hope you approve," Lucy said.

"Oh, I do. Most assuredly. You must tell me more about it."

After the requisite round of pleasantries, the talkative Lady Strange dominated the conversation. Stroking the spoiled Precious, she told Lucy that when she was young the main interests of her circle of friends were gala balls, marriages, foods, wines, horses, gaming, and seaside villas in the South of France.

Her eyes disappearing in laugh lines, she happily boasted, "My name had appeared in *Town Topics*--New York's most widely read tattle sheet--a dozen times before I turned twenty."

"Your life in New York sounds very exciting," Lucy graciously remarked.

"It was," said Lady Strange. "And in London as well." She sighed softly. "But do forgive me. I've been prattling on about myself, as usual. I want to hear about you. I really do."

"There's not much to tell, I'm afraid," said Lucy.

Blackie spoke up, "Lucy's too modest. She was appointed to her position at the Colonias post office by President Benjamin Harrison himself. She was just eighteen years old. The youngest postmistress in America and she..."

Lucy gently interrupted, "Blackie, I'm sure they don't want to hear..."

"But we do," said Lady Strange and she urged the younger woman to talk about her important work.

At their coaxing Lucy related, with modesty and quiet authority, her extensive knowledge of the post office system. She knew its operation inside out and was indeed very proud to be one of the more than 170,000 people presently employed by the United States post office.

The Colonel said, "Wasn't Honest Abe a postmaster at one time, Lucy?"

"He was, yes, he was. When Abe Lincoln was young," she said, smiling at the Colonel, "he was the postmaster in Salem, Illinois in 1833. He considered one of the main attractions of the position to be that he could educate himself by reading the many newspapers and journals before delivering them to his patrons." Lucy laughed melodiously and admitted, "I do the very same thing. I read every magazine and newspaper and bulletin that comes through my post office."

"Good for you," said Lady Strange. "A well informed woman is an interesting one."

"I just hope my box holders don't find me out," said Lucy.

"I'm sure they wouldn't object," said the Colonel, fully approving.

"Lucy Hart, I do believe you're one of the smartest young ladies I have ever met," praised Lochlin.

Lucy smiled at him, glanced at the cards spread out on his wooden tray. Gesturing, she said, "Black five to the red six."

Lochlin looked down. "Now how did I miss that?"

He began to struggle manfully to maneuver the weightless card across the few inches of space. Watching, her heart going out to him, Lucy automatically leaned forward a little, started to help. Blackie touched her forearm. Shook his head.

She sat back.

Lady Strange asked about Lucy's family. Lucy spoke freely and fondly about her handsome, silver-haired father who had been a Civil war hero and Colonias' first postmaster. She disclosed, without sentimentality or emotion, that her dear mother had suffered through a long, debilitating illness; had finally, mercifully, passed away two summers ago.

Blackie, listening intently, gazed at Lucy in amazement and admiration. He'd had no idea--until this minute--that Lucy had lost both her parents.

"No, no, I'm not alone," Lucy quickly assured Lady Strange. She went on to say she had plenty of family. Two older brothers. One in Texas. The other in California. And she had a half dozen nieces and nephews. She was blessed as well with a number of dear friends. Her face lighted when she told the attentive Lady Strange about the darling four-year-old girl who lived next door and came over to visit at least once a day.

When she concluded, Lady Strange said, "You're certainly a more resourceful woman than I was at your age. Why, you must not be more than twenty-five or twenty-six."

"A bit older than that," Lucy said without hesitation. "On the last day of August, I will turn thirty." She made a slight face, shrugged.

"Why, that's only a week away," exclaimed Lady Strange. "So you will be here in Atlantic City on your birthday?"

Lucy nodded. "Yes. I'm staying through Labor Day." She glanced at Lochlin, gave him an embarrassed smile. "I told you I was leaving, didn't I? But here I am."

"Well, we're all glad you stayed," he said, smiling broadly. "We will celebrate your birthday," said the Colonel.

"You bet we will," agreed Lochlin, the self-appointed, widely recognized activity director and chief party planner of the Atlantic Grand. "We'll throw a big wing-ding in the Blue Room with an enormous birthday cake and an orchestra and..."

"Hold on a minute," Blackie coolly cut in. "That's really thoughtful of you all, but Lucy and I have already made plans." He looked at her. "Tell 'em, Lucy."

Caught off guard, she gave him a quick questioning look. He grinned and his black eyes twinkled. He hadn't known, until just now, that her birthday was coming up. She hadn't told him. They had made no plans. But she played along.

She said, looking from Lochlin to Lady Strange to the Colonel, "Can you believe it? Blackie won't even tell *me* how we're going celebrate. Wants it to be a surprise."

"How wonderfully exciting," enthused Lady Strange, ever the romantic. "I love secrets and surprises." She looked directly at Lucy. "You'll tell us afterward?"

"Maybe she will," said Blackie before Lucy could answer. "If she doesn't," he paused, gently squeezed Lucy's shoulder, and winked at Lady Strange, "don't ask."

Lady Strange clasped her hands to her pillowy breasts and swooned.

Lochlin chuckled merrily.

The Colonel cleared his throat.

CHAPTER EIGHTEEN

The buzz along the Boardwalk, that warm Friday evening the 25th of August 1899, was of the grand opening of yet another big amusement pier. This one was at the foot of Pennsylvania Avenue and contained a large indoor auditorium meant for theatricals and musicals.

Hence its name, the Auditorium Pier.

Blackie and Lucy were part of the animated crowd that swarmed out onto the brand new pier that sultry August night, eager for an exciting evening of entertainment. After a ribbon cutting ceremony and a couple of brief speeches by visiting state dignitaries, young and old alike streamed into the new auditorium, quickly filling every available seat.

The houselights dimmed.

The footlights came up.

The expectant crowd applauded.

The curtain rose on a performer who was billed as 'America's Greatest Comic Juggler'.

A smiling, ruddy-faced young man, with light brown hair and a bulbous nose, stood alone at center stage. He reached into the pocket of his baggy brown trousers and withdrew a red rubber ball. He held it up, showed it to the crowd, then tossed it into the air with his right hand. He caught it with his left while pulling a second red rubber ball from his pocket. He tossed the second ball into the air and out of his pocket came a

137

third. He dexterously juggled the three red rubber balls to the wonderment of the approving audience. After putting aside the red rubber balls, the young man expertly juggled three heavy white bowling pins. Then three china plates. Finally, three dangerously sharp butcher knives.

The juggling portion of his act came to end and the comedian stood in the spotlight and told jokes, one right after another. He was hilarious. He held the crowd in the palm of hand with his funny, offbeat stories. Loud, riotous laughter rocked the new auditorium and echoed out over the water.

The audience absolutely loved him.

Young W. C. Fields triumphantly concluded his act to deafening applause and the spirited shouts of 'encore, encore'.

Lucy clapped as enthusiastically as anyone, the palms of her hands stinging like fire, tears of laughter brightening her shining, green eyes. The dry, outlandish wit of the juggling comedian left her in stitches.

A barbershop quartet garbed in matching brightly striped jackets, white trousers, and fashionable straw boaters followed the comical juggler on the evening's program. Their first number was a rousing rendition of *Hello My Baby*. The crowd had quieted and calmed by the time the quartet went smoothly into their second offering, the slower paced romantic ballad, *When You Were Sweet Sixteen*.

Listening to the rich male voices harmonize on the beautiful love song, Lucy was suddenly overwhelmed with the burning desire to steal a secret, admiring glance at Blackie's handsome face. The need was incredibly strong to get at least a fleeting glimpse of the clear, olive skin, the fine cut features, the sensual lips.

Lucy cautiously turned to look at Blackie, only to meet his wickedly laughing, black eyes. She quickly looked away as if she'd been caught in some deviant act. Face warm, she stared straight at the stage, her heart beating fast.

It beat faster still when the smiling Blackie captured her left hand, drew it down, and held it tightly imprisoned between his trousered thigh and her full skirts.

If anyone had told Lucy that the simple act of holding hands could be so thrilling, so unsettling, she would never have believed it.

Blackie's hand was much larger than her own and there was firm masculine strength in the lean fingers that were closed around her palm. Lucy was vaguely aware that the back of her hand rested against Blackie's thigh. But she thought nothing of it, until he deftly turned her hand over so that her soft palm was pressed against the hard muscle straining the flannel of his white trousers.

Lucy was well aware that she shouldn't be sitting in a public place--or a private one for that matter--intimately touching a man's thigh. She should immediately snatch her hand away and shoot a threatening look at Blackie. She should do more than that. She should inform him in no uncertain terms that she would not tolerate such familiarity.

Lucy turned to tell him.

But she didn't follow through. His hauntingly beautiful, night-black eyes were on her again. Or still. She wasn't sure which. At the sight of him gazing fixedly at her, her heart skipped a beat. Several beats. Partly because she was afraid of him, and partly because he so fascinated her.

Blackie LaDuke was the sensual symbol of all the wickedness, passion, and libertine living of which she knew nothing about. He was everything she was not. Maybe that's why she felt an excitement in his presence like no other in her life.

His dark smoldering gaze holding hers, Blackie coolly guided Lucy's captured hand up and down the outside of his long thigh, forcing her soft palm to press flush against the fine flannel fabric of his trousers.

And the hot, hard muscle and bone beneath.

Lucy's fingers tingled at the intimacy. She felt half dizzy. She could hear her heart beating. Could feel it throbbing beneath her left breast. She couldn't believe that she, Miss Lucy Hart, old maid postmistress of Colonias, New York, was actually sitting in a dimly lit auditorium in Atlantic City, New Jersey, touching a darkly handsome stranger in the intimate manner a devoted wife might touch her beloved husband.

And then only in the privacy of their bedroom.

Snatches from a long forgotten newspaper article flashed into Lucy's mind, unnerving her, accusing her. The column had warned that 'women, who in their home towns are wholly decorous and would never go to anything more exciting than an ice cream sociable, would, in Atlantic City become absolutely careless about minor mores.'

Lucy realized with sudden alarm and nagging shame that she had become one of those women.

Forcefully she tugged free of Blackie's grasp and clasped her hands tightly together in her lap. She heard Blackie's teasing chuckle and wanted to smack him a good one.

But not for long.

Her attention was drawn to a troop of flamenco dancers who took the stage, castanets popping, booted feet stamping. When the last flashing-eyed, colorful skirted señorita had swirled away through the exit, the curtain was lowered.

When it rose again, a company of talented New York actors performed a lively one-act play. A clever, fast paced comedy, which had the audience laughing again.

It was a full evening of splendid entertainment. When the final curtain rang down and the house lights again came up, everyone went away happy.

Back out on the Boardwalk Blackie, again holding Lucy's hand, said, "I know the perfect way to top off the evening."

Lucy shot him a warning look. "If it's having a highball at one of the beer gardens you can just forget it. Take me back to the hotel at once. You know how I feel about you drinking alcoholic beverages."

"You're a doubting Thomas, Lucy Hart," Blackie said, smiling. "Not a single drop of hard liquor has touched my lips for the past seventy two hours and that's the truth."

"My, my. That long?" she said, as if impressed. "That must surely be a record of sorts."

"For me it is," Blackie admitted, nodding his dark head. "And it's all thanks to you."

"Well, I'm glad I could be of help," she said pertly, her smile now playful.

Blackie abruptly stopped walking, drew her back, smiled down at her. "We can get high without liquor."

"Oh?"

"Know how?"

"I'm afraid to ask."

"A ride on the Ferris wheel."

Lucy's smile fled immediately. Her nervous glance left Blackie's face, shifted to the two mammoth, lighted wheels looming high above the Boardwalk. A mixture of terror and temptation flashed for a brief second in her expressive green eyes.

"No. No I won't...I can't." She shook her head violently, looked back at Blackie. "It's dangerous."

"Everything's dangerous," said Blackie. "My old aunt broke her leg at the cake walk."

Lucy's quick, responsive laughter was as much a product of anxiety as amusement and Blackie knew it. He also knew she would enjoy the exhilarating ride immensely if he could get her on it. He slid a possessive arm around Lucy's slim waist and propelled her along the crowded walkway directly toward the pair of turning, lighted wheels, assuring her as they went that it would be fun.

"Blackie, I don't know," Lucy weakly protested, reluctant to get on one of the frightening wheels.

"Do it this one time for me," Blackie coaxed. "If you don't like it, I'll have the operator stop the wheel immediately and let us off."

Lucy swallowed with difficulty. "What if I scream and embarrass you?"

His black eyes twinkling merrily, Blackie gave her trim waist an affectionate squeeze. "*You* embarrass *me*? Now that would be switch."

Lucy laughed, despite her mounting dread. "Alright then, what if I scream and embarrass myself?"

"That won't happen."

"It won't? How can you be so sure?"

Blackie's heavy eyebrows arched, giving him demonic look. He said, "I know how to keep you from screaming." His penetrating gaze traveled slowly over her upturned face, deliberately settling on her lips. "Want to hear what it is?"

"No, thanks," Lucy replied as the two of them joined the long queue of eager patrons waiting for a spin on the giant, lighted Ferris wheel.

There were dozens, perhaps a hundred people in line ahead of them. They would have to wait at least a half hour, maybe more. The wait began, and the longer they waited, the more apprehensive Lucy became.

Slow minutes passed.

Squeals of fear and pleasure resounded from the twin turning wheels. The line moved steadily forward, sweeping the jittery Lucy along with it. At last she and Blackie reached the front of the line. They were next.

The wheel was stopping. The operator stepped forward, swung the safety bar aside, and a glowing, laughing couple leapt up out of the wooden seat and rushed away.

"Our turn," Blackie said above Lucy's ear and handed her into the wooden seat. Her eyes were wide, and her pulse pounded in her ears, as he sat down beside her. The wheel's leathery-faced operator swung the heavy bar down across their knees, snapped it into place, stepped back, and signaled to his helper.

The chair began to slowly lift away from the platform.

Lucy felt her stomach falling away along with the ground and wondered why she had ever agreed to this foolish feat of derring-do. When the wooden seat she shared with Blackie was eight or ten feet off the ground, the wheel again stopped, discharged a chattering trio of young girls, picked up a pair of teenage boys.

And went into motion again.

When all seats were vacated and filled once more, the big revolving wheel swiftly picked up speed. Lucy's eyes were closed, had been closed from the beginning. She was too terrified to look.

Eyes squenched tightly shut, hands gripping the safety bar, she hastily offered up a silent prayer for their safety, concluding with the promise that if the Almighty would just get her back to earth, she would *never* climb on a Ferris wheel again for as long as she lived.

Lucy heard Blackie's low, deriding chuckle and said without opening her eyes, "It isn't funny, Blackie LaDuke! I'm scared to death."

"No need to be," he murmured in low, modulated tones and put a long arm around her. "I've got you. You're as safe as a baby in her cradle."

"I am not," Lucy wailed miserably, so tense she was literally frozen in place, her back straight and poker stiff, her hands clutching the bar so firmly her knuckles were turning white.

Blackie squeezed her rigid shoulders and gently commanded, "Lucy, open your eyes and you'll see a sight so breathtaking you'll no longer be afraid."

"I can't," Lucy whispered miserably, shaking her head, "I just can't."

"Sure you can," Blackie soothed, one hand cupping her slender shoulder, the other at her waist. Very slowly, very carefully, he pressed her back against him.

Still clinging tenaciously to the bar but cradled in Blackie's protective arms, Lucy finally got up the nerve to peep out through lowered lashes. Her lashes fluttered, then lifted. She looked about and her eyes slowly widened with wonder. She saw a fairyland of twinkling lights, silvered waters and tiny people moving about far below.

Enchanted, she slowly lifted her gaze to the skies above where a quarter moon sailed lazily in and out of the low lying clouds.

"If you let go of the bar," Blackie said in a warm, caressing voice, "you can reach up and touch heaven."

Fingers curled around the bar, Lucy said, "We aren't quite that high, LaDuke."

"Wanna' bet?" was his response. "Go on. Give it a try. You'll see."

"If I let go of the bar, do you swear to me you won't rock this chair?"

"Cross my heart."

Lucy took a deep, calming breath. Reluctantly she released her death grip on the safety bar, and sank slowly back against Blackie. He took one of her chilled hands in his and pressed it to his chest. Lucy could feel his rhythmic heartbeat beneath her icy, perspiring palm. The slow, steady cadence pulsing through her fingertips was reassuring. He wasn't afraid, so why should she be? They stayed like that for three of four full revolutions of the turning wheel.

Then abruptly, just as the wooden seat in which they rode reached the highest point, the giant wheel jerkily stopped.

They hung suspended, rocking gently back and forth, high atop the unmoving wheel. Lucy trembled. She turned her head, looked into Blackie's dark eyes, and asked fearfully, "What is it? What's wrong?"

"Nothing's wrong. Everything is right." He smiled reassuringly at her, wrapped both arms more snugly around her, and drew her closer into his embrace. He said, "We've stopped so that you can lift your arms, reach up and touch heaven."

"Don't be absurd. I can't reach heaven from here."

"Sure you can. Try it and see."

"You won't let me go? You won't stop holding me?"

"No. Never."

"Very well. This is silly, but..."

Lucy's hands reluctantly left his shirtfront. She hesitantly lifted her arms up, up until finally they were stretched out full length above her head. She waved her slender fingers about, as if attempting to touch the heavens.

Head thrown back, looking straight up at the night sky, she said, "You lied, LaDuke. I can't reach that far." She started to lower her arms. He stopped her.

"Wait," Blackie commanded. "Don't give up too soon."

"My arms are getting tired." Lucy obediently kept them lifted over her head, but lowered her eyes to look at him. "When do I touch heaven?"

"It's about to happen," he said, his black eyes flashing in the shadows, as his dark face moved closer to hers. When his lips were an inch away from her own, he said, "Lucy, I'm going to kiss you."

CHAPTER NINETEEN

Lucy wasn't given an opportunity to say no. She didn't even have time to lower her raised arms before Blackie's mouth was on hers. He kissed her squarely on the lips, but it was nothing more than an amiable, closed-mouth kiss. The harmless affectionate kind that he might have bestowed on an old friend or relative whom he hadn't seen in some time.

At the very most it was an innocently playful kiss, a teasing caress not intended to stir any real emotions. Either hers or his own.

But Lucy was stirred.

His unexpected kiss produced an immediate weakness that left her without the strength to keep her arms raised. They fell weakly to Blackie's wide shoulders. The momentary pressure of his warm, smooth lips on hers took a toll on her senses. She *was* affected by his harmless, hasty kiss. More than he would ever know.

Lucy didn't let on.

She didn't dare allow the worldly, wise cracking Blackie to guess that she was so pitifully inexperienced it took nothing more than one quick, meaningless kiss to put her in a dither. She'd have died a thousand deaths rather than have him know that the touch of his lips on hers evoked a sweet yearning that startled and dismayed her.

Blackie's lips left Lucy's and slid over to her ear. "A touch of Heaven?" he queried cockily, a grin in his voice.

Lucy pushed him away and decisively shook her head. "Not so much as a hint of paradise," she sassily informed him, hoping he wouldn't detect the rapid beating of her pulse, the glassy look in her dazzled eyes.

"You didn't feel a thing?" He pulled back to look at her.

Shrugging her slender shoulders, Lucy sighed dramatically. "No. Sorry. Absolutely nothing happened. Not a thing."

"Wanna' try again?" he asked, leaning closer.

"You had your chance," said she, turning away, crossing her arms over her chest.

Blackie laughed, amused and enchanted. He liked it when she insulted him. He got a kick out of it. It was novel. Different. Enjoyable and challenging. He was tempted to wipe the smug little smile right off her composed face. He was of a good mind to take her in his arms, press her back against the chair seat, and kiss her good. Really kiss her. Kiss her like she'd never been kissed before.

He didn't do it.

An hour later, when they said goodnight at the door of Lucy's third floor hotel room, Blackie put his hand to her chin, tilted her face up to his, and brushed his lips lightly back and forth on hers. That's all he intended to do.

But he forgot himself for a second. He opened his mouth slightly and nipped at Lucy's full bottom lip with sharp teeth. Then sucked her soft lip into his mouth while his hand moved from her chin to cup the side of her neck. His long thumb gently stroked the delicate hollow of her throat. Lucy softly sighed.

Blackie lifted his head and looked into her shining, emerald eyes. His thumb continuing to lightly caress her bare throat, he said, "Meet me in the lobby at nine a.m. sharp tomorrow."

"And if I don't?" She could hardly speak her heart was beating so.

"I'll get a key from the front desk, come up here and haul you out of bed." He grinned wickedly and his night-black eyes gleamed with devilment. "Maybe you'd like that."

Lucy gave him a wilting look. But before she could say anything smart, he clasped her upper arms, drew her up on tiptoe, bent and pressed his lips to the spot his thumb had caressed. Lucy shuddered involuntarily when she felt his warm mouth open on her sensitive flesh. Her head fell back and her heart pounded when he kissed the hollow of her throat, his lips gently plucking, his tongue stroking the tender flesh.

"Blackie," Lucy murmured weakly, breath short, senses reeling, "Don't...don't do that. Stop."

Blackie stopped. His moving mouth immediately stilled. He raised his handsome head and smiled at her.

"Tell me something, Lucy," he said. "Were *don't* and *stop* the first words you learned as a baby?"

"It's too bad you were never taught their meaning," she was quick to reply. "It's obvious no one ever said no to you. And Lord knows you could have benefited from a few *don'ts* and *stops*. You're spoiled, self indulgent."

"I am what I obviously am and I have no problem with that," Blackie said with a shrug. "Do you?"

He touched a springy lock of curly chestnut hair, which lay against her check. He carefully tucked it behind her ear with his little finger. Lucy brushed his hand away.

"I guess not, but we don't see eye to eye."

"Hell no, I'm taller than you."

Lucy couldn't keep from laughing. Then she sighed and said, "You are hopeless and I am tired. I have to go in now and get some sleep. Goodnight."

"Dream of me," Blackie said.

"I never have nightmares, LaDuke," she said flippantly.

Blackie laughed. Then he quickly threw her words back at her, "It's cruel of you to entertain yourself at my expense."

Lucy laughed and hit at him. Dodging, he caught her hands in his, drew them up, and Lucy was struck by how white and slender her fingers were against the olive of his warm palms.

"Let me go," she warned.

"Or you'll what?"

"I'll...I'll hide from you tomorrow."

"No, you won't," Blackie said, cocked his head a trifle to one side, and grinned. "You're looking forward to spending the day with me."

"Your conceit is colossal."

As if she hadn't spoken, Blackie told her in a low, soft voice, "Just as I'm looking forward to being with you." He released her hands. "Goodnight, sweetheart."

Blackie kissed her cheek, turned, and was gone, whistling as he walked down the silent corridor.

Smiling, Lucy went into her darkened room and once inside, sighed dreamily. Then she spun dizzily about in circles, flinging her arms out and dancing gaily around, giddy, happy, on top of the world.

The Last Dance

The room was cool and quiet. A stiff breeze off the ocean billowed the heavy curtains and drew the starry-eyed Lucy out to the small balcony. Yanking the pins from her curly, chestnut hair as she went, Lucy shook her head about and let the heavy locks spill down around her shoulders.

On the balcony she laughed into the sea scented wind. It blew her hair about her face and pressed her summer dress against her slender frame. The strong, moisture-laden breeze caressed her flushed cheeks and coolly stroked the heated hollow of her throat where Blackie had kissed her.

Lucy's fingers lifted to touch the magical place where his lips had so thrilled her. In her entire life, no one had ever kissed her throat. It felt wonderful. Lucy's eyes closed in vivid recollection. She tingled, just as she had during the actual kiss. Then she laughed in nervous anticipation, as she guiltily considered all the sensitive spots where she had never been kissed. She wondered. Before she left this oceanside paradise would Blackie leave no part of her unkissed?

The wicked thought swiftly flooded her body with intense heat and Lucy was thankful for the soothing balm of the strong cooling breezes blowing in off the ocean.

***

While welcome ocean breezes pleasantly cooled the Atlantic City seaside resort that hot August, there was no relief for those still in the city. The stifling heat in New York was intolerable. Manhattan was sweltering under a long siege of ninety-five degree days.

Lilly Styvestant, the Park Avenue goddess, was miserable. She went about her plush penthouse apartment wearing nothing but a frown of displeasure.

A chilled glass of iced gin constantly in her hand, her heavy golden hair pinned atop her head, the long legged Lilly paced restlessly about in a pair of satin, high heeled bedroom slippers, as naked as the day she was born. Refusing to put on clothes, Lilly cursed the horrid heat, snapped at the servants, and complained about what a callous cad her lover was.

At sunset on yet another long, sticky day, a bored, unhappy Lilly stalked irritably about her spacious bedroom, muttering to herself, envisioning the deeply bronzed Blackie frolicking freely on the beach with a bevy of pretty female playmates.

The inconsiderate bastard!

Lilly downed the last of her gin, made a face at the empty glass, and dropped it angrily to the carpet. She walked determinedly to the living room and went directly to the heavy liquor cabinet. She poured straight gin into a tall, fresh, crystal glass, reached into the silver ice bucket, and scooped up a handful of ice, dropping it into the freshly poured drink.

She started to walk away, stopped, and turned back. She picked up the silver ice bucket by its curved handle and carried it into her bedroom. Lonely, miserable, hot, sorry for herself, Lilly kicked off her satin bed slippers and dropped down onto a cream-hued chaise lounge. The long satin couch rested directly before a pair of tall floor-to-ceiling windows, which afforded a breathtaking view of the park and the city.

Lilly set the bucket of ice on the floor by the chaise. She stretched out on the shimmering sofa before the sparkling plate glass windows and waited impatiently for the electric lights to start coming on across Manhattan. One by one the tall buildings and the street lamps far below blazed to life in the gathering August dusk.

The Park Avenue Goddess watched the spectacle from her sky-high bedroom as she thirstily sipped her gin. More than a trifle tipsy, and bored to tears, Lilly Styvestant dipped her hand into the silver bucket, picked up a small piece of ice, touched it to her chin, and trailed it wetly down the bare column of her slender throat.

She dabbed at the hollow of her throat with the ice and felt a faint stirring of familiar desire. Her breath caught in her chest when she allowed the melting ice to glide over the swell of her pale right breast. Lilly bit her bottom lip with growing excitement when she pressed the ice to her sleeping nipple. Then sighed deeply as she rubbed the frozen ice back and forth over the nipple until it budded into a rigid peak, so tight, so sensitive, so in need of a man's skilled hands or heated lips.

Lilly laughed huskily and held the ice against the taut crest until it was stinging with sensation. She took a long slow, swallow of gin, purposely relaxed, reached for more ice, and began to play a prolonged, pleasurable game. While she gazed dazedly at the skyline of Manhattan, perfectly framed in the tall, uncurtained windows, Lilly stretched and arched and purred with feline satisfaction, trailing varying sized bits of ice over her bare, straining body.

Her slender arms and long silken legs soon shimmered wetly. Her flat belly glistened. Her full white breasts with their hard, wine-hued nipples were moist. The thick growth of golden curls between her pale thighs was beaded with diamond drops of water from a generous sprinkling with the melting ice.

Lilly smiled wickedly as she placed a sizable chunk of fresh ice at her left knee and began to slowly, seductively, slide it up the inside of her tingling thigh. She watched the progress with growing fascination and accelerating heartbeat.

She suddenly giggled naughtily, pretending that the entire city was observing her amorous acrobatics. Quickly warming to the naughty fantasy, she imagined that behind each one of those thousands of lighted windows were eager voyeurs. And who could blame them? She was, after all, quite beautiful. Her pale, bare body was an exquisite work of art, a priceless treasure that men longed to look at and touch.

So she would let them.

Let them imagine it was their unworthy hands touching her body, worshipping her, arousing her. She imagined it as well. She preened and panted and pretended that dozens of pairs of strong male hands were touching her, tempting her, toying with her.

It was a lovely, lascivious game and Lilly played it with a passion. Hers was an uninhibited and highly erotic performance Framed there in the plate glass windows high above Central Park, the Park Avenue Goddess played her part with such expertise she soon had herself--and hopefully her vast audience--so hot and excited she could stand it no longer.

With an apologetic moan to her hard breathing voyeurs, she anxiously drew the melting ice up between her parted thighs until it reached its throbbing target. In seconds she was writhing in orgasmic ecstasy.

But the bliss didn't last.

It never did.

No sooner did her breathing slow to normal than Lilly sighed wearily. She was unhappy. Miserable really. She wanted Blackie. She needed him. Nothing else would do her.

Lilly abruptly sat up on the water-dampened chaise, as an idea popped into her mind. She started to smile as she rose to her feet and rushed across the room to ring for Marie.

In neat black uniform with white cap, cuffs, collar, and apron, Lilly's personal maid, Marie, momentarily appeared. Embarrassed, politely averting her eyes, the gray-haired servant stood before her tall, naked mistress.

"A towel! Get me a towel, Marie," Lilly ordered. The little woman scurried into Lilly's large bathroom and returned with a pair of fluffy, white towels. Without being told to do so, Marie began toweling dry her mistress' curiously wet body.

Lilly grabbed the towel. "Never mind that. Go find William and tell him to contact Captain Weems. The captain is to be informed that he and the crew are to ready the *Temptress* for a midnight departure."

"Midnight?" asked the surprised Marie. "You're going out on the yacht tonight?"

"I most certainly am!" Lilly said, and laughed, gesturing toward her dressing room. "Start packing, Marie. I'll need something suitable for the beach and evening gowns for hotel dances and..."

"Where exactly are you going, Miss Lilly?"

"To Atlantic City to surprise Blackie LaDuke!"

CHAPTER TWENTY

END-OF-SUMMER DANCE
Monday, September 4th, 1899
Nine P.M.
The Blue Room
Don't miss The Last Dance of the Season!

Lochlin MacDonald struggled for several long minutes before he was successful at placing the large, white poster up on the easel. The smile never left his face, but his forehead perspired from the tremendous effort, and he was so tired when the task was completed he could barely roll his wheelchair back to admire his handiwork.

The poster announcing the upcoming Labor Day Dance was but one of several that were going up around the Atlantic Grand. This particular one was positioned next to a grouping of wine-colored easy chairs in the lobby, directly across from the elevator. Any and all hotel guests exiting the elevator could not miss seeing the large, white billboard with its fancy gold lettering.

Lucy Hart didn't miss it.

Lucy, rested, happy, and so eager to see Blackie she could hardly wait to get downstairs, stepped onto the elevator at ten minutes past nine on that sunny Saturday morning.

Davey, the young muscular operator with the perennial wide, teeth-showing smile, courteously greeted Lucy, then did a quick double take, and blurted out with unthinking honesty, "My gosh, Lucy. You look so pretty this morning, I almost didn't recognize you." Lucy laughed when he immediately turned red and, shaking his sandy head, stammered, "I...I...didn't...mean that the way it sounded. What I meant was..."

"...that I look quite different then when I first arrived in Atlantic City a week ago," Lucy finished for him.

"Well, yeah. That's it," Davey said and put the car in motion. "You look...ah. different. *Is* something different? Your clothes? Your hair?"

"Just my heart."

"Huh?"

Lucy laughed, shook her head, bid the puzzled Davey a good, good morning, and stepped out into the marble floored, atriumed lobby. The first thing her sparkling, green eyes fell on was the huge, white poster with the gold script lettering announcing the End-of-Summer dance.

A sudden spasm of doubt gripped her. Would she, in her beautiful white tulle evening gown, be at the Last Dance with Blackie? Or, would he have tired of her long before then?

"Lucy, good morning!" Lochlin MacDonald's cheerful voice shook her from her tortured reverie. "What do you think of my poster? Is it well placed here in front of the elevator? Did I forget anything I should have said on it?"

Lucy, glancing anxiously about for Blackie and not seeing him, walked directly toward the seated, smiling Lochlin. Greeting him warmly, she touched his shoulder lightly and then, thoughtfully studying the large placard, mused aloud, "Seems to me it says it all."

"Good, good." Lochlin was pleased. "It's going to be a grand occasion. We've engaged not one, but two orchestras for the big dance. And, of course, there will be garlands of fresh cut flowers and plenty of good food and chilled champagne."

Excitement flashing in his eyes, he eagerly related how everyone agreed that the Atlantic Grand's End-of-Summer dance was unfailingly the best of the entire season. He reminisced about last year's dance, laughingly admitting that he'd drunk so much champagne, he had merrily wheeled around attempting to kiss all the pretty girls.

"Sounds like it was a wonderful dance," Lucy remarked.

"It was, it sure was," said Lochlin, remembering. "But this one will be even better."

Lucy smiled and said, "Lochlin MacDonald, I'll bet you said that last year."

"I did for a fact."

"And," she predicted, "you'll say it again next year." She laughed then.

Lochlin laughed too. "I'm sure I will," he said and carefully kept to himself the inescapable knowledge that he *wouldn't* be saying it again next year. He would never be saying it again. Not after this year.

Lochlin MacDonald knew that, this year for him the Last Dance would really be the Last Dance. He would not live to see another summer. His only hope was that he would live to see the end of this one.

That he would be alive for this last, Last Dance.

His unchanged expression betraying nothing, he said again, "Yes, I'm sure I will. Then; "Now, listen here, you're coming to the dance, aren't you, Lucy?"

Lucy hesitated, uncertain what to reply.

"Yes, she is," came a deep, pleasing voice. Both Lucy and Lochlin looked up. Blackie joined them. He smiled down at the man in the chair, clamped a firm hand on his thin shoulder, slid a possessive arm around Lucy's slender waist, and said to Lochlin, "She's coming to the Last Dance with me." Only then did his gaze shift and his brilliant black eyes meet hers as he asked, "Will you come to the dance with me, Lucy?"

"Yes. Yes, I will," she managed, momentarily mesmerized by the firm line of muscle that went from his beautiful cleft chin up to his well shaped ear. She had such a compelling, inexplicable urge to reach up and touch that handsome, olive face, her fingertips tingled.

"Yes, she is," Blackie told Lochlin. "And now that that's settled, you ready to go to work?"

"Ready," said Lochlin. "This was the last of the posters. They're all up."

Blackie again shifted his attention to Lucy. "What about you?" His smile was so disarming, she realized suddenly that a world without him in it was unthinkable. Unbearable. "You ready for the day *and* night with me?" he asked softly.

She couldn't speak. Could only nod. Blackie never noticed. Lochlin MacDonald did. He saw what was happening. Before his eyes Lucy Hart was growing younger. Prettier. There was healthy color in her cheeks. Youthful vitality in her movements.

In just a week, she had come alive.

Blackie and Lucy wheeled Lochlin down to the Boardwalk, to his tall Toledo standing scales. They left him there with the promise they'd be back for him around two thirty p.m., at which time the three of them would retire upstairs to Lochlin's apartment for a pleasant hour of rest and relaxation on his balcony.

Customers were already crowding around the seated Lochlin when Blackie took Lucy's hand and gently pulled her away. They had gone but a few yards down the Boardwalk when Blackie said, "You were ten minutes late coming down this morning."

"Was I?" She tilted her head to one side. "And what about you? You were nowhere in sight when I got off the elevator."

He stopped short, drew her back. "I was hunting you." A delicious chill of joy skipped up Lucy's spine when he said, "I was about to come up there and haul you out of bed." His lean fingers gripped hers warmly, and his black eyes danced with devilment when he leaned down and whispered suggestively, "Or else climb in with you."

Pretending to be angry, Lucy freed her hand from his, shook her finger at him, and said, "I'm warning you, LaDuke."

"About what?" He was all little boy innocence.

Under her breath, "I've told you before I will not tolerate vulgarity."

"Who's being vulgar?" He looked around for the guilty culprit.

"You are," she said, but she was smiling at him. "Either you promise to behave yourself, or I'll go right back to the hotel."

"No, you won't."

"I will. So help me."

Shaking his dark head, he arrogantly stated, "You couldn't last a whole day without me."

"I beg your pardon. I've lived twenty-nine years without you," she informed him, "so I guess I can make..."

"Thirty," he interrupted, correcting her. "Come Thursday, you'll have lived thirty years without me. And you know what? That's too damned long. Let's go somewhere quiet and get to know each other better." Lucy's cheeks flushed with warmth. His black eyes twinkled and he added, "Relax. I don't mean in the biblical sense. Unless, of course you'd like to..."

"Shhh!"

Lucy frowned, looked anxiously about. Sure enough, several pairs of eyes were on them. But instead of being embarrassed, Lucy experienced--as she always did--a heady rush of vanity at being seen with Blackie. She had told herself it was childish and silly that she was proud of being seen with a rogue and a rounder.

But every time she saw the look of undisguised envy in the eyes of women far more beautiful than she, she felt privileged to be the lucky woman with whom Blackie LaDuke chose to spend his time. There was little doubt in her mind that every eligible female in Atlantic City--and some who were not so eligible-- would have given their eyeteeth to trade places with her.

The frown left Lucy's face. Knowing they were being observed, she slipped a possessive hand up around Blackie's hard biceps, smiled up at him, and said, "What are we waiting for? Aren't we going out to the Turkish Pavilion this morning?"

Blackie's heavy eyebrows shot up quizzically. "Did I miss something here?" He looked about as if hunting for an answer. "What happened all of a sudden to sweeten your mood?"

Lucy laughed girlishly. "Forgive me if I seemed a bit of a sour puss." She squeezed his arm. "I guess I got up on the wrong side of the bed."

"There you go, talking about beds again." Blackie grinned wickedly. "Are you trying to shock me, Lucy Hart?"

"If only I could."

Blackie threw back his dark head, laughed, and impulsively hugged Lucy close. Then, holding hands once more, they headed happily down the Boardwalk with Blackie promising today was going to be 'a perfect day'.

They breakfasted on the Boardwalk and afterward rented a pair of bicycles. They road all the way down to the south end of Absecon Island. Once there, Blackie pointed out the huge, grotesque building in the shape of a giant elephant. Lucy refused to believe him when he told her the elephant's name was Lucy.

But when they ventured inside the huge monstrosity and encountered other visitors, Blackie said loudly, "Can anyone tell us what this place is called? Does the elephant have a name?"

"Lucy," came the quick response from a dozen helpful people at once. "Lucy, Lucy," echoed throughout the building.

"Sorry you doubted me?" Blackie asked Lucy. She nodded. "Think you should apologize?"

"Don't hold your breath," she said, shrugging slender shoulders.

Blackie smiled. He stood with his feet apart, arms folded over his chest, while she circled slowly around him, looking at the strange building. He told her the giant, Margate elephant had been a major attraction since being built by a real estate promoter years ago.

162

"Hmmm," Lucy murmured, stopping directly in front of Blackie. Her hands went to her hips and she asked, "Did you bring me here because I resemble her?"

Blackie's arms came unfolded. "I brought you here because I don't want you leaving Atlantic City without seeing and doing everything there is to see and do." He reached out, curled a long forefinger around the top edge of the boat-necked bodice of her dress, and gently drew her toward him. His voice lowering, he said, "The only similarity between you and this other Lucy," he inclined his dark head to encompass the interior of the huge elephant, "is that you--like her--are a 'major attraction' to me."

Lucy didn't believe him for a second, but her knees weakened just the same and it was all she could do not to helplessly sway into him. She could almost feel herself melting against his tall, lean frame. Oh, how she longed to lay her head on his chest and wrap her arms around him.

Instead she rolled her eyes skyward, brushed his hand from her bodice, turned and walked away. Laughing now, Blackie watched her a moment. Then he went after her.

Lucy squealed her surprise and outrage when he swept her off her feet, lifted her up against his solid chest, and told the startled tourists who turned to stare, "Pay us no mind. We're on our honeymoon."

The statement elicited aaahs and ooohs and even a round of applause from the approving, romantic crowd. Shouts of congratulations and best wishes followed them as Blackie carried the laughing Lucy toward the exit.

Struggling in his arms and kicking her feet, Lucy said, "Put me down! Now, I mean it, Blackie. Put me down. People are staring!"

"Kiss me and I will."

"Are you insane? It's broad daylight and we're in a public place and there are crowds all around and we..."

Blackie's lips silenced her protests. He kissed Lucy right there in broad daylight in that very public place with crowds all around. Holding her high in his arms, he kissed her until she quit struggling.

Lucy stopped gripping and twisting at his shirtfront when his mouth opened on hers. Her hand flattened against the hard muscles of his chest when his tongue parted her lips, skimmed over her teeth, then slipped between. Her heart tried to beat its way out of her chest when his tongue touched hers.

The broad daylight, the public place, the crowds all around them quickly faded away and were forgotten by Lucy. There was no one and nothing but Blackie. Only Blackie. Blackie's strong hands beneath her knees and at her waist. Blackie holding her so close her breasts were flattened against his chest. Blackie's marvelous mouth molding her trembling lips to fit his own.

Blackie. Blackie. Blackie.

Slowly, gently, his lips never leaving hers, Blackie lowered Lucy to her feet. When her toes touched the ground, his hands settled on her hips and he turned her more fully to face him.

As she had wanted to do earlier, Lucy swayed helplessly into him. She melted against his tall, lean frame, wrapping her arms around his trim waist.

Lucy swallowed and blinked when at last their lips separated. She caught the flash of sultry heat in his night-black eyes before it vanished and Blackie set her back, as if mentally shaking himself.

He gave her a grin and, as if nothing had happened, said, "So what do you say, Lucy? The Steel Peer for lunch and then the Sousa concert?"

Lucy nodded, dazed.

Back on the Boardwalk they lunched on hot dogs and ice-cold sodas. Then they held hands at the early afternoon concert and Blackie whispered to Lucy that Sousa's wife was from Atlantic City. That's why the maestro played here every summer.

It was a wonderful, spirited concert and both Lucy and Blackie were humming the lively marches when they made their way down the long wooden walk to meet Lochlin MacDonald.

Lochlin was humming with them by the time they reached the Atlantic Grand. The trio made it up the hotel's back steps. Out of breath, stumbling and laughing, Blackie wheeled Lochlin through one of the double beachside doors Lucy held open wide.

They were happily headed for the elevator when the desk clerk called out, "Blackie! Excuse me a moment, please. A message came for you."

Blackie waved to the desk clerk. "Take over the driving for a minute, will you, Lucy? I'll meet you at the elevator."

Lucy nodded and stepped behind Lochlin's wheel chair. Blackie crossed to the marble topped front desk. The beak nosed desk clerk with the bushy eyebrows and large prominent ears handed Blackie a small envelope of heavy blue parchment paper. "When did this note arrive?" Blackie asked.

"A messenger clad in sailing clothes delivered it an hour ago."

Blackie frowned, tore the blue envelope open, and read the brief message.

Darling,

Just arrived on the Temptress. Hurry aboard or else I'll come straight to the hotel. The champagne is cold and I'm hot!

Lilly

CHAPTER TWENTY ONE

Jesus God Christ!

Blackie swore under his breath and reflexively crumpled the note into a tightly wadded ball in his fist.

"Sir?" said the desk clerk. "Did you say something?"

"What?" Blackie looked up. "Oh. No. No, I didn't say anything." He glanced anxiously over his shoulder, then back, pushed the crinkled note and matching envelope across the marble counter. "Throw this in the trash for me, will you, Sims?"

The desk clerk nodded politely.

Blackie turned away. For the first time in days he wanted a drink. Needed a drink. Bad. He cast a longing glance toward the hotel bar. He could almost taste a soothing shot of bourbon. His mouth watered. A vein throbbed on his forehead. He swallowed hard and crossed back to Lucy and Lochlin.

"Hey, folks," he said, smiling easily now, rubbing his hands together, "I've got this minor problem."

"We don't want to hear it," Lochlin quickly cracked, "do we, Lucy?"

Lucy smiled, but looked worriedly at Blackie. "Has something happened?"

Blackie shrugged wide shoulders. He answered imperturbably, "No, no. Nothing like that. Actually, I had completely forgotten about a previous engagement...ah...a...business appointment I have this afternoon. Right now as a matter of fact. I'm already a half hour late."

"A business appointment?" Lucy immediately brightened. Hopefully; "An opportunity for a position at some reputable firm perhaps?"

"Blackie LaDuke seeking gainful employment?" Lochlin said, then burst out laughing. "Now that'll be the day."

Blackie laughed as well, and offered no further information. He looked at Lucy. "I'll be back in an hour; two at the most." He laid the back of his hand against her cheek, took it away. "Lady Strange and the Colonel should be joining you two around three." He pressed Lochlin's shoulder and whispered to Lucy, "Say you'll miss me."

"I'll miss you."

"Go on. Get out of here," ordered Lochlin.

Blackie turned and hurried back toward the beachside double doors. Once outside on the hotel's wide veranda, he exhaled loudly, then gritted his teeth and shook his dark head with frustration. He skipped down the steps muttering oaths, wishing to high heaven he had a good stiff drink, wondering how the hell he was going to get himself out of this fine mess.

***

Short minutes after Lucy pushed Lochlin's wheel chair out onto his sunny fifth floor balcony, Colonel Mitchell and Lady Strange arrived. The tall, silver-haired Colonel was, as usual, friendly, charming, and considerate, a strong reassuring presence of fatherly authority.

On his arm was the short, rotund Lady Strange. And resting in Lady Strange's plump arm was her spoiled, overweight Persian, Precious. The huge, black tom was cradled comfortably against his mistress' pillowy breasts, the extended claws of his right paw tangled in a rope of priceless pearls. Precious flopped his long tail languidly back and forth in lazy contentment, and made low rattling sounds deep in his throat as he dozed with his golden eyes slitted half open.

Warm greetings were exchanged and Lady Strange, looking about, frowning, immediately asked, "Where's my sweet boy, Blackie?"

"He had a prior engagement, Your Ladyship," Lochlin calmly explained, "some sort of business meeting."

Puffing, lowering herself--with the aid of the mannerly Colonel--down onto the long white settee, Lady Strange said, "He'll be joining us shortly?"

"He hopes to," said Lucy.

Just then a white jacketed waiter from the hotel kitchen stepped out onto the balcony carrying a silver tray atop which was a tall crystal pitcher of iced tea, a half dozen glasses, a porcelain sugar bowl, a small silver dish containing sliced lemon, and a plate of freshly baked miniature cakes and assorted cookies.

Lady Strange's short, bejeweled fingers were the first to reach for the tempting sweets. Lochlin and the Colonel drank their iced tea in easy companionship as Lady Strange eagerly began devouring the rich desserts. Neither thirsty nor hungry, Lucy was fidgety. Unable to sit still. She told herself Blackie's absence was not the cause of her restlessness. But she knew better.

Lochlin's balcony seemed empty on this sunny Saturday afternoon.

Blackie was not here.

Inwardly sighing, impatiently counting the minutes until his return, Lucy ventured over to the powerful telescope mounted on a tripod at the balcony's railing. She pulled the telescope around, leaned to it, closed one eye, peered through the lens, and looked out at the array of ships and boats on the water.

She attempted to entertain herself silently for a time. Then, pointing to a vessel far out on the horizon, wondering what kind of ship it was and where it was headed, she enlisted Lochlin's help.

The former seaman was eager to share his vast knowledge of all ocean-going vessels. His eyes immediately flashed and he strained against the confines of his unresponsive body. The Colonel was aware that Lochlin's condition was worsening so rapidly now he was incapable of rolling the wheels of his chair. Mitchell rose to his feet. He stretched, yawned, acted as if he himself wanted to move about. He pushed Lochlin's chair to the mounted telescope where Lucy waited, then unobtrusively stepped aside, and leaned on the balcony railing for a time, staring wordlessly out to sea. Momentarily he turned away, reclaiming his chair near Lady Strange.

Beaming, in all his glory now, Lochlin eagerly identified for the interested and impressed Lucy the various kinds of craft moving about in their line of vision. He could spout chapter and verse as to the make, the tonnage, the speed, and the cost of every vessel--sail, steam, and tug--that ever plied the choppy waves of the shallow coastal waters and deep seas beyond. Lochlin would peer through the telescope, zero in on a particular ship or boat, pull his head away, and allow Lucy to look while he told her exactly what she was seeing.

Making a wide, slow sweep from right to left with the telescope, teacher and pupil enjoyed themselves tremendously while Lady Strange, stroking the purring

Precious, greedily finished the cakes and cookies. Colonel Mitchell, quietly observing his strange assortment of treasured friends, smiled to himself and steepled his long fingers.

Lucy said, "Oh, Lochlin! Look at this. It's a big private yacht, isn't it?" And she turned the telescope over to him once again.

Lochlin squinted through the lens, focused on the sleek white yacht bobbing gently up and down.

"It sure is and it's a fine one, too. I can read the name on the stern. It's the yacht *Temptress*, out of New York City." Lochlin suddenly whistled through his teeth.

"What? What is it?" Lucy asked.

"A beautiful blond with long hair just appeared on deck."

"Really? I want to see," Lucy said.

"Alright. Just a minute and I...I..."

Eye pressed to the lens, Lochlin was watching as a small motor launch came up alongside the large white yacht and a tall, lean, black haired man stood up. Lochlin blinked, stared, swallowed. And watched as Blackie LaDuke stepped out of the launch, agilely climbed the yacht's side ladder, and lithely swung aboard.

"Let me look now," Lucy was growing impatient. "I want to see the blond lady."

"She's gone below," Lochlin lied. He pulled back from the telescope, but did not relinquish the lens to Lucy. "I'm a little tired now," he said quickly. "Think you could wheel me to the table and pour me an iced tea."

"Oh, of course," Lucy said.

***

"Darling! Oh, darling! I missed you so!"

The Park Avenue Goddess threw her arms around Blackie's neck and kissed him the minute he stepped onto the deck of the yacht, *Temptress*. Her wrists clasped firmly behind his head, she leaned back from the waist, pressed her pelvis to his, and began to thrust slowly, rhythmically against him.

"Lilly, for christsakes," Blackie took hold of her arms, and attempted to free himself.

She clung for dear life. "What? What's wrong? Aren't you glad to see me?"

Blackie reached up, gripped her wrists, and pried her hands from his neck. He set her back a little away from him and said, "What are you doing here?"

"Well, what kind of welcome is that? I was lonely without you." She smiled and informed him, "It's all planned, darling. We'll go on down to Cape May this afternoon and tomorrow..."

"No, Lilly. We won't. *I* won't."

She laughed and shook her gleaming blond head. "I love it when you're stubborn, Blackie. You're so adorable." She clasped his rib cage, dug her long nails into his flesh, leaned forward, and pressed her lips into the V of his open collared shirt.

Again he set her back. "Lilly, we have to talk."

"Later, darling. We'll talk later. First let's..."

"No. Now. We'll talk now. I'm not staying."

She looked at him as if he was speaking a foreign language. "What do you mean? Of course, you're staying. I want you to stay and I..."

"Lilly, you aren't listening." He shook his head in annoyance.

She frowned. "But, I am. You want to talk, let's talk." She smiled at him, crossed her arms.

"That's better," he said. "I came out to tell you..."

"We can't talk here, Blackie." Lilly's arms came uncrossed. She glanced around, gestured to a half-dozen crewmembers, uniformed in starched white, all within earshot. "Let's go below where we have a little privacy." She tugged on Blackie's hand.

Blackie considered flatly refusing. He was uncomfortable with the idea of going down to her cabin. He knew this spoiled, determined woman all too well. Once she got him below, she would do everything in her power to keep him here.

He knew himself, too. Knew his own weaknesses. Knew if he held still for a couple of drinks, a couple of kisses, he'd be a goner. The afternoon would quickly turn into one of those heated sexual frolics that might well last into the night.

He couldn't let that happen.

He had promised Lucy he'd take her to the rooftop dance at the Ritz Carlton and he meant to keep that promise.

"Come on, darling," Lilly coaxed, honey dripping, "we'll have one teeny-weeny little drink and we'll talk."

"Too early in the day for a drink," Blackie said, reluctantly following her down the stairs to the opulent main cabin.

Lilly gaily laughed as if he'd said something hilarious. "Darling, since when is any hour too early for a drink?"

Below deck, Blackie ducked his head and went through the teak framed hatch of Lilly's private cabin. He advanced a couple of steps, blinking blindly. It was very dim inside. The curtains were closed over the portholes. The lamps were unlit. Blackie stood unmoving, waiting for his pupils to adjust. Lilly's

173

laughter filled the shadowy room as she kicked off her shoes, danced around in back of him, then closed and locked the door. She swiftly stepped up behind him, wrapped her arms around him, and pressed herself against his back. She nipped at his left shoulder through the fabric of his shirt and slid a bent knee up the outside of his long, right leg.

"Give you any ideas?" she asked seductively, hooking her raised leg around his hard thigh, slithering her bare heel toward his groin.

Blackie caught her slim ankle with his hand, staying her foot. "Cut it out, Lilly. I told you, I'm not staying."

Lilly lowered her bare toes to the floor, released him, and moved around to face him. Fingers toying with a shirt button at the middle of his chest, she pouted like a spoiled child, puffing out her bottom lip, then whining, "You are too staying! Pleasssse. Darling...pleasssse."

"No," he was inflexible. "No. I'm sorry you've come all the way down here when..."

"Look around you," she interrupted, a sharp red fingernail circling a flat brown nipple through his white lawn shirt. "And it's all for you."

Blackie's eyes were now adjusted to the dim light. He glanced around, saw that the lavish cabin had been readied for a tryst. White satin sheets shimmered on the turned-down bed, and a couple of bottles of champagne were stashed deep down in the icy depths of a silver bucket beside the bed. On the bedside table was a silver bowl of sun ripened fruit and a tray of cheeses and breads.

And placed squarely on the satin sheeted bed was yet another silver tray, this one holding perfumed oils in sparkling crystal vials, a half dozen long, white feathers, and an impressive array of toys and trinkets for taunting and tickling an aroused, unclothed body. It was evident she had planned well for an adventure in prolonged sexual pleasure.

Blackie was tempted.

A sensual man by nature, he was tantalized by the prospect of whiling away the long August afternoon in erotic play on that inviting white bed with the luscious, uninhibited Lilly.

A muscle danced in his lean jaw when his dark eyes returned to her upturned face and he said, "No, Lilly, I really have to get back to the hotel."

Lilly read the indecision in his eyes and knew it was time to move in for the kill.

"If you must," she murmured softly, "then you must."

Holding his gaze, licking her lips, she took a quick step back, reached down and grabbed up the hem of her dress. With amazing speed and deftness, she lifted the loosely flowing dress up over her head and tossed it aside.

She was totally naked beneath.

Blackie's dark eyes widened, then narrowed. Lilly laughed seductively, trailed one hand across her flat white belly and cupped and lifted her full ivory breasts with the other.

She said, "It's all yours, Blackie. Don't you want to touch anything? Kiss anything?" Her hands dropped to her sides, then lightly caressed her pale, strong thighs. "Don't you want to have my legs wrapped around you?" She saw him swallow convulsively and quickly pressed her advantage. She began to anxiously unbutton his shirt; he stopped her.

"No," he said weakly, "don't do that."

Lilly was beginning to get a little nervous. By now he should be reaching for her, crushing her to him, filling his hands with her flesh, kissing her senseless. Lilly gripped his shirtfront and tore it open, sending buttons flying. She pressed her naked breasts against his bared chest and whispered, "Make love to me, Blackie. You know you want me."

Her hand went between them, found his groin. He was half hard. She had him now. A smile of triumph touching at her lips, Lilly's hand eagerly cupped him, caressed him. She leaned into him, put out her tongue, and licked his broad, naked chest, inhaling deeply of his clean, masculine scent.

Against the dense black, tickling chest hair, Lilly murmured provocatively, "Mmmm, darling, I'm going to eat you up."

Blackie shuddered involuntarily. He was tempted to stay. Snared by the lure of lust, he wanted to shed his clothes, join this beautiful, naked woman in the cool, white bed, and let the rest of the world--including Lucy Hart--go to hell.

But he couldn't do that.

An unfamiliar sense of duty, or something akin to it, made him mentally shake himself and stop short of surrender. His hands lifted, clasped Lilly's bare arms, and set her back.

"Not this time, Lilly," he said to her. "I told you, I can't stay."

Stunned, hurt, realizing he actually meant it, she said, "But why? I don't understand. I came all the way down here to see you and now you tell me..."

"You shouldn't have come without letting me know. Without asking me first."

"Asking you?" Her eyes began to spark with anger. "Asking you? I don't have to *ask* you for permission to visit a public resort!"

"No. No, you don't. But had you told me you were coming, I might have been able to join you this afternoon. As it is, I can't."

"That's nonsense. What could you possibly have to do that is better than what I am offering?" With her hands she gestured to her voluptuous body.

"It's not that. It's...well...I have obligations."

"Obligations?" she snorted derisively. "You? Why, you don't know the meaning of the word!"

Blackie exhaled wearily. He bent, picked up Lilly's discarded dress from the carpet, held it out to her. "You're probably right about that. I'll amend that; I have a prior commitment."

Lily angrily snatched her dress from his hand, but did not put it on, or bother to cover her nakedness with it. "You have a prior commitment?"

"Yes." He nodded. "I'm sorry you've come all this..."

"You're seeing another woman!" Lilly cut in, her voice lifting. She swatted at him with her discarded dress, then dropped it to the carpet again. "So, that's it! That's it, isn't it? Isn't it? Answer me, Blackie LaDuke!"

Calmly, he said. "I promised a young lady I'd take her dancing this evening."

"Well, darling," Lilly's hands went to her bare hips and she gave him a knowing smile, "it won't be the first time you've broken a promise to a woman, now will it?"

"This is one I intend to keep."

Lilly was growing really worried now. "Who is she? What's so special about her?"

"I have to go, Lilly." Blackie turned away.

Lilly grabbed for his arms, spun him around. "You think you can take some trollop to a silly dance while I sit here alone? Do you? How dare you treat me this way! I won't have it!" She was starting to shriek, shaking her doubled up fist in his face. "Do you hear me? I will not have it!"

"Good-bye, Lilly," he said, and again turned away.

"You come back here!" she screamed and when he ignored her, she flew at him in a rage.

"Jesus Christ, behave yourself," he warned, easily shaking her off. Turning to face her, he said, "Get dressed and pour yourself a drink, Lilly. You need to calm down."

"Don't you tell me what I need to do," she wailed. She reached out to a rosewood bookcase nearby, picked up a one-of-a-kind porcelain figurine, and whacked him hard across the jaw. The glass statue shattered. Blood flew. Blackie raised a hand, wiped it away.

"I hope you're really hurt," Lilly screamed hysterically. "I hope I hurt you as badly as you've hurt me, you...you...shitheel!"

CHAPTER TWENTY TWO

Moments after Lucy pushed Lochlin's wheeled hospital chair back to the table and poured him a tall glass of iced tea, Colonel Mitchell rose to his feet. Nonchalantly he sauntered over to the mounted telescope, swung it slowly around, leaned down and pressed his right eye to the lens.

He focused on the sleek white yacht.

Blackie LaDuke stood on the teak deck, the brilliant summer sunlight glinting on his blue-black hair. He was not alone. A beautiful blond woman was with him. Her slender body was pressed intimately against Blackie's tall frame; her hands were clasped behind his head. She was smiling up at Blackie and her smile was almost as suggestive as the manner in which she was grinding her pelvis to his.

The silver-haired Colonel straightened, coughed needlessly, shoved the telescope aside, and drew a slow, deep breath.

Mitchell was not surprised by what he had seen. Not at all. Blackie LaDuke had been an unrepentant rogue and insatiable womanizer for as long as he'd known him. Which was, in the Colonel's view, nobody's business but Blackie's. So long as Blackie stayed with his own kind. Like the rich, beautiful blond on her private yacht.

If Blackie wanted to spend all his time and energy drinking and carousing with women as jaded and experienced as he, that was his look-out. More power to him. Live and let live. Eat, drink, and be merry and who cared? The Colonel didn't. Did not give a hoot in hell.

But he *did* care about the tender feelings of the genteel, unsophisticated Lucy Hart. He was deeply offended by the notion of Blackie spending the afternoon in bed with the glamorous blond and the evening dancing with the unsuspecting Lucy.

Mitchell frowned as he squinted out to sea, but carefully composed himself before turning around. No hint of concern showed on his face when the Colonel came away from the railing, and sat back down near Lady Strange.

Lady Strange, having finished the last of the cookies and cakes, was mellow and uncharacteristically quiet. She sat languidly stroking a contented Precious as the black tom catnapped on her lap. She noticed Lucy lifting and looking at the brooch watch pinned to her bodice. Again. Lucy had glanced at the watch a half dozen times in the past hour.

Lady Strange smiled to herself.

The younger woman was counting the minutes until Blackie joined them. Lady Strange wasn't surprised. Nor could she say she blamed Lucy. In all likelihood, the naive postmistress from Colonias, New York had never known a man half so handsome and charming as Blackie. Much less have been courted by such a dashing rascal.

Lady Strange's romantic heart was warmed by the thought as she studied Lucy's face.

Unlike her overprotective friend the Colonel, Lady Strange wasn't worried about what might or might not happen between Lucy and Blackie. She was just glad that the dynamic Blackie, for whatever his reasons, had chosen to spend so much of his time with the dazzled Lucy.

Every woman should have a Blackie LaDuke once in her life. Even if only for a brief two-week interlude.

Lady Strange had learned years ago that life was more the re-living of it than the living. Long after this lovely summer had ended, the spinster postmistress would--time and time again--relive the treasured hours she had spent here with the exciting Blackie LaDuke.

Fanned by a cooling ocean breeze, Lady Strange sighed deeply, closed her eyes, and half dozed like the contented cat on her lap.

***

A little more than an hour after leaving Lucy and Lochlin in the lobby of the Atlantic Grand, Blackie was back at the hotel. He raced up the beachside steps, hoping he wouldn't run into anyone he knew. He was in luck. The spacious lobby was almost empty at this quiet hour of the afternoon. Blackie made it to the elevator without attracting attention.

Holding his torn and bloodied shirt together over his dark chest, Blackie waited impatiently for the car to descend and the heavy elevator door to slide open. He heard he clanking of machinery signaling the elevator's descent. He was in luck again. The door opened and no one was inside except the operator, the grinning Davey.

"Wow!" Davey exclaimed, eyes and grin widening as Blackie stepped inside. "Look at you!" Davey admired Blackie's cut and badly bruised cheek as though it were a badge of honor. Noting the torn shirt as well, Davey said, pleased, "I was beginning to think you weren't going to get into any fist fights this summer." He closed the elevator door.

"Now you know me better than that," Blackie said, smiling, touching his purpling cheek with two fingers. "Have I ever failed?"

"No, Siree," said Davey happily, and both men laughed in easy comradeship as the car lifted.

At the penthouse floor, Blackie hurriedly exited the elevator, rushed down the silent corridor to his northern tower suite. The minute he stepped inside the door, he began undressing. By the time he reached the black marble shower, he was stripped to the skin.

He stepped into the roomy enclosure, twisted the silver faucet handles, and lifted his bruised, bloodied face to the pounding needles of water. Blackie soon bent his dark head under the spray, braced both open palms against the black marble shower wall before him, closed his eyes, and reviewed the events of the past hour.

He saw again Lilly throwing her arms around him when he stepped on deck. Kissing him and thrusting her pelvis to his while white-uniformed crewmen stood only a few yards away. Lilly leading him down the ladder to her dim stateroom. Locking the door and climbing all over him. Removing her dress and standing there naked and eager in the cool cabin darkness, begging him to make love to her.

Blackie's dark head sagged lower. The force of the water pounded on his bare, brown shoulders.

He wondered at himself.

Lilly was a beautiful woman. She had been undeniably desirable standing there naked, offering herself to him. He had wanted her--but not with the hunger she usually evoked. Her wanton behavior seemed almost repugnant. He had never found it so before. He'd always liked her aggressive and vulgar and shocking ways. Had thought it appealing that she was delightfully lewd and shameless and immoral.

Just like him.

Blackie's eyes opened. He lifted his head. He pushed away from the shower's black marble wall. He rubbed water from his thickly clumped eyelashes and began to smile.

Jesus, he knew what it was.

It was the contrast. The glaring difference between Lilly and Lucy. Lilly had acted no more unorthodox than usual, but her behavior seemed somehow scandalous when compared with Lucy's proper demeanor.

Lucy was the reason he hadn't gone to bed with Lilly, not Lilly. If Lucy was like Lilly, he could have made love to Lilly, then come back and made love to Lucy an hour later.

But she wasn't.

And he couldn't.

Even to a *shitheel* like him, it would have seemed somehow unforgivably obscene to make love to Lilly in the afternoon and take Lucy dancing the same night.

Blackie soaped his body from head to toe and scrubbed himself vigorously to make sure none of Lilly's scent clung to his skin. Then he turned round and round in the shower, allowing the jetting sprays of water to wash away the thick suds. He turned off the shower, stepped out, and hurriedly toweled himself dry.

Blackie checked his face in the mirror above the black lavatory.

An inch long gash directly below his bruised and blackened right cheekbone was hardly visible on the discolored flesh. He looked as if he had been in fight and that his opponent had gotten in a well-placed left hook to his jaw. No one would have any trouble believing that was exactly what had happened.

Blackie quickly threw on some fresh clothes. He was buttoning his shirt when he got back on the elevator and told Davey to rush him down to the fifth floor.

His night-black hair still damp from the shower, Blackie stepped out onto Lochlin's balcony. Every head immediately turned. Every eye came to rest on him He offered a cheery hello and stood smiling confidently in the sunshine.

"Hey, Slugger," teased Lochlin. "How does the other guy look? Hope you got in a couple of mean punches."

"Oh, Blackie, honey! You've been at it again," said Lady Strange worriedly, pressing a plump hand to her bosom.

Colonel Mitchell said nothing. Just nodded coolly.

"Blackie," Lucy's lips formed his name but no sound came.

Her face pale, she instinctively moved to him. She wanted to reach out and touch him, to cradle him protectively to her and kiss away his hurt. Instead she calmly checked his bruised cheek with chilly, assessing eyes. As soon as she was satisfied he wasn't badly hurt, her hands went to her hips and she scolded him.

"Fighting like a school boy or a waterfront ruffian. I really must tell you that..."

"I know, I know," he interrupted, grinning mischievously, "...that such philistine behavior is totally inexcusable and I should be ashamed of myself and if I insist on continuing to act a demented fool you will have nothing more to do with me and neither will anyone else who cares one whit about decorum and decency." He paused, inhaled dramatically, and asked, "That about it? Have I left anything out?"

Lucy tried not to laugh, but couldn't quite manage.

CHAPTER TWENTY THREE

Despite a faint lingering reluctance to associate with a man of his dubious reputation, Lucy found the debonair, determined Blackie impossible to resist. She had never known anyone like Blackie, and it was more than just his striking good looks and strong sexual magnetism that snared her.

He was mischievous. He was exasperating. He was exciting. He was funny and he was fun. He was cynical and mysterious, as if he was the keeper of intriguing secrets. At the same time he was playful and boyish, as open and as honest as a guileless child.

Lucy found herself relaxing with him, letting down her guard, opening up, allowing the dark, engaging charmer to steal into her lonely heart. Fascination had turned quickly into infatuation.

Lucy knew, deep down inside, that she was making a foolish mistake, but once she had fallen under his spell, there was no turning back. Moreover, she didn't really want to turn back.

Or away.

She just wanted to get closer. Her days were now filled with laughter, and fun of a kind she'd never known before. Her nights were a romantic dream come true. A cherished, longed for dream from when she never wanted to awaken.

The two of them were inseparable. Every warm, sun drenched day together was a new adventure to be eagerly shared. Every sultry, moon-silvered night was a fanciful fairy tale.

Blackie LaDuke had easily, effortlessly awakened Lucy Hart from a decade long slumber. She came alive when he came along. And it was wonderful.

Lucy realized that life, as it really was, lay back in Colonias, waiting for her. But life as it should be was right here in Atlantic City.

With Blackie.

Even as she was living these long lovely days of this last summer of the century, Lucy knew that nothing this side of Heaven would ever be quite so sweet, quite so perfect, again.

It didn't matter.

She was happy *right now* and she refused to think about tomorrow.

***

After a wonderful weekend, Lucy found herself with an hour to spend alone on Monday afternoon. Blackie had been saying for days that he badly needed a haircut. She whole-heartedly agreed. So after a late, leisurely lunch, Lucy left him just outside the hotel barbershop.

She glanced through the barbershop's plate glass window, saw Colonel Mitchell seated in one of the red barber chairs, and waved spiritedly to him. He waved back. She watched as Blackie walked inside, dropped down into the chair next to the southern Colonel, and two men spoke.

She heard the Colonel say, "Glad I bumped into you, Blackie. There's something I've been meaning to discuss with you."

Blackie shrugged and nodded. Then he ran a tanned hand through his too-long black hair as the barber stepped up behind him.

Lucy, sighing with contentment, turned and walked away.

She considered a solitary stroll on the Boardwalk, decided instead to take this opportunity to avail herself of the standing invitation to visit the royal reader of tea leaves, Lady Strange.

Not that she believed in fortune-tellers. Of course, she didn't. Still, she saw no harm in hearing what Lady Strange had to say.

In the quiet corridor directly outside the door of Lady Strange's Southern tower penthouse suite, Lucy lifted her hand to knock, but hesitated. A hint of a chill suddenly skipped up her spine. She shuddered involuntarily. She lowered her hand, deciding not to knock after all. Not to go inside.

She didn't want to know the future.

She was afraid to learn what might happen to her.

Lucy started to turn away.

The door slowly opened and the mountainous Lady Strange stood framed in the opening, smiling. Lucy blinked at the obese woman who was grandly garbed in a loose, long, flowing robe of shimmering cream brocade, shot through threads of gold. Her thick, mahogany hair, which Lucy had only seen elaborately dressed atop her head, was brushed out straight, flowing around her shoulders and down her back to her waist. The dark, lustrous locks were held back off her plump, youthful-looking face with combs of gold studded with precious jewels.

"Don't leave, Lucy," Lady Strange gently entreated. "Come in, please. I've waited for you. I've been looking forward to this visit." Her blue eyes were warm and friendly. "All is ready."

Nodding nervously, wondering how Lady Strange had known she was coming--that she was standing outside the door--Lucy, half reluctantly, stepped inside.

From the marble floored entry, the rotund, little woman led Lucy into a spacious drawing room. Lucy's eyes widened as she glanced around at the elegant and comfortable room. Silken wall coverings of deep, rich, beige complimented the down-filled sofas of pristine white. Priceless antiques filled the large, lovely parlor where the centerpiece of the room was a gilt framed picture of a young, beautiful Lady Strange with Britain's Queen Victoria.

"The opening of the Crystal Palace," Lady Strange commented, "It was quite a celebration."

Nodding, Lucy detected the faint aroma of freshly brewed tea.

Lady Strange waddled toward an overstuffed easy chair that looked out of place in such lavish surroundings. It was somewhat wider than a normal chair and although it was upholstered in a handsome navy blue silk, the cushions were lumpy, loose threads abounded, and a couple of tears in the fabric looked as if it had been slashed with a razor sharp knife.

Lucy soon saw the reason.

"You get down this minute!" Lady Strange shook a short finger at the huge black Persian presently making himself at home on the soft, lumpy seat cushion of the oversized chair.

Stretching, yawning, rolling over on his back and exposing his belly, Precious, who wore a gold collar studded with semi-precious jewels, clearly wanted to be petted. Demanded to be petted.

Lady Strange affectionately stroked him, admitting to Lucy, "He's a little spoiled, I suppose, but what's the harm?" She smiled and said, "Watch this."

The one hundred-ninety-five pound Lady Strange turned about and backed up to the chair. She lifted the long shimmering skirts of her brocade robe with one hand, braced the other on a chair arm, and began laboriously lowering her great girth down into the chair.

Precious hissed loudly, made a loud screeching sound, flipped over onto his belly, leapt up onto the chair back, and shot to the floor as if he'd been fired from a cannon.

Lady Strange giggled with delight and said, "He's smart enough to know it would be catastrophic if he failed to move quickly enough." She exhaled heavily, settled herself in the chair, tried to put her dimpled knees together beneath the flowing brocade robe. And failed.

She indicated the long white sofa across from her. "Sit there, Lucy." Lucy sat. Lady Strange immediately asked, "Shall we see what your future holds?"

A tight smile. "Yes, why not."

On a low table between them rested a porcelain teapot, one fragile teacup, and an empty bowl. No sugar, no lemon, no cream. This tea was not for drinking.

Lady Strange instructed, "Pour tea into the cup, dear."

Lucy nodded, did as she was told. She noticed, as she poured, that the tea had not been strained. Tea leaves spilled from the spout with the hot dark liquid. The cup brim full, she set the teapot down and looked to Lady strange.

"Now," said the fat fortune-teller, "wait a moment or two and very slowly pour the tea from the cup into the bowl."

Lucy nodded.

When that was done, Lady Strange said, "Are there tea leaves clinging to the sides of the cup?"

"Yes. Yes, the leaves are clumped together and..."

"Hand the cup to me, please."

Lucy complied. Then she sat back down and waited while Lady Strange carefully studied the tea leaves sticking to the sides and bottom of the cup. Long minutes passed. A clock ticked loudly in the silence. Lady Strange said not a word; continued to stare unblinkingly at the tea leaves in the china cup.

At last her round face lifted. Lady Strange looked directly at Lucy for a second, then back at the tea leaves. Finally she began to speak

She said in an unfamiliarly low, soft voice, "You came here to Atlantic City alone and you will leave alone."

Lucy nodded, shrugged slender shoulders. This was no news. She had never expected Blackie to go with her.

"But," Lady Strange continued, "when you leave this place, you will be very different. You will be a changed woman." She paused dramatically for several seconds, then continued, speaking so softly Lucy straightened and leaned a little forward on the white sofa, straining to hear. "When you have been back home for several weeks you will learn of yet another change that occurred while you were here." Her eyes slowly lifted, met Lucy's. "And this change will forever alter your life."

"How? What do you mean? How will it change my life? Please," Lucy pleaded, "tell me more."

Lady Strange shook her head, setting her unbound hair to dancing about her rounded, brocade draped shoulders.

"No more." She set the teacup on the side table near her dimpled elbow. "I can say no more."

Disappointed, Lucy sighed, started to rise.

Lady Strange quickly lifted a plump hand to stop her. "Don't go just yet." Diamonds on her short, fat fingers flashing, her round cheeks dimpling deeply in a smile, she said, "I *can* tell you a great deal about Blackie."

Consumed with curiosity, Lucy's well-arched eyebrows lifted. "You know a lot about Blackie?"

"I do." Lady Strange bobbed her head. "Will you promise never to repeat what I tell you?"

"Oh, yes, I would never...I promise."

"Very well then." She sat back, placed her hands on the chair's armrests, and reached into the past.

She began; "There was a time when Blackie LaDuke's parents moved in the same social circles as Lord William Strange and I..."

Lady Strange told the attentive Lucy that Blackie was sent away to boarding school at the tender age of seven. He rarely saw his mother or father, and he received very little demonstrated affection during his formative years. Lonely and rebellious, he was a little boy in trouble all the time.

"The pattern continued when Blackie grew up," confided Lady Strange. "Seeking attention, he got it the only way he know how; by causing mischief. You see, when he behaved nobody noticed him. No matter how hard he tried to please his distant parents, he was constantly told what a terrible disappointment he was, unlike his two older brothers."

Lucy listened silently, not daring to interrupt, longing to learn all she could about Blackie.

"Since nothing Blackie did pleased his parents, he went out of his way to annoy them. As a young man he was sent home from Princeton. 'Blotted his copybook' as the British say. He was taken into the family real estate firm, but got into some sort of trouble and within months of joining the firm he found himself cast out and cut off from the sizable LaDuke fortune."

Lady Strange continued to tell Lucy about Blackie, her tone of voice and the expression in her eyes revealing the affection she had held for him since he was a child.

"Blackie LaDuke is not without a heart," she concluded at last, looking Lucy squarely in the eye, "but when he was a boy, his was such a tender, aching heart that I'm afraid he locked it safely away forever."

CHAPTER TWENTY FOUR

The long sunny days and sultry summer nights continued to pass swiftly by in a sweet haze of contentment. Lucy and Blackie were together every waking minute. They took long strolls down the busy Boardwalk, or glided along the wooden walkway in one of the swan-necked wicker rolling chairs.

They looked through the Boardwalk's coin operated viewing telescopes pointing out to sea. They rode on the merry-go-round, and Blackie even persuaded Lucy to give the Ferris wheel another try. They went barefoot on the beach. They watched the sand artists create all manner of sculptures.

They went to numerous band concerts. They roller-skated at the Seaview. They went to vaudeville shows and dances. They sampled pickles on the Heintz pier. They bought scads of one-cent view cards at Hubin's Big Post Card store.

Then never mailed a single one.

They took long walks in the moonlight, holding hands, harmonizing on the their favorite popular songs. Blackie liked *The Band Played On*, while Lucy's choice was *After the Ball*.

From the bustling Boardwalk stalls, Blackie bought nonsensical trinkets for Lucy. Over her laughing objections, he bought her a pair of beaded leather moccasins which both knew would never be worn. He bought her a Kewpie doll. Some Swiss woodcarvings.

Pearl shells with landscapes painted on them. A tinsel brooch. And a dozen other sentimental, totally useless little items.

They stuffed themselves on deviled crabs and lemonade and soda pop and tutti-frutti and Fralinger's Salt Water Taffy and Gage's ice cream and Smith's cream java coffee. They crammed as much living as possible into the fast fleeting days of the century's last summer.

They were good friends who laughed and had great fun together. But affectionate goodnight pecks on the cheek had swiftly changed to long, heated kisses on the lips, which now occurred in broad daylight as well as at night. Lucy's slumbering passions had been awakened, and from the way she kissed him, looked at him, Blackie knew she was his for the taking.

But as far as he had fallen, something--some imperishable last glimmer of his once better self--had survived. He cared for Lucy too much to take any pleasure in the knowledge and did not seduce her. Not that he didn't want her. He did. He couldn't remember when he had desired a woman more.

But he knew Lucy Hart deserved more than a few meaningless nights of passion with a no-good guy like him. Lucy wasn't like all the others. She wasn't like *any* of the others. She was a fine, trusting woman of sterling character and high morals. She needed love and marriage while he wanted only sex and freedom.

***

Sunset.

August 30, 1899.

It was hot and muggy on the Jersey Shore as that long lazy Wednesday came to its close. Blackie and Lucy had spent the entire afternoon at the beach. Even now with the sun going down, they lingered. Most of the bathers had long since gone inside. A few stragglers, like the two of them, were scattered up and down the long stretch of sand. Reluctant to leave.

Unwilling to let go of the day.

In and out of the water throughout the steamy afternoon, Lucy now waited for him on shore as Blackie took one last swim. Sighing, feeling incredibly peaceful and happy, Lucy sat on her heels on their spread blanket and watched Blackie. She picked up a towel and languidly dried her curly chestnut hair while her eyes continued to cling to the dark man slicing skillfully through the incoming, white-capped waves of the Atlantic.

She loved to watch Blackie swim. He was an excellent swimmer, graceful and lithe and strong. And his physique, which was quite magnificent, was almost indecently exhibited in his snug fitting bathing costume of ebony knit. The shirt pulled taut across his wide chest. The knee-length trunks hugged his lean thighs like a second skin.

The black knit suit revealed the masculine beauty of his body, a body more perfect than any she had ever seen.

He was more beautifully formed than any of the muscular men who made up Atlantic City's Beach Patrol. Lucy only wished she was half as finely built a woman as Blackie was a man.

Her gaze momentarily shifted from Blackie.

She looked down at herself and smiled recalling that first occasion--less than a week ago--when she had timidly come out of Jackson's bathhouse in this new, never before worn, bathing costume. Fashioned of light-brown linen, it had tiny puff sleeves, a white sailor suit collar, and a daringly short skirt under which she wore the conventional long black stockings.

The walk from the bathhouse to the water's edge was excruciatingly long and she had felt like every person at the beach was staring at her, noticing all her imperfections, talking about how silly she looked. Anxiously she had rushed into the water to eagerly sink down in the depths and hide herself.

But it was when she came out of the surf that she'd almost died of embarrassment.

To her horror the new linen suit, once it had gotten wet, was plastered to her body, accentuating every curve and hollow of her slender form. She was mortified. She felt naked and ashamed. She wanted to bury herself in the sand.

Now as Lucy's eyes slowly lifted to once again target Blackie, she felt reasonably comfortable in her damp bathing costume. She had seen no aversion in Blackie's dark eyes that first day when he'd closely examined her. Just the opposite. She had detected a spark of new interest in the depths of his beautiful black eyes when he looked at her. And he had assured her that she was stylish and pretty in the linen bathing suit. The way he had said it, the firm conviction in his deep baritone voice, had made her feel pretty.

She felt pretty now. Confident. Attractive. Feminine.

And it was splendid.

At this late hour there were no lifeguards on duty. There was no one within fifty yards of Lucy. No one would be coming close. Except Blackie. Shaking her damp, curly hair about, she dropped the towel and rose to her feet.

And in an act that was decidedly daring for an old maid postmistress from Colonias, New York, she calmly peeled off her soggy, black stockings, brazenly exposing her long, pale legs. She had noticed several young women do so in the past few days. Some of the pluckier ones had abandoned the stockings all together; appearing bare legged on the beach in broad daylight.

Feeling bold and liberated and naughty all at the same time, Lucy rolled the damp, black stockings into a ball and carelessly dropped them to the blanket. She laughed into the rising ocean breezes, inhaled deeply of the heavy salt air, and saw Blackie swimming back to shore.

Back to her.

Suddenly weak-kneed, Lucy sagged down to the blanket, knelt there for a second, then sat back on her bare heels and waited expectantly, her heart beating fast beneath the damp beige fabric clinging to her bosom.

Blackie emerged from the pounding surf like some sensual god of the sea. He came running toward her, the last rays of the dying sun striking him full in the face. Awed, Lucy watched him approach. Black hair, black eyes, black suit; all were wet and gleaming in the late lilac dusk. He raced across the sand with the grace and agility of an athlete, power and beauty in motion.

With a shout he skidded to a sand flinging stop directly before Lucy, lifted his tanned hands, and pushed his thick wet hair straight back off his handsome, smiling face. Lucy raised a towel up toward him.

Before he took it, Blackie's hands went to the sides of his black knit shirt. He yanked the tail of the soggy garment free of his swim trunks and shoved it up his chest. And in a purely masculine gesture, he reached up behind him, grabbed hold of the wet, bunched-up shirt, pulled it impatiently over his head and off, tossing it carelessly aside.

Shocked, Lucy worriedly looked around and warned, "Blackie, you know it's against the law to be bare chested on this beach!"

He grinned impishly. "After sunset we make our own laws."

He took the offered towel and haphazardly dried himself. Then he dropped to his knees, sat down flat on the blanket, and turned about so that he was facing away from Lucy. Then he quickly scooted up close and leaned back against her, taking her by surprise.

Her breasts were flattened against the wet, smooth flesh of his back and Lucy felt her nipples instantly harden and tingle from the contact. Her breath short, she laid a loving hand on his glistening shoulder and bent her head forward a little. His thick, wet hair ruffling against her chin, Blackie sighed and made himself comfortable, wiggling, stretching his long legs out before him, crossing one bare ankle over the other.

Smiling, loving this new kind of closeness, Lucy allowed her hand to slip over his shoulder and inch down across his chest. Her palm opening against the hard muscle and bone, she dipped the tips of her fingers into the crisp wet hair covering his broad chest.

She closed her eyes and sighed.

Blackie sighed too.

And he reached for her free hand, drew it down under his arm and around his ribs, guiding it to his water-beaded stomach.

Lucy's eyes came open and she winced at such unfamiliar intimacy; automatically she started to move her hand. But Blackie's lean fingers captured hers, kept her hand where it was, pressed against his wet, washboard stomach. He turned his dark head outward, kissed the inside of her pale arm, and said, "God, you're skin's so soft and fair."

"Mmmm," she murmured, staring, entranced as he was at their arms folded together over his taut middle. His was so dark and muscular. Hers so slim and white. "I'm so light," she mused aloud, "and you're so dark."

"Know why?" he asked, coolly maneuvering her spread hand a little lower down on his drum tight belly.

"No. Why?"

"Well, I don't know if it's gospel, but it's always been whispered that Granny was raped by a wild Apache chief when she took a trip out west as a young woman. All the LaDuke men have black hair, dark skin, and high cheekbones. I suppose these distinguishing features are the result of our Indian blood."

"Blackie LaDuke," she was highly skeptical, "are you lying to me?"

Blackie laughed, tapped his fingertips against his open lips and give a war whoop. Lucy pinched him.

"Just telling you what I've heard," he said and Lucy had no idea if he was teasing her or not. Probably he was.

She said, "So, Chief, am I safe alone with you?"

"You never know," he said matter-of-factly. "My entire family considers me an untamed savage, not fit to associate with respectable people like you and themselves."

"Now, Blackie," said she, "you don't mean that."

Blackie's covering hand lifted from hers. Lucy's stayed where it was, pressed against his belly. And her fingers, of their own volition, gently caressed his slick, bare flesh.

"Do too," he said, the muscles of his belly tightening beneath her teasing, feather soft touch. "You don't know my family, Lucy."

"No, I don't know *your* family," she said, "but I *do* know families. The old that adage that 'blood is thicker than water' is really true."

She laughed softly then and immediately began to talk about her own family, telling him about her happy, carefree childhood and how she'd been absolutely certain that her big, tall, silver-haired papa was the handsomest, bravest, smartest man on earth. She said her mamma was sweet and pretty, and never once in her life raised her voice. She talked about her brothers, said they wrote regularly and that both had invited her to come and live with them.

Lucy continued to talk fondly about her family, but her real purpose was to learn more about his. She never revealed anything Lady Strange had told her about him, but she carefully, cleverly drew him out by talking about her own childhood instead of asking questions about his.

Until finally, almost without realizing it, Blackie began to casually talk about his parents, his brothers, his early life, revealing insightful glimpses into his past.

"...and I thought for the longest time that my name was really 'that little upstart'," Blackie said, laughing easily. "'You naughty boy' was another way I was frequently addressed. It seemed like no matter how quietly or carefully I tried tiptoeing into a room I attracted unwanted attention and I..."

Speaking in a low, dispassionate voice, Blackie lying comfortably back in Lucy's arms, told her things he had never talked about with any one else. He told her he had never fit in with his family, that they had never considered him one of them. He had been in the way from the very beginning, had been raised almost exclusively by servants, had gone for weeks at time without seeing either his mother or father.

He confessed to being terrified when he was sent away to boarding school at age seven and said his teachers had immediately labeled him backward and precocious. They complained to his parents that he was troublesome and naughty. His parents, naturally, had taken the professors' side, scolding him for being such a problem to everyone.

Blackie endearingly admitted that he wrote long, sappy letters to his elegant mother, begging her to come for him, to take him home, to let him live with her and his father.

The letters went unanswered.

He didn't hold it against her. Likely as not, she never even saw the letters. Hers was a busy life filled with social obligations and frequent travel, and there wasn't much room in it for a trouble-making, stubborn child.

Her arms tightening protectively around him as he spoke, Lucy listened, carefully concealing her shock at what she was hearing. Calmly she asked an occasional question or made a comment, and all the while her heart hurt for the lonely little boy shuffled off to boarding school so he'd be out of everyone's way.

Unemotionally, Blackie told Lucy that he was the undisputed black sheep of the LaDuke family and that even his brothers, who were both serious-minded, successful businessmen, found excuses to keep him out of their lives. Not that he blamed them.

He told of being expelled from Princeton. After which his father had, against his better judgment, reluctantly taken Blackie into the family real estate business. But that had lasted only a few short months. Blackie had gotten into some serious trouble and, as had always been the rule, no one cared to hear his side of it. He was the guilty one. Everyone agreed. It was unanimous.

Case closed.

Blackie continued to talk dispassionately about his checkered past as the sun went completely down, and a deep summertime dusk settled over the deserted Atlantic City beach.

"No question about it," he said after a long pause, "I attract trouble the way some people attract great wealth."

Left unsaid was that he knew exactly what he was and who he was, a thirty-three year old failure without home. Without hope. Without family. Without future.

Lucy couldn't trust her voice. The muscles in her throat had constricted and almost pinched off her breath. So she said nothing. Just hugged him tighter, harder.

The night air had cooled dramatically, and the winds off the ocean strengthened. Crashing breakers rolled into shore as the high tide of evening approached.

A long moment passed in silence.

Then a wry smile lifted the corners of Blackie's mouth and his droll sense of humor came back to him.

"So, Lucy Hart, from Colonias, New York," he asked with a smile in his voice, "aren't you the lucky one, running into me?"

"Yes, I am," she said without hesitation, "Very lucky. And so are you."

She gave his bare torso a squeeze, then slid her hand over his naked chest, up his tanned throat and captured his firm chin. She gently turned his head toward her, ran tender fingertips over his bruised cheekbone, looked into his flashing back eyes, and said his name softly.

"Blackie."

"Mmmm?"

Her lips lowering to within an inch of his, Lucy whispered, "I'm going to kiss you."

CHAPTER TWENTY FIVE

Blackie's promise that Lucy's thirtieth birthday would be special was no idle boast.

Even the day's beginning was extraordinary, with Blackie banging on Lucy's door well before dawn and calling out to her to let him in. Bare-footed, a robe hastily thrown on over her nightgown, Lucy opened the door, frowning groggily.

"Has something happened?" she asked, pushing her wild chestnut hair out of her eyes.

"Not yet," he told her, "but if we don't hurry, we'll miss it." He barged inside.

Lucy took a couple of steps backward.

"Miss what?" she asked, puzzled, still half asleep.

"Why, sunrise, of course." He flashed her a quick and dazzling grin, walked past her. Hurriedly crossing the room, he said over his shoulder. "Don't you want to see the sun come up on your thirtieth birthday?" He stepped out onto the tiny balcony in the dawn darkness and called to her. "Hey, you coming?"

Shaking her head, finally starting to smile, Lucy followed, holding the lapels of her robe tightly together at the throat. She glanced appraisingly at herself as she passed the mirror, and frowned again.

How could Blackie look so incredibly handsome at this early hour while she looked so awful?

Shrugging resignedly, she stepped out onto the balcony. Blackie turned from the railing and came quickly to her. He put his arms around her, buried his dark face in the curve of her neck and shoulder, kissed her clean, sleep-warm skin, and murmured, "God, you look so cute this morning. You sure you're not just turning twenty?"

Before she could reply Blackie released her, backed over to the armed wicker chair, dropped down into it, and sat down with his knees spread wide apart.

"Come here," he said.

"No. I'll just stand at the..."

"No, you won't." He reached for her hand, and drew her to him. He patted a knee and said, "Sit right down here and make yourself at home."

Lucy laughed then. Joyful, feeling playful as if she *was* only twenty, she jumped on his lap and rumpled his hair. Blackie grinned at her, tapped his bottom lip with a lean forefinger and said, "Kiss me. Kiss me, birthday girl."

Lucy kissed his lips, smoothed his raven hair back with both hands, then said softly, "Good morning."

"Yes, isn't it," he said, kissed the underside of her chin, put an arm beneath her knees and drew her bare feet up into the chair. Covering her toes with his spread hand, he said, "Better cuddle up *real* close, it's cool this morning."

Lucy nodded, lifted an arm up behind his head, draped it around his wide shoulders, and folded the other across his chest. She clasped her wrists together atop his shoulder and laid her head against his head. Blackie hugged her close, his arms around her, one hand pressing her bent knees against his chest, the other cupping her robed bottom.

Lucy started to protest the familiarty.

Blackie's kiss silenced her.

When the kiss ended, they looked at each other for a long moment, then turned their eyes eastward. In companionable silence they watched the summer sun come up over the Atlantic Ocean on Lucy's thirtieth birthday.

When at last the big, red, ball of fire had cleared the watery horizon and began climbing rapidly up into a cloudless sky, Blackie tugged on a lock of Lucy's uncombed hair and said, "Spectacle's over."

She sighed happily. "It was wonderful."

"So are you," he said. "Now get dressed, lazy bones, and let's start the celebrating."

"Mmmm," Lucy sighed, reluctant to move, certain that any celebrating he had planned for the rest of their day couldn't compare with this hour they'd spent watching the sun rise.

She was wrong.

After a big birthday breakfast with their friends Lady Strange, the Colonel, and Lochlin MacDonald, Blackie bade them good-bye, whisked Lucy out of the dining hall, and across the hotel lobby. He ushered her through the Atlantic Grand's front revolving doors, down the front steps, and to a waiting motorcar he had leased for the occasion.

Lucy had never ridden in an automobile and she said so. Blackie told her that the horseless carriages were the thing of the future so it was high time she rode in one.

He handed her into the gleaming Daimler, climbed in himself, drove her away from the Grand, and out of Atlantic City. Hanging on for dear life, Lucy shouted to Blackie over the engine's noise, warning him to slow down.

But he didn't and she was secretly glad. She liked the thrilling sense of speed. It was frightening, but it was fun. She liked the excitement. She liked the automobile's comfort. Most of all she liked watching Blackie drive the big motorcar.

She liked watching his night-black hair toss about in the wind. And looking at his strikingly perfect profile. And at his beautiful hands, so masterful on the steering wheel. And at the powerful muscles pulling in his tanned forearms.

Miles out of town, Blackie braked to stop. As if by magic, he produced a fully stocked wicker hamper complete with red and white checked tablecloth. They picnicked in the deep shade of an Elm tree on the green banks of a brook that trickled noisily over a bed of smooth rocks.

Sharing figs, grapes, cheese and bread and wine and laughter, they spent the summer afternoon in the country. The seclusion was peaceful and they were lazy. Tired from rising before daybreak, they stretched out on the tablecloth after the meal. Lying on their sides, they held hands and faced each other. Full. Content. Sleepy. Lulled by the sound of the brook spilling over the rocks and the droning of the katydids, soon both were dozing. Then fast asleep.

The sun was beginning to wester when they roused and returned to the hotel. Blackie left the rented Daimler with the doorman, rushed Lucy through the revolving doors, straight across the lobby, out the back beachside doors, and down to the Boardwalk.

"Hurry," he urged. "We have to hurry, Lucy."

"Why? Where are we going?"

"You'll see."

The next thing she knew, he was leading her down the steps to the beach. She immediately felt sand sifting into her shoes, but said nothing as Blackie eagerly led her toward a stretch of the beach where a gathering of bathers stood together in a semi-circle. All were talking and looking down.

"Please, excuse us, folks," Blackie said and the polite crowd parted to let them through. But first Blackie turned to Lucy and commanded, "Close your eyes."

"Now, Blackie..."

"Do it for me."

Lucy closed her eyes and clung to his hand. He lead her a few steps further, then stopped abruptly, warning her to 'keep her eyes closed'. Blackie gently drew Lucy around directly in front of him. He put his hands on her shoulders and said, "You may open your eyes."

Lucy's eyes opened. While the group of onlookers watched and applauded, she stared, open-mouthed, at the sand below her. *Happy Birthday, Lucy* was written in huge, fancy, scrolled lettering directly above a giant, framed, oval cameo inside of which was an amazing likeness of her own face! The lettering and the sculpture were created entirely of sand.

Lucy's hands went to her cheeks. Her face flushed. Her heart skipped several beats. She felt for all the world as if she was going to cry. She had never been so surprised in her life. Never in a million years could she have imagined a birthday present half so special--half so thoughtful--as this one.

Happiness causing her throat to ache, she longed to whirl and fling her arms around Blackie's neck. But she couldn't do that. There were people around. She was too embarrassed even to tell him how much she liked the unique gift. So she simply stood there, mute, overcome with emotion, while everyone else laughed and whistled.

Lucy became aware of Blackie's deep, rich laughter just above her ear. She sagged back against him. She felt his strong hands clasp her shoulders and he gently turned her to face him. He smiled into her eyes, put his arms around her, and drew her into his embrace.

As if he knew exactly what she was feeling, he said softly so that only she could hear, "You don't have thank me, sweetheart. I know you like it, so you're very welcome."

Over her head his black eyes implored as he gestured for the onlookers to go away and give them a minute. The crowd reluctantly dispersed, leaving them alone.

"Everybody's gone," he said against her ear, continuing to hold her. "It's just you and me now, Birthday Girl."

Lucy's head slowly lifted. She looked at him, making no attempt to keep the adoration from showing in her expressive green eyes.

"Thank you so much, Blackie," she said. "You have made my thirtieth birthday so special, I know I will never forget it."

Blackie smiled warmly at her. Then he said, "It's not over yet."

And it wasn't.

An hour later Blackie, dressed handsomely for the evening in a custom cut summer suit, was knocking on Lucy's third floor door and handing her a fragrant corsage of ivory gardenias to wear on her summer lilac dress.

"Ready for your birthday party?" he asked. Radiant, she nodded. "Then come, it's going to be a grand affair."

It was indeed a grand affair.

A glittering gala made wonderfully unique by the total lack of guests.

No one had been invited.

The elegant party--arranged down to the last detail by Blackie--was solely for the two of them.

Lucy loved it.

Her birthday party was held in a small, private dining room on the hotel's mezzanine floor. When she stepped inside, Lucy's green eyes sparkled like the gleaming candelabra lighting the cozy, intimate room. She had heard, or perhaps read, that some of the finest luxury hotels boasted exclusive little dining salons such as this one where secret trysts were conducted.

A shiver danced up her spine.

She looked beyond the candle-lighted table and saw, as suspected, a chaise lounge of rich, white velvet. The elegant sofa was partially concealed by a sweep of tied-back velvet curtains draping the alcove.

"Shall we?" asked Blackie.

Lucy, staring fixedly at the half hidden sofa she supposed was meant for engaging in forbidden carnal pleasures, looked up sharply. Then immediately laughed at herself when she saw that Blackie stood at the table, holding out the chair for her.

But he had read her thoughts. He smiled devilishly, and said, "If you've other hungers, dinner can wait."

"I'm starved," she said, hurriedly sat down in the chair he held for her, and quickly added, "For food I mean!"

Blackie laughed.

Lucy blushed.

He took the chair across from her, rang for service. The party began. The attentive host entertained his happy guest royally.

Unobtrusive waiters served a sumptuous, five-course meal after which a giant, white birthday cake was placed before Lucy. The waiters vanished. Lucy cut the cake as Blackie splashed chilled champagne into fragile long stemmed flutes. Toasts were proposed. Happy Birthday was sung. Cake was consumed. Laughter filled the candle-lighted room.

At just the right moment Blackie placed a carefully wrapped gift on the table in front of Lucy. She looked at it. She looked at him.

"What are you waiting for?" he said, leaning back in his chair.

She took a deep breath, tugged impatiently at the gold ribbon, and eagerly tore away the white paper. Her green eyes glowed with pleasure when she saw the exquisite tortoise shell music box with one perfect porcelain ivory gardenia gracing its fragile lid.

"Blackie," she murmured, eyes lifting to meet his, "it's the most beautiful thing I've ever seen."

"No, it's not. You are. Open it," he urged, his enthusiasm endearingly boyish.

Carefully Lucy lifted the lid. A tiny golden couple popped up to spin about on a miniature mirrored circular dance floor. The music box played Lucy's favorite song, *After the Ball*.

"You like it?" Blackie asked hopefully.

"Oh, Blackie," was all Lucy could say and he nodded, pleased that she was pleased.

They danced then, just like the golden couple in the dainty music box. Each time the music box ran down, Blackie rewound it and they danced again. As they danced they kissed. Finally they no longer danced. They just kissed. As they kissed they gravitated toward the long, white velvet chaise in the partially-curtained alcove. At last they were seated on its softness.

And then Lucy was conscious of nothing but the pressure of Blackie's lips, the hardness of his chest against her breasts, and the wild, wild beating of her heart. Blackie moved his hand caressingly up and down her back, let it rest on the curve her hip, touched her lightly on the knee. Lucy sighed, tilted her head to one side, and opened her mouth a little wider.

Blackie shuddered and deepened the kiss. His hand slipped around her knee, stroked slowly up the inside of her slender thigh, through the folds of her skirts.

He felt her tremble against him, knew he had erotic control of her. He started to press his advantage, realized what he was doing, what he was about to do, and stopped. He tore his burning lips from Lucy's, set her back from him.

He heard her breath catch. She blinked at him in confusion. Her lips were puffy from so much kissing and the curves of her breasts and nipples were outlined against the soft fabric of her lilac dress. She was as beautiful as a provocative dream, and he wanted her. He fought the compulsion to take her, to have her, to make her his own.

Blackie swallowed hard, took Lucy's head in his strong hands, looked into her trusting eyes, and resisted the temptations that welled up in him.

She broke the spell by asking, "Are you alright?"

He exhaled with relief, laughed, hugged her, and said, "Hell no, I'm thirsty. What about you?"

"Me, too."

"Let's go down to the Boardwalk and drink an ice cold soda pop."

The moment and the danger had passed.

Both were totally relaxed and getting sleepy when they stood outside Lucy's door, saying their final goodnights sometime after midnight. Holding the fragile tortoise shell music box in her hands as if it were the most valuable treasure on earth, Lucy said, "You've outdone yourself, LaDuke. You made this day the most special of my life."

Blackie grinned, reached up and wrapped a wayward chestnut curl around his little finger. "Nothing to it. We'll make tomorrow just as special. And the day after. And the day after that."

And so they did.

The remaining days were all special. Too special to last. Those special days waned rapidly away until only one remained.

One last golden day--and night--of summer.

CHAPTER TWENTY SIX

September 4th, 1899.

The Labor day crowd swelling the population of Atlantic City on that first Monday in September was the largest of the season. Of any season. Larger even than the holiday hordes who'd poured into the seaside resort for the Fourth of July.

Every hotel and rooming house was filled to capacity. Long lines formed at the front desks of every inn, large and small, up and down the Jersey Shore. Latecomers desperate to find lodging for the night. Everyone reaching for that one last fling of summer.

The hotel dining rooms and fine restaurants and outdoor cafes could hardly cope with the swarms of hungry Labor Day revelers. The Boardwalk was so crowded that the famed rolling chairs couldn't maneuver up and down the long wooden walkway. Business was phenomenal for the stalls and shops, the beaming proprietors managing to hear the sound of their cash registers ringing above the din.

Below the busy Boardwalk the sandy beach was a solid sea of humanity. Only those who'd wisely gone down very early in the morning had enough room to spread a blanket on the sand. As the sun climbed higher and hotter into the sky, there was barely space to stand or sit, much less stretch out in the sun and relax.

Blackie had warned Lucy what this day would be like. He'd spent holidays here before. He told her it would seem like every man, woman, and child in America was in Atlantic City for Labor Day.

It proved to be true, but Lucy didn't mind. Not at all. The crowds only added to the sense of excitement in the air. She was glad she was here. Right in the middle of it all. It was a good feeling. A wonderful feeling. That satisfying feeling that comes from knowing that, without any doubt, this was *the* place to be. And that Blackie LaDuke was *the* man to be here with. That *she* was the lucky one who was here at *the* place with *the* man.

All week, Blackie had tried to persuade Lucy to eschew the Boardwalk and the beach for the holiday. He had suggested that they spend the day being lazy up on his penthouse terrace. There they could look down on all the activity, but not be a part of it.

Lucy declined. She wanted to be a part of it. She wanted to mingle with the mobs on the Boardwalk and visit the amusement piers and hear the band concerts and swim in the ocean.

And she wanted Blackie to do it with her.

Please, Blackie, this one last time. Please.

Easily swayed, he granted her wish.

***

END-OF-SUMMER DANCE
Monday, September 4, 1899
Nine P.M.
The Blue Room
Don't miss The Last Dance of the Season!

Blackie stood directly in front of the large poster when Lucy stepped from the elevator around eight that Monday morning. His dark head was turned. He was looking away, his classic profile to her. She had a moment to examine him while he was unaware of her scrutiny. The sight of him took her breath away. He stood with his feet apart, his hands jammed deep into the pockets of his white duck trousers. The shirt he wore was navy-and-white striped cotton, open at the collar. His black hair glistened as if not quite dry from his morning shower. Unsmiling, he looked dark and dangerous, as though he might actually be the descendant of a proud Apache war chief.

Blackie's head swung around.

He saw her and smiled.

Lucy hurried to him, saying, "Am I late? I'm terribly sorry if I am. I've always considered it unforgivably rude to be tardy for an appointment and I certainly don't want to..."

All the while she chattered, saying what she knew were trivial, idiotic things, she was thinking how much she loved him, loved everything about him--his dark, olive coloring, the broad shoulders, the flat narrow waist, the proud nose, the sensual mouth, the beautiful midnight eyes, the curly, jet black hair.

Grinning mischievously now, he looked like a bad little boy. A bad, charming, spoiled little boy who was a lot more fun to be with than any well-behaved child.

"Want to go outside and play, little girl?" Blackie asked, and wrapped his lean fingers loosely around the back of her neck.

"I do," she said, and gently tapped his chest with the bamboo tip of her colorful silk umbrella, a birthday gift from Lady Strange.

Blackie stepped away from the easel-mounted poster. Lucy's eyes fell for a second to the large placard. She felt her heart squeeze painfully in her chest.

She needed no reminder that today was the end of summer.

Her eyes swiftly lifted and she pushed the poster and its meaning from mind. Blackie guided her through the crowded lobby to the beachside doors and out into the warm September sunshine.

They played hard throughout the long hot day, behaving like two boisterous, carefree kids. They were constantly in the middle of the crowds, yet were jealously possessive, sharing themselves with no one but each other.

As sundown approached, the huge crowds finally began to thin. The tide had drifted out and gulls were scavenging for food along the shore.

Blackie and Lucy stood at the Boardwalk railing, looking out to sea, and placidly licking ice cream cones. Blackie finished his ice cream first. Lucy generously shared hers, smiling when he devoured the last bite of the crunchy cone.

At last Lucy sighed and said lazily, "If I'm to look presentable for the End-of-Summer dance, I'd better go in and start getting ready."

Blackie's dark head turned and he pinned her with his eyes. A devilish gleam appeared in their black depths and he said, "Jesus, Lucy, maybe you should have started sooner."

"Why you...!" She laughed, doubled up her fist and hit him on the shoulder.

"Owwww!" Blackie howled and caught her wrist.

He laughed, too, tucked her hand around his arm, and they headed back toward the Atlantic Grand in the summer twilight.

CHAPTER TWENTY SEVEN

Lucy luxuriated in a suds filled tub as the summer dusk deepened. Her treasured oyster shell music box rested on a footstool directly beside the tub. The tiny, gold couple danced on their miniature mirrored dance floor while Lucy hummed along. As they danced, she languidly soaped herself, enjoying the bath and the music.

Once she was out of the tub and had carefully dried off, Lucy did something she had never done before. She dropped the damp towel to the floor, picked up the delicate music box, and walked back into her room wearing nothing but a smile.

She carefully placed the music box on the night table, then went about laying out all the articles of clothing she would wear tonight. She took the new underthings she'd saved for this special occasion from a drawer of the tall bureau.

The cream, ribbed linen, waist-length bust support. The daring, thigh-high knickers trimmed with broderie anglaise. The ice blue satin-and-lace garters. And finally, a pair of sheer white silk stockings.

Lucy spread each item out on the bed. She took from the closet a new pair of white leather shoes with openwork detail and louis heels. These too, she placed on the bed.

She rewound the music box. Then she picked up the small crystal vial of expensive *Bal Versailles* perfume that the Colonel had given her for her birthday. She padded over to the long aqua sofa across from the bed. She sank down into the sofa's softness and went about the pleasant task of applying smudges of the costly perfume to her clean, bare skin. She touched the tiny, crystal stopper to the sensitive spot behind her right ear, then her left. To the insides of her elbows. And the outsides of her ankles. Behind her dimpled knees.

She carefully began to place the tiny, glass dauber back into the neck of the carved perfume bottle. Then all at once a wicked, un-lady-like, un-Lucy-like smile came to her lips and she blithely rose from the sofa. She moved with feline grace to the mirror, stopped, and stared. She whipped her head back, sending the abundance of unfettered, curly, chestnut hair off her face. She watched herself, fascinated, as she trailed the gleaming crystal perfume stopper down between her pale breasts.

Her breath grew labored as she drew a criss-cross over her flat stomach, then delineated the faint line of wispy hair leading downward from her naval. Bottom lip caught between her teeth, Lucy turned about, and reaching around, touched the tiny perfume dauber to the top of the cleft in her buttocks.

Lucy laughed gaily then, feeling wonderfully feminine and risqué.

She set the perfume bottle aside, rewound the music box, and began to skillfully dress her hair. She swept the thick, curly, chestnut locks atop her head, using a half dozen plain, functional hairpins which she cleverly concealed beneath the glossy curls. She turned her head this way, then that, checking her handiwork. Satisfied, she picked up the decorative, pearl encrusted, gold hairpin that Lochlin MacDonald had given her for her birthday.

Lucy slid the pearl pin into the left side of her hair. Generally she wore her hair adornments on the right side. But not tonight. Tonight she would be in Blackie's arms, dancing the evening away. Her right temple would be pressed to his tanned cheek. She didn't want her hairpin scratching his face.

Lucy took one last appraising glance at her hair. Convinced it looked as good as possible, she went to the bed, sat down on the edge of the mattress, and began drawing on the sheer white stockings. Slender right leg extended, toes pointed toward the ceiling, Lucy carefully drew the sheer, shimmering silk up over her knee, wondering at herself.

She was doing everything backwards this evening.

Shoes and stockings were always the very last thing she put on, after she was fully dressed. Yet here she was, totally naked, pulling on her stockings. It seemed almost sinful. It seemed even more sinful when both stockings were on, the ice blue satin-and-lace garters encircled her knees, and the new white leather shoes with the louis heels were on her feet.

And she was still naked.

Sinful, yet strangely delightful.

Exhaling softly, Lucy rose from the bed, ventured back to the mirror. She gazed at the shameless woman reflected there. This naked wanton before her couldn't possibly be the spinster postmistress from Colonias, New York. Miss Lucy would *never* have been guilty of parading around in nothing but shoes and stockings. And she wouldn't have dared admire herself in this state of provocative undress.

Lucy smiled.

Miss Lucy wouldn't do such a thing. But then she was no longer Miss Lucy. She was Lucy. Simply Lucy. Lovely Lucy at the moment. A free spirited, daring, seductive Lucy who wasn't afraid of admiring the slender feminine beauty of her own undraped body.

A resounding knock on the door caused Lucy to jump and attempt to cover herself with her hands.

"Yes?" she called, anxiously crossing the room to the closed door, throwing out her hands lest anyone should attempt to open it.

"You decent?" came Blackie's low baritone. "Let me in, Lucy."

"No," she called to him, her face growing hot at the thought of Blackie, fully dressed, standing barely a foot away from her while she was naked. Only the door separated them. Helplessly obeying some erotic impulse, Lucy suddenly pressed her bare body flush against the door, pretending she was pressing herself against Blackie.

"Lucy," he said, "are you alright?"

"Ahhh, yes, yes, I...my dress is not entirely fastened."

"My hands are deft," he said, "I'd be happy to loan them to you."

Lucy's bare belly involuntarily tightened. She swallowed convulsively. "Thanks all the same, but I can manage. Give me five minutes."

"They're yours," said Blackie.

Lucy flew into action, snatching up her underthings and hurriedly putting them on. In seconds she was pulling the new, never-before-worn evening dress over her head and struggling to fasten it down the back. Successful at last, she put on her pearl drop earrings.

She hurried back to the mirror where she'd stood naked moments ago.

Her green eyes sparkled when she saw herself. She was *so* glad she had bought this special white tulle evening dress.

The ball gown was exquisite, fashionable and flattering. A lace-edged off-the-shoulder neckline, large puff sleeves, fitted bodice, V-shaped panel, deep pleated cummerbund, and a flared skirt decorated with wide lace frills around the hem. She credited the dress with being so stunning it made her look pretty.

And feel pretty.

Lucy took a deep breath, crossed the room, and opened the door.

Blackie stood framed in the portal, handsome in a tropical, off-white suit, a white gardenia in his lapel. He said nothing. But the way he looked at her sent an electrical charge through Lucy's slender body. Her fingertips tingled when he handed her a fragrant corsage of ivory gardenias. Her hand began to tremble.

"Allow me," said Blackie, took the gardenias from her and pinned them to the low cut bodice of her evening gown, directly above her heart.

He bent his dark head, inhaled the pleasing fragrance of the corsage and of her. Then he brushed his warm lips to the swell of her pale bosom, attractively revealed in the low cut gown.

Lucy's breath caught in her throat. She felt the overpowering urge to lay a gloved hand on the back of his dark head and press his handsome face against her breasts. To hold him close forever and...

"God, you're pretty," Blackie murmured as he lifted his head and gazed at her. "And sweet. So sweet." A muscle jumped in his lean jaw and he added, nearly inaudibly, as if thinking aloud, "Almost too sweet and pretty for me to...to..."

Abruptly, he stopped speaking, cleared his throat. And Lucy could have sworn that he flushed slightly beneath his tan and a little shudder of emotion surged through his tall, lean frame before he grinned and said, "Let's go to the dance."

CHAPTER TWENTY EIGHT

They were all there.

Lochlin MacDonald in his wheeled chair was stationed near the ballroom's entrance, smiling, greeting people. Hair slicked back, a blood-red rose in the lapel of his white dinner jacket, his eyes, if not his failing body, were alive with excitement.

Lady Strange, in a flowing silver satin ball gown and sparkling diamonds, was comfortably seated on a long blue sofa against the wall. A pair of mother-of-pearl opera glasses, suspended from a silver chair around her fat neck, rested on her enormous, silver-draped bosom. In one plump hand was a glass of chilled champagne; in the other was a shrimp canapé. A plate filled with exotic, edible tidbits was balanced on her dimpled knees. Precious, in a diamond-decorated collar, dozed peacefully on the couch beside his mistress.

The indulgent, attentive Colonel Cort Mitchell stood beside the sofa. The tall, impeccably groomed, silver-haired Colonel was an imposing figure in a superbly fitting dark suit that had been tailored in London. Lingering glances were being cast his way, lonely matrons and rich widows hoping the dapper southerner might favor them with a dance or two before the evening ended.

The starry-eyed newlyweds from Pittsburgh were on the dance floor. Still starry-eyed. The prominent New York City physician and his sour, complaining wife bickered as they waltzed. The loud, boisterous family of eight--the mother and all six children with their flaming red hair--had arrived early, the rambunctious, redheaded youngsters descending like a cloud of locusts on the long, food-laden buffet table.

Then there was the wealthy railroader and a widowed lady friend he had met at a Boardwalk arcade. The hypochondriac banker, complaining about his bad back. The fading stage actor, telling anyone who would listen that he would soon be going into rehearsals for a starring role in a big New York City theater production. The circus clown, minus his make-up. The recluse writer, who rarely ventured out of his room.

Ninety percent of the registered Atlantic Grand guests had come down for the dance. Dozens of vacationers from the other hotels up and down the Boardwalk were also in attendance. The Grand's last dance of the season had gained the much deserved reputation of being the season's best; entertaining and exciting and enjoyable, an event above all others which was not to be missed.

The costly grandeur of the hotel's Blue Room made it the ideal setting for the End-of-Summer dance. Not only was it the largest hotel ballroom in Atlantic City, it was by far the most luxurious. Walls of rich, royal blue paneling soared twenty feet high to a ceiling of the same hue upon which thousands of tiny, incandescent silver stars twinkled magically.

A half dozen glittering chandeliers hung suspended from the blue and silver ceiling, their tiny, electric-lighted prisms casting intricate patterns on the dancers spinning below. The floor was of the finest parquet, polished to high gleam with not one spec of dust or dirt on it. Gilt chairs with plushly padded seats of rich, royal blue brocade lined the walls, and garlands of fresh cut flowers sweetened the air.

A twenty-piece orchestra in full evening attire played from a raised dais, while white-jacketed, white-gloved waiters popped champagne corks and poured generously for thirsty guests.

Well before the appointed hour of nine, the vast ballroom had begun rapidly filling with eager dancers. It was a happy, handsome crowd. Elegantly clad ladies in cool, pastel gowns and glittering jewels with well-heeled gentleman in custom-cut summer suits and starched dress shirts. Laughter and music filled the beautiful blue ballroom. And Lochlin MacDonald, the dance's self-appointed host, beamed with pleasure as a steady stream of glowing guests gathered around his chair to compliment him, declaring this to be the best dance ever!

***

Blackie and Lucy were as eager as the rest to get downstairs to the dance. They hurried to the elevator, waited impatiently. When the elevator door opened, the broadly grinning Davey greeted them, telling Lucy she looked extra pretty tonight.

She graciously thanked him and said, "This isn't your regular duty time, is it, Davey? Will you be coming to the dance?"

"No. I mean yes." Davey shook his sandy head, closed the elevator door, and explained. "This isn't my shift, but I agreed to work 'til ten since it's my last day on the job." Massive shoulders lifting slightly and grin widening, he said, "I get to go the dance tonight because, after ten I'm no longer by an employee of the hotel."

"Good for you," said Blackie. "You going to college this fall?"

"Sure am. I'll be registering at Columbia University the end of the week," Davey said proudly. He was half turned, looking at them. "Lucy, you're leaving tomorrow aren't you?"

She nodded. "At noon."

"How about you, Blackie? You going or staying?" Davey turned back to face the front of the car.

"Leaving on the dawn train," Blackie said. And looking only at Lucy, added, "Tomorrow."

The elevator stopped. Davey opened the door. He said, "Gosh, since it's the last night for all of us, I hope we have a really good time." His grin stretched from ear to ear.

"Count on it," said Blackie, and Lucy nodded her confidence. Out of the elevator, they crossed the lobby and followed the sound of music down the long, carpeted corridor. When they reached the Blue Room, they paused for a moment at the entrance. They stood on the threshold, holding hands, looking over the crowd.

And being looked over as well.

Heads turned. People stared. Dancers whispered. And Lucy was struck by how different it was to be examined now than when she had first arrived. Then she had hated being noticed, had felt awkward and embarrassed and was sure everyone was pitying the plain postmistress who looked so lost and out of place.

Tonight Lucy, smiling confidently, experienced that fabulous, now-familiar feeling of vanity that came from being the woman with the handsome Blackie LaDuke. Lord, was she the lucky one!

"There's Lochlin," Blackie directed Lucy's attention to the man in the wheel chair.

"Yes!" Lucy said, waving madly, expecting Lochlin to wheel eagerly over to them.

Lochlin's smile was brilliant, and his eyes lighted, but he stayed where he was, as he was. Didn't move; didn't wave.

Lucy leaned close to Blackie and whispered, "Something's wrong. He sees us, but he..."

"Nothing's wrong," Blackie smoothly cut in, propelled her forward. "Let's go say hello."

When they reached him, Blackie placed a hand on the seated man's thin shoulder while Lucy leaned down and gave Lochlin's cheek a quick kiss.

"Looks like your dance is a huge success," she said.

"What did I tell you!" Lochlin replied. "Everybody who's anybody will be at this dance tonight."

"I believe you," said Lucy.

She turned her head slightly so he could see the gold and pearl hairpin in her hair. He was pleased.

"I see a couple of somebodies," Blackie said, nodding to Colonel Mitchell and Lady Strange. "Want to go over with us for a minute?" he asked Lochlin.

"Better not desert my post," Lochlin told him. "Still lots of people coming in."

"Aye, aye, sir," said Blackie.

"We'll see you again later," Lucy promised, touching Lochlin's thin, white-jacketed shoulder.

They made their way through the crowd to Lady Strange and the Colonel. The Colonel, taking Lucy's hand in his, looked her over thoroughly and commented on how exceptionally pretty she looked.

"Almost too pretty," he added as an afterthought, the expression in his gray eyes puzzling, and Lucy was struck by the thought that Blackie had said much the same thing a little earlier. It made no sense. Too pretty? Who could ever be too pretty? Too pretty for what?

Blackie leaned down, kissed Lady Strange on the forehead, and warned, "If those opera glasses are for spying on me, I'll take them away from you."

"Don't be silly," she said, but she looked sheepish.

The four talked a few minutes, but when Lucy started to sit down beside Lady Strange and the sleeping Precious, Blackie stopped her.

Taking her hand, he said, "If you'll excuse us, it's time Lucy and I showed them how to dance."

"Oh, yes, do," said Lady Strange.

"Save a dance for me, Lucy," said the Colonel.

"I will."

Blackie led Lucy onto the crowded floor as the orchestra went into an extraordinarily fast tempoed offering of *The Band Played On*. Lucy laughed with delight as Blackie wrapped a long arm around her waist and spun her dizzily about on the polished, parquet floor. She was breathless and over warm when the upbeat music ended, her face tinged with color, her eyes aglow.

The orchestra immediately began to play once more. This time a slow easy ballad. Lucy sighed with relief and moved back into Blackie's arms. The two of them danced effortlessly, moving gracefully together on the smooth parquet floor beneath the glittering chandeliers and silver-starred, blue ceiling.

During one of the numbers, Blackie kissed her lightly on the forehead and it brought Lucy a flush of good feeling. They danced every dance, caught up in each other, unaware and uncaring of the looks and whispers they drew. A number of envious women did everything they could think of to attract Blackie's attention. Glamorous, expensively gowned socialites yearned for an opportunity to dance with Blackie LaDuke. To step into his long arms and let the handsome New Yorker know they were ready and willing to do a great deal more than just dance with him.

Desperate for an opening, several clever, conniving women manipulated their dance partners into maneuvering close to the tall, dark object of their interest so that they could pretend to accidentally bump into Blackie, then stop and express their apologies, hoping it would bring about introductions and a change of partners.

It didn't work.

Each time it happened, Blackie accepted their 'oh, excuse me' without taking his eyes or his arms from the dazzled Lucy.

From her vantage point on the blue sofa, Lady Strange licked her lips with delight as she watched the fascinating drama, fueled by desire, unfolding on the dance floor. She was neither shocked nor surprised by the lengths to which beautiful, respectable women would go in an attempt to make Blackie notice them.

She was, however, a little puzzled by Blackie. His potent animal magnetism was--as usual--luring the ladies to him like moths to the flame. Yet he showed no interest in anyone but Lucy.

Lady Strange still found it difficult--nearly impossible--to believe that Blackie LaDuke, lovable bad boy and alley cat rogue, had spent almost his entire two week holiday with the pretty, but straight-laced Lucy Hart. She was a dear, sweet young lady, but she was hardly Blackie's type.

It occurred to Lady Strange that the constantly changing parade of beautiful, liberated women were not the only vice he had seemingly given up. Since meeting Lucy, Blackie hadn't once been falling down drunk. Had he been, she'd have heard about it. Nor had he gambled the night away in the rough joints down on Kentucky Avenue or gotten himself into numerous barroom brawls. Save for somebody landing a lucky punch to his jaw that Saturday afternoon before last, he had stayed out of mischief.

The clean living had already begun to show. His dark face had lost the harsh lines of dissipation and had become young and handsome again. His lean, lithe body rivaled any twenty-five year old and, as he spun the enchanted Lucy about the dance floor, he was as sinuous as a leopard. He exuded so much maleness he set every feminine heart aflutter, drawing women helplessly into his orbit, as the sun attracts the earth.

Colonel Mitchell's eyes also rested on the dancing pair. It was clear to see that Lucy, since arriving in Atlantic City, had experienced a metamorphosis, an initiation into a new state of being. Her transformation went beyond the physical; her spirit had changed. She was a new woman, a woman eager to embrace and explore every new emotion.

Even without the aid of opera glasses, Mitchell could read the look of love and longing in Lucy's eyes. She gazed at Blackie as if he was a god.

Blackie's eyes betrayed him as well. Want and desire shone from their depths, a rising passion for the pretty woman in his arms.

Watching, worrying, the Colonel heard Lady Strange say, "Cort, let them be."

"I have no idea what you're talking about."

"You know exactly what I'm talking about," she said.

The Colonel shifted his attention from the couple on the dance floor to Lady Strange. He smiled, stepped in front of her, plucked at the sharp creases in his dark trousers, and sat down on the sofa.

He said, "I haven't said one word to..."

"But you're considering it," Lady Strange accusingly interrupted. "Don't. Don't do it."

"You have those opera glasses," Cort gestured. "Can't you see what's happening? Lucy is in love and Blackie is...is...Well, dammit, he's taking advantage of her."

"Taking advantage of her? I think not. I think he's going to make love to her tonight."

"Exactly!" The Colonel's face grew instantly red.

Lady Strange smiled and touched his arm. "Cort, Cort," she said affectionately, "Lucy could do with a bit of passionate lovemaking. Rather one night of heaven than a lifetime of boredom."

"One night of heaven can cause a lifetime of hell," Cort reminded her.

"Perhaps. But as you like to say, you cannot live a risk-free life and know any real happiness."

"You're forgetting that I also say if you're prepared to take risks, then you must be prepared to suffer losses."

"How do you know Lucy isn't?" said Lady Strange. "You know what your trouble is? You've forgotten what it's like to be young. For you there are no longer any illusions. That's sad, Cort."

A half wistful expression appeared in Cort's gray eyes. "I suppose you're right. We're getting old, my dear. Our generation is passing from the stage now." He exhaled slowly. "It was a more innocent time then."

Lady Strange's laughter made him turn his head sharply and frown. She said, "When we were young, our elders were saying that same thing. And when these young people are old, they'll being saying it too." Cort's expression softened immediately; he nodded his agreement. Lady Strange continued, "I'm fortunate, as are most women. I can recall exactly what's it's like to be young. You should try to remember. Think back to how you felt then. Surely you can recall those feelings from out of your past, out of a youth that was surely romantic and restless."

Cort made himself try and reach way back into his sixty-six years to see if he could remember exactly how it felt to want somebody so much it hurt. But it had been too long. Try as he might, he could not duplicate the longing, the yearning, the aching need of passionate, hot-blooded youth.

So, later that evening, when he claimed Lucy for their promised dance, the Colonel's intent was to gently warn her about the dangers of a fleeting summertime romance. To remind her of the high price which all too often had to be paid. Of the regrets to be suffered. Of the pain that could last for a lifetime.

That's what he meant to do.

But when Lucy, looking so young and happy, stepped into his embrace, he couldn't do it.

Instead he said honestly, "Lucy, a time like this may never come again in your whole life. Enjoy it, my dear."

Lucy did enjoy it. Every bit of it. The music. The dancing. The champagne. As she whirled about under the silver-starred ceiling, she marveled at Blackie's smooth athletic grace. She thrilled to the feel of his lean muscles rippling beneath his clothes. She was hypnotized by his beautiful, dark, half-sleepy eyes.

Lucy wished the End-of-Summer dance would never, ever end. That it would go on forever.

The Last Dance

"Ladies and gentlemen," said the orchestra leader and dancers turned their attention to where he stood at the center of the raised dais, baton in hand. "Where has this evening gone?"

A loud groan went up from the dance floor.

"My friends," said the conductor. "It's one o'clock in the morning and time for the dance to end." He gave a very brief speech, praising the Atlantic Grand and Lochlin MacDonald for making the evening such a success. Concluding, he asked, "Did you all enjoy this year's End-of-Summer dance?"

Shouts and whistles were his answer.

"Then come back again next year." He raised his baton in the air. "Until then, get that special partner out on the floor for one Last Dance."

He brought his baton down.

CHAPTER TWENTY NINE

The Last Dance.

The last chance for love.

The orchestra began to play.

Violins rose and the hauntingly beautiful strains of *After the Ball* filled the crowded Blue Room. Blackie looked at Lucy for a long moment before lifting his hands to span her narrow waist. Neither spoke. It was an electric moment.

Lucy's breath came out in a rush when Blackie slowly drew her to him. Eyes locked with his, she slid her hands up over his chest and looped her arms around his neck.

They stood unmoving for a time as the lights dimmed and the music swelled and other dancers glided past. Lucy's lips parted slightly when Blackie's strong hands applied the gentlest of pressure, bringing her slender body in closer to fit intimately against his own.

She felt his hard thighs brushing her legs through their clothes, felt his firm, flat abdomen against her fluttering stomach. A tiny gasp escaped her lips when Blackie laid a spread hand to the center of her back to urge her even closer.

His midnight eyes were on her mouth. She felt herself flush and her tongue made a circle of her lips, wetting them so that they shone in the light from the chandeliers above. Her soft breasts met the hard muscles of his chest and Lucy anxiously exhaled. Her eyes closed helplessly, and she trembled against him.

They began to move.

To sway in rhythm to the sweet music. Their feet slid slowly on the polished parquet, their bodies undulating to the tune's languorous tempo. Lucy's temple was pressed against Blackie's smooth jaw. She could feel his heart beating through the fabric that covered his broad chest.

She felt the instinctive pressure of his tall, hard body, the strength of his leanly muscled arms. His knee was between her legs, his pelvis sliding and pressing provocatively against her own. Lucy's whole being responded to the indisputable message his sent.

Their closely pressing bodies silently expressed emotion and sensuality with an extraordinary potency. Affection was growing. Ardor was escalating. Each was helplessly attracted to what the other represented. The innocent Lucy was a model of well-bred yearning, of idealistic devotion, of passion repressed. The worldly Blackie was her exact opposite; the dark, seductive man, the great lover, his sexual power barely held in check.

Oblivious to everything but the rising heat of their swaying, yearning bodies, the physical attraction between them was strong and growing stronger as they slowly, sensually danced the Last Dance.

Both blinked in confusion when the music stopped and the dimmed lights came up. They broke apart as if they'd been caught in some deviant act, laughed nervously, and reluctantly returned to the real world. Remembering their manners, they bade their friends goodnight, assured Lochlin the dance was a huge success, and drifted toward the exit with all the others.

Not wanting the evening to ever end, Lucy quickly agreed to Blackie's suggestion of a walk on the beach. They took a chilled bottle of champagne, rushed out of the hotel to the Boardwalk, and hurried to the very south end of the long wooden walkway, leaving the crowds behind. At the bottom rung of wooden steps leading down to the beach, they stopped.

Blackie insisted, so Lucy took off their shoes, handed them to him.

He shoved them into his jacket pockets and gestured, "Stockings too."

Lucy turned her back to him, removed the ice blue satin garters, and peeled down the long, white silk stockings. She felt naked without her stockings; a delicious chill skipped up her spine. When she turned to face him, Blackie was barefooted, his trouser legs rolled up to mid calf. He turned his right shoulder toward her, indicating the breast pocket of his suit jacket. Lucy laughed and stuffed her hose and garters into it.

His shoes in one hand, the champagne in the other, Blackie said, "Let's go."

Lucy lifted the skirts of her white tulle gown and stepped down onto the soft sand. They strolled down the beach, wandering farther and farther from the lights of the Boardwalk.

The stars were out. The ocean was beautiful. The night air was warm and sweet. They found a secluded spot far down the deserted beach. Blackie dropped his shoes, handed Lucy the champagne, and shrugged out of his suit jacket. He spread the jacket on the sand and seated Lucy on it. While she hugged her knees and watched, Blackie gathered driftwood and built a small fire.

He uncorked the champagne, handed the bottle to Lucy, and moved around in back of her. He sat down directly behind her, trapping her inside his spread knees. He drew her back against his chest, wrapped his arms around her, and said, "Know what I want to do, what I've wanted to do all evening?"

"Tell me," she whispered, lifted her arms and clasped her hands behind his head.

"I want to kiss you," he said, his hands spanning her ribs. "I want to kiss you all night long."

Blackie shifted then and, turning her a little in his arms, lowered his mouth to hers. He kissed her with such devastating tenderness Lucy felt her bones melt. She sighed and cuddled against him, praying he really would kiss her all night long.

They stayed there on the beach in the moonlight until the champagne bottle was empty, and Lucy was a more than a little tipsy. Blackie was stone sober but he was more than a little aroused.

"Lucy, Lucy," he murmured, pressing her back across his bent arm, bending to her, his hand sweeping her white tulle skirts up her bare legs, exposing her pale thighs to the night air and to his hot touch.

Lucy felt an overpowering rush of helplessness, a surging warmth that left her limp as Blackie kissed her again and again. The warm, soft kisses had swiftly graduated in intensity until she clung to him, the world spinning, he the only solid thing in it.

Her head cradled in the crook of his strong arm, she sighed and squirmed while his hot, insistent mouth pressed kiss after kiss to her parted lips and his hands caressed her barely covered breasts and naked legs. Dizzy with desire, Lucy moaned softly when his searing mouth sank into the pale softness of her throat and his thumb rubbed back and forth over an erect nipple through the soft fabric of her dress. Her head fell back and she could hardly breathe as his hot, open mouth slowly spread a trail of fire from the sensitive hollow of her throat down over the exposed swell of her breasts.

When the low-cut bodice of her white tulle gown finally stopped the downward progress of his questing lips, her heart was beating so fast it frightened her and she felt faint. Blackie laid his dark cheek against her rapidly beating heart and held her quietly while she calmed a little.

"Blackie," she whispered breathlessly, "Oh, Blackie."

"I know," he murmured, raised his dark head, and looked at her with passion-glazed eyes. He shuddered deeply, exhaled heavily, and kissed her again.

A thousand heated kisses were inadequate and Blackie was tempted to snatch Lucy from the sand, carry her straight up to his hotel suite, and make love to her.

But he was trapped with a good girl, so he took her back to the Atlantic Grand to her own third floor room.

Lucy put the key in the lock, opened the door, and turned slowly to face him, unsure exactly what to do or say.

Blackie smiled at her, returned her shoes, stockings, and one ice blue garter. The other he kept, with her permission, for a souvenir.

They stood making small talk for a long, awkward moment, Blackie with his hands in his trouser pockets, Lucy clutching her shoes and stockings to her breasts.

At last Blackie exhaled, took his hands from his pockets, touched her cheek, and said, "We had some fun, didn't we, Lucy?"

Her throat suddenly so tight she could barely swallow, Lucy smiled weakly, "Yes, we did. We had some fun."

Then, his beautiful, midnight eyes reflecting some of the torture she felt, Blackie moved a step closer, gently cupped both of her pale cheeks in his tanned hands, and kissed her. A light, quick brush of his tongue across her lips.

"Goodnight, sweetheart," he said, turned, and walked away.

CHAPTER THIRTY

Lucy watched him walk down the silent corridor. He didn't look back. She was sure he would turn to wave and smile when he reached the elevator. He didn't. He disappeared into the waiting car and was gone.

Stunned, dejected, Lucy went inside and slowly closed the door. She deposited her shoes and stockings on the round drum table beside the porcelain vase that held a huge bouquet of gardenias. Every morning since that first day he'd sent them, Blackie sent a fresh bouquet of gardenias. Lucy looked at the velvety petaled flowers and sighed. She unpinned the wilted gardenia corsage from the low bodice of her white dress and laid it beside the shoes.

Edgy, unnerved, she left the lamps unlit, the room in a patchwork of deep shadow and bright moonlight. Barefooted, she moved across the deep-piled aqua rug, stepped out on the tiny balcony, and drew a slow, deep breath of the heavy misted air. She stared unblinking at the moon-silvered sea. Great ocean waves were rising, breaking, then rising again.

Lucy told herself she was glad that Blackie had gone. Glad nothing really happened. But she couldn't quite convince herself that she was.

She loved him.

Loved him without condition or expectation. Loved him intensely, completely, passionately. Loved him now and forever.

242

Lucy's chest was so tight she could hardly stand the pain, and that great empty feeling which had been so much a part of her life for too many years already was returning.

She turned and went inside.

She paced fitfully in her bare feet, agonized by the knowledge that she would never, for as long as she lived, see Blackie LaDuke again. Tonight would be the last night he spent upstairs in the north tower penthouse suite. The last night she stayed in this third floor room.

With the dawn, Blackie would be gone. Gone for good. Gone forever. She couldn't let him go without...

Suddenly all Lucy knew for sure was that if she didn't take this one chance to grab at life--real life--she was going to explode! Shatter into a million pieces that could never be put back together again. Just *once* in her life she had to live. Really live.

***

Blackie stepped inside the darkened drawing room of his penthouse suite and closed the door. He didn't bother with lighting the lamps. He didn't bother taking his shoes from the pockets of his wrinkled, sand-dusted suit jacket. He shrugged impatiently out of the jacket and, in a fit of frustration, wadded it up and threw it as hard as he could across the room. Jacket and shoes struck the wall with a loud thud and fell to the carpet below.

Immediately ashamed of his infantile behavior, Blackie exhaled wearily, took off his wrinkled shirt, and hung it neatly over a chair back. He took a cigarette from the silver box on a nearby table. He stuck the cigarette in his mouth, cupped his hands, lighted it, and shook out the match. He inhaled deeply, drawing the smoke down into his lungs and holding it before slowly releasing it.

Bare-chested, smoking in the darkness, he paced the shadowy drawing room like a caged animal, his lean body straining against invisible bonds.

He abruptly stopped pacing and his black eyes closed in pain when the knock came on his door. His naked belly tightened reflexively and a deep shudder passed through his body. He knew it was Lucy. He knew he had to turn her away. Not answer the door. Keep silent until she gave up and returned to the safety of her own room.

Nerves raw, every muscle in his tall, lean body taut with agony, Blackie stayed where he was as she knocked again, a little louder, more insistent this time. A vein throbbing on his forehead, he stubbed the cigarette out in a crystal ashtray and ground his even white teeth.

A long minute passed.

Again she knocked, a rapid-fire rat-a-tat, her fist forcefully pounding on the solid door. And slamming into his aching heart.

Blackie stood his ground.

I'm doing it for your own good, sweetheart, he murmured soundlessly, miserably. *Go away, Lucy. Run for your life!*

He held his breath and waited.

Finally the knocking stopped. All was silent. She had given up. She was leaving.

Oh, God, she was leaving!

Unable to stop himself, Blackie tore across the darkened room and yanked the door open.

Lucy, half-way down the hall, stopped, whirled about, and saw him. Wordlessly they raced toward each other. Laughing, crying, Lucy eagerly threw herself into

Blackie's outstretched arms and felt those powerful arms close firmly around her. She drew his handsome head down and kissed him. And in her kiss was all the love she had saved for a lifetime.

When finally their lips separated, Blackie swung Lucy up into his arms, marched back down the corridor and into his suite, kicking the door shut behind them. Continuing to hold her high against his naked chest, Blackie stood in the darkened drawing room, kissing Lucy hotly, hungrily, like he'd never allowed himself to kiss her before.

At last he raised his dark head and gazed into her adoring eyes. A pulse throbbed in his tanned throat and his chest constricted.

His voice a gentle caress, he said, "Are you sure, Lucy? I don't want to hurt you, sweetheart. I don't want you regretting..."

"My only regret," she interrupted, "will be if I allow you to leave without making love to me." Her arms tightened around his neck. "Love me, Blackie. Just this once, love me."

"Oh, God, Lucy. Sweet Lucy," he said and carried her straight to the bedroom.

No lamps burned in the spacious bedroom, but bright moonlight streamed in the open balcony doors and fell across the turned down bed. Shimmering sheets of pale white silk looked silver in the moonlight. A half dozen silk-cased, down pillows rested against the bed's tall, black walnut headboard.

Lucy looked at the vast bed without any indecision or apprehension.

She loved him with all her heart and soul and she trusted him with both. And if she never saw him again this side of Paradise, it didn't matter.

Tonight he belonged to her. No one was going to take this moment or this man away from her. There was no past, no future, no fears. Only this night. And there was nothing she wanted more than to lie in the moonlight and make love with Blackie.

Blackie walked directly to the bed. He sat on the mattress' edge and drew Lucy down to sit his left knee. His arm tightened around her waist and he hugged her close.

She pulled away just a bit and, looking at him with such total devotion he felt his heart kick against his ribs, said, "You do desire me a little, don't you, Blackie?"

"Oh, honey, yes," he told her honestly. "I want you more than you'll ever know."

Satisfied, she squeezed his bare shoulders and leaned her forehead against his. "I'm so glad. I was afraid maybe..."

"Lucy, Lucy," he murmured and his mouth captured hers in a kiss that assured her he really wanted her.

As he kissed her, the tips of his tanned fingers lightly stroked her face, her throat, then swept slowly over the pale flesh exposed above the low cut bodice of her white evening dress. When the long, drugging kiss finally ended, Blackie's fingertips were inside her dress, gently caressing her left breast.

"Lucy," he said again, very softly, and Lucy thought she had never known her name was so beautiful until she heard him say it.

Her blood was stirring, her heart beating fast, she felt flushed from head to toe. Her hand played nervously on Blackie's naked chest, her fingertips raking through the crisp, black hair, palm spreading on the bare bronzed flesh. He was hot to the touch and that thrilled her, pleased her beyond words.

His smooth lips brushing kisses to her to face and throat, Blackie lifted a hand to her hair, carefully removed the pearl studded pin Lochlin MacDonald had given her, and laid it on the night table. In seconds he had dexterously removed all remaining hairpins and Lucy's curly, chestnut hair cascaded down around her face and shoulders.

Blackie put his hands in her hair, running his fingers through the thick, curly locks. When Lucy looked into his eyes, his lean fingers tightened and he drew her mouth down to his. With deliberate slowness, he kissed her, his spread fingers clutching her hair.

His burning lips so dazzled her, Lucy never knew when his hands left her hair. But soon she found that just as the pins had easily slipped from her hair, her clothes easily slipped from her body. Masterfully enclosing her in a world that reached no further than the tightness of his arms and the heat of his kisses, Blackie undressed Lucy as she sat there on his knee in the moonlight.

Dizzy with desire, consumed with a kind of hot mysterious longing that was totally alien to her, Lucy sighed and swooned and felt her clothes being taken away. It registered vaguely somewhere in the passion fogged recesses of her mind that Blackie was doing the same thing she had done earlier as she had dressed for the dance. She had dressed backwards, now he was undressing her backwards. He was taking off her underwear first. She felt her lace trimmed knickers slide down her quivering stomach and over her hips. One-handed, Blackie coaxed the undergarment from beneath her and it whispered down her legs and over her bare feet.

Lucy shivered.

"Kiss me, Baby," Blackie murmured. "Kiss me good."

Tingling all over, hot and cold at once, Lucy cupped his tanned jaw in her hand and lowered her lips to his. This was different from the preceding kisses. Blackie allowed--made--Lucy become the aggressor, forced her to be the dominant one.

Lucy kissed him hotly, urgently, feeling the rise of her feminine power as she commandingly took the lead. Molding his mouth to hers, she kissed him with complete abandon, holding nothing back. It was a fiery, sexual, prolonged kiss to which she gave her all, her lips eagerly drawing on Blackie's, her tongue thrusting into his mouth to tease and torment his.

She kissed him good.

Caught up in the lusty, open-mouthed kiss, Lucy was hardly aware that as she kissed him, Blackie was calmly unfastening the hooks going down the back of her dress. That wasn't all. His hand had moved up under her dress, was gently stroking her knee.

Feverish, Lucy finally tore her kiss-puffy lips from his. Gasping for breath, heart pounding, she hugged his dark head to her breasts. She sighed when Blackie sat her back and lowered her loosened dress, pulling the sleeves down her weak arms, pushing the white tulle bodice to her waist. Whispering her name and looking into her eyes, he lifted a hand to the small bow at the top edge of her lace-trimmed camisole. He gave it a gentle tug. It came undone. Using only his curled little finger he managed to unhook the tiny clasps going down the center of the wispy camisole.

Lucy shuddered involuntarily when he pushed the camisole apart and her small, pale breasts were exposed. She held her breath as he gazed at her bared flesh, a hot light burning in his dark hooded eyes. She murmured his name when Blackie slowly bent his head and kissed the undercurve of her right breast. Then her eyes closed in rapture when his hot mouth enclosed the aching nipple. With his strong arm supporting her back, Blackie's plucking mouth stayed at her breasts while his hand moved up the inside of her pale thigh beneath the white tulle dress.

Lucy winced softly when his fingertips raked through the tight chestnut curls between her thighs and touched her where she'd never been touched before. Her eyes opened and closed in wonder and her nails dug into Blackie's bare shoulder as he began to slowly, seductively caress her. Lucy bit her lip and squirmed, unsure if she liked what he was doing.

She was undecided for only a moment.

"I have wanted," she heard Blackie say in a low voice, rough with emotion, "to touch you this way all night."

CHAPTER THIRTY ONE

"You looked so beautiful tonight, Lucy," Blackie continued, his breath hot against her flushed cheek, "while we danced I dreamed of holding you like this, loving you like this."

His smooth baritone voice, his shocking words sent a new injection of heat through her entire body. Lucy's heartbeat again accelerated. Waves of erotic impulses surged inside her, pressing her pelvis up and forward to meet the increasingly pleasurable touch of Blackie's long, skilled fingers.

Calm down, she silently screamed at herself, but found it impossible to do.

Then Blackie's mouth was back on hers and she knew his blood was racing, too, from his devastating kiss, a kiss almost savage in its hot urgency. She felt the same urgency, an intense yearning that was rapidly escalating.

Lucy could no longer think clearly, no longer wanted to think. She surrendered totally to the sweet new passion consuming her. She thrilled to every intimate touch of Blackie's hands and mouth. She arched and sighed and moaned while Blackie held her on his knee and patiently, expertly prepared her for total lovemaking.

Lucy didn't know exactly when the white tulle dress came completely off and was cast aside. She did become dreamily aware, at some point, that she was totally naked, but she couldn't quite remember how it came about. And she didn't care. The heat and need of her bare body was all, was everything.

On fire, Lucy whimpered softly when Blackie took his loving hand away from that burning spot between her legs, the spot which had become her entire universe.

"Blackie," she breathed her objection, desperate for him to continue.

"I know, Baby," he whispered as he rose to his feet with her in his arms.

He turned and gently laid her in the middle of the bed. Lucy sighed gratefully, delighting in the soothing caress of the soft, cool sheets against her hot, bare skin. Her hands sweeping anxiously over the shimmering silk, her bare belly contracting, she saw the play of moonlight on Blackie's rippling muscles as he hastily stepped out of his trousers.

Enthralled with his physical beauty, she had only a second to admire him before he was in bed beside her, holding her close, every inch of their naked bodies touching. His hand sweeping down her back, Blackie held Lucy to him, purposely giving her the opportunity to become acquainted with his fully aroused male body. He pressed his pulsing erection to her, letting her feel the throbbing hardness against her bare belly. His hand cupped and caressed her soft buttocks, then his fingers slipped between the crevice to touch and fondle and keep her in a state of hot excitement. Trembling, burning up, Lucy arched anxiously to him, so Blackie smoothly pressed her down onto her back.

His mouth covering hers, he nudged her slender legs apart and agilely moved between. He lay very still atop her for a moment, his weight supported on his stiffened arms, his mouth fused with hers. Their lips finally separated. Blackie raised his dark head.

He spoke her name and Lucy gazed into his dark, flashing eyes as he thrust swiftly into her. Her hands clutching his hard biceps, she winced at the sharp, stabbing pain and bit her lip to keep from moaning. Her eyes closed, she fought back the tears.

"Baby, I'm sorry, I'm sorry," she heard Blackie whisper and his mouth pressed soothing kisses to her closed eyes, her feverish cheeks, her trembling lips. "Try to relax. The pain will soon pass, I promise. Don't be afraid, Sweetheart."

Lucy was not frightened. For this shining hour, for these glorious moments, she was complete, as happy and as fulfilled as it was possible to be on this earth.

It was pure heaven to lie here in the arms of this magnificent man whom she loved more than her own life. There was nothing she would have changed. It was perfection, all of it. Even the pain was beautiful because with it, she became his. She belonged to him, now and forever. And in her heart of hearts, he would always belong to her.

So Lucy laid in the arms of Blackie LaDuke, learning, loving, living. This, she knew, was life--real life--and she wouldn't have missed it for the world.

Soon the pain gave way to pleasure, and pleasure turned to sheer ecstasy. Blackie took her with deep, slow thrusts and Lucy's pelvis lifted and lowered to match his languid driving rhythm.

It was good for Lucy.

It was fantastic for Blackie.

They moved together in slow, graceful splendor as if they'd been made for each other. Moonlight silvering them and the bed on which they made love, they undulated sensuously, their damp bodies slipping and sliding together until the sweet, sexual joy Blackie found in Lucy propelled him into the fast, frenzied rhythm that led toward blinding release.

Lucy's eyes widened with wonder when her orgasm began. Her nails dug into the smooth skin of Blackie's back, as the bliss spiraled steadily upward until wave after frightening wave of nearly unbearable ecstasy buffeted her. When the feeling became so incredibly enjoyable it actually hurt, there was a long, fierce explosion of heat that caused her to cry out and call Blackie's name in delirium.

It was the sweetest sound he'd ever heard.

Blackie let himself go then, driving savagely into her with deep, fast thrusts until his own release came on the heels of hers. He groaned as if in great pain and the tendons in his neck stood out in bold relief while his spasming body spurted hot, thick, semen deep inside Lucy.

Panting, breathing hard, Lucy let herself fall back onto the pillows. Blackie collapsed against her.

"You alright, baby?" Blackie murmured, his perspiration slick face buried in her damp curly hair.

"Wonderful," Lucy whispered, wrapping her arms around him to hold him close, to keep him on her and in her for as long as she possibly could.

Silence came then, and peace.

The sweetest kind of peace known to humans.

But sooner than either could have imagined, the total peace gave way to gentle stirrings of new desire. Affectionate touches changed to arousing caresses. Quick brushes of the lips turned to long, drugging kisses of passion. Hands and mouths became insistent. Naked flesh responded to sensual stroking and lusty licking.

They made love again.

This time Lucy was seated astride the reclining Blackie. It was even better than before. Her hands clasping his rib cage, unbound hair whipping wildly about her head, she quickly caught his rhythm, moved to meet his deep, driving thrusts with slow, erotic rolls of her hips.

They looked into each other's eyes while they made love. The pleasure was incredible, awesome. Lucy gazed steadily into Blackie's fiery, night-black eyes while her breasts swayed and danced and she gyrated her bare bottom. Grinding and bucking against him, she felt him expand and throb within her.

It was pure heaven.

So pleasurable she wished she could stretch it out, make it last, but she was such a novice she had no idea how to go about it.

His mind as well as his body totally in tune with hers, Blackie murmured hoarsely, "Just slow it down a little, baby. Easy, sweetheart...easy...yes, yes...that's better...that's it..." He took his hands from her hips, folded them beneath his head, and let her learn how to love him languidly.

Lucy learned fast.

Encouraged by Blackie and guided by her own innate sexuality, Lucy eagerly experimented, playing at this new delightful game, bent on discovering how to best prolong and increase their pleasure. She made love with total abandon, watching Blackie's handsome face for response, asking questions, taking instructions.

And when finally it came, their climax was so awesome, so draining, it left them both fully satiated. Tired and happy, Lucy fell asleep in Blackie's arms almost immediately.

She slept serenely while the bright moonlight slowly inched away, leaving their entwined naked bodies in darkness as the moon went down and the dawn approached.

Blackie never closed his eyes.

Shortly before daybreak he slowly, carefully, untangled himself from Lucy, moving her slender arms from around him, sliding her bent knee off his belly. She shivered slightly in her sleep, sighed softly, turned over onto her stomach.

And slept on.

Blackie eased across the mattress and slipped from the bed. Silently he went into the black marble bath, quietly closed the door, and stepped into the shower. Out after only five minutes he hurriedly dressed. He skipped the morning shave.

Back in the bedroom he eyed the stacked luggage, ready to be taken downstairs. One suitcase remained open for last minute items. Blackie glanced around. His discarded suit trousers were on the floor beside the bed. He picked them up and frowned, wondering where he'd left the matching jacket. He went into the drawing room, turned about in a circle, and spotted it. His shoes sticking out of the pockets, the jacket lay on the floor. Sheepish, recalling how he'd thrown it against the wall last night, he went to retrieve it.

A dainty, lace-trimmed, blue satin garter fell out of a jacket pocket. Blackie bent and picked up the garter, held it for a second in the palm of his hand, staring at it. Then he exhaled, shoved it into his trouser pocket, and rushed back into the bedroom.

Blackie stuffed the wrinkled clothes into the open suitcase, closed the valise, and looked around to see if there was anything he had forgotten.

He saw only Lucy.

He moved silently to the bed and looked at her. She slept peacefully, her bare body relaxed and half turned toward him, her features soft and sweet in repose, like those of an innocent child. Blackie went down on one knee beside the bed and leaned closer. He stared at her, memorizing each line, each plane and angle of her pretty face. Then soundlessly, he rose and walked away.

Blackie never considered waking her to say goodbye. He hated goodbyes. He never said goodbye. Never had. He'd learned that little trick when he was just a child and had been shipped off to boarding school. If you didn't say goodbye, it didn't hurt so bad.

The first gray light of dawn began spilling in through the open balcony doors. Blackie knew he'd better hurry if he was going to make his train. He picked up the heavy, black suitcases and headed for the door. He eased it open, carried the luggage through, set them down, and turned back to close the bedroom door.

His hand shook slightly on the gold knob and a muscle spasmed in his beard-stubbled cheek.

Blackie pulled the door shut, lifted the luggage, crossed the spacious parlor, and stepped out into the hall. He walked down the silent corridor whistling softly.

CHAPTER THIRTY TWO

The Boardwalk was deserted. The white wicker rolling chairs were parked in neat rows out of the way. Awnings on the Boardwalk stalls were pulled down and tightly fastened. The booths were empty. Closed for the winter.

It was a resort out of season.

A pervasive gloom had settled over the place. There was no sun. The sky was a bleak, gun-metal gray. Low lying clouds looked like rain. A strong wind whipped in off the dark, restless ocean. White capped breakers crashed loudly on the desolate Jersey Shore.

Summer was over. Blackie was gone. And Lucy was thirty years old.

Sand blew into Lucy's face as she strolled aimlessly down the abandoned Boardwalk. She told herself that the irritating grains of sand were responsible for her stinging eyes. Blinking back the tears she refused to let herself shed, Lucy walked almost a mile on that dismal Tuesday morning.

Heading in a southerly direction on the long wooden promenade, she considered going down to the beach. Down to where she and Blackie had drunk champagne and kissed in the magical moonlight.

She decided against it.

Lucy paused, ventured over to the Boardwalk's waist high steel railing. She rested her hands on the damp metal and looked out at the nearly empty beach. A handful of people were milling about. But they were mostly the clean up crew, collecting the mountains of refuse left by yesterday's massive crowd.

No squealing, laughing bathers rushed into and out of the surf. No sun worshippers lolled lazily on the sand. The big, muscular lifeguards were no longer on duty. The sand artists had departed.

Lucy turned suddenly and hurried back up the Boardwalk. When she was sure she had located the right spot, she stopped and leaned out over the railing. She squinted down at the site where a few short days ago her Happy Birthday sand sculpture had graced the beach. No part of the sculpture remained. It was gone. Trampled by thousands of bare feet and carried out to sea with the tides.

Lucy's chin sagged down onto her chest. She closed her eyes. Her hands gripped the solid steel railing and she stood there motionless, lost in thought. Only a few seconds had passed when a soft, almost inaudible sound, which she couldn't identify, attracted her attention.

Lucy's eyes opened and she looked curiously around. She heard the sound again. A soft plaintive moan or the whimpering of a small child. Frantically she looked about, searching for the source. She saw nothing, no one.

She felt a tug on the hem of skirts and glanced down. Her lips fell open in astonishment. Lucy immediately went down on her heels and put out her hands.

"Precious, what in the world are you doing here?" She picked up the heavy black Persian and rubbed her cheek against his head. "I can't believe Lady Strange would allow you to...to..."

She stopped speaking. Her eyes lifted, swept searchingly out over the beach.

***

Laboring to keep up, Lady Strange was short of breath as she waded through the soft sand of the beach. She had been short of breath since Cort Mitchell had banged on her door a half hour ago, waking her from a deep slumber.

"Beatrice, wake up!" He had shouted loudly, his fist hammering on the solid door of her penthouse suite. "It's Cort, Beatrice, get up!"

Her heart had started pounding before her feet touched the floor. Cort never called her Beatrice except in times of an emergency. And he knew better than to awaken her before ten thirty in the morning unless it was absolutely necessary. She glanced at the porcelain clock on the marble mantle. Five minutes to ten.

Anxiously hiking the long tails of her flowing nightgown up around her dimpled knees, Lady Strange lunged out of bed, rushed frantically into the parlor, and opened the door.

"It's time, Bea," Cort said gently.

"Oh, dear god," she murmured and her plump hands flew up to cover her mouth.

"Get dressed, my dear," Cort patted her rounded shoulder soothingly. "He's asked to go down to the beach. He wants the ocean to be the last thing he sees on this side."

Nodding, she gave no reply. Just turned and hurried back to her bedroom. Ten minutes later she was puffing and trying to keep up with the long legged Cort as he pushed Lochlin MacDonald's wheel chair down the deserted, wind-swept Boardwalk. Worrying and wondering how Cort would be able to get Lochlin down from the Boardwalk and onto the sandy beach, she trotted along beside Lochlin's rolling chair. Wheezing and chattering nonsensically, Lady Strange, for once in her life, scolded the spoiled Precious when the big, black tom kept getting in their way.

The trio reached the nearest set of wooden steps to the beach. The winded Lady Strange watched in awe and admiration as the sixty-six year old Colonel Cort Mitchell lifted Lochlin's chair--with Lochlin in it--and carried the dying man across the lonely stretch of sand almost to the water's edge. There, Cort carefully set the chair down.

Lochlin MacDonald could no longer move a muscle. Nor could he speak. But a dim light still burned in his expressive eyes and it said to Cort, 'thank you, good friend, for letting me spend my last minutes here beside this old briny sea I so love'.

"Don't mention it," Cort said aloud.

"Is there anything we can get you, sugar?" Lady Strange asked, taking one of Lochlin's useless hands in both of hers. He blinked no. "Well, you just tell us and we'll get it for you," she said as calmly as if she were asking him if he'd care for another glass of iced tea.

Lochlin MacDonald gazed wistfully out at the ocean, his eyesight fading as death drew ever nearer. Still, those dim eyes lighted slightly when he caught the ocean's heavy scent and felt the sea breeze ruffle his lank, perspiring hair.

One lone tear formed in the corner of his left eye.

***

Lucy stared in disbelief when she spotted the three people far down on a lonely stretch of beach. The tall, silver-haired Colonel Mitchell and the short, mountainous Lady Strange flanked Lochlin MacDonald in his chair.

Lucy was dumbfounded.

She had never seen any of the trio on the beach before and couldn't imagine what they were doing there on a bleak, sunless morning such as this.

Puzzled, Lucy nonetheless started to smile, feeling her spirits lifting a little. What difference did it make what they were up to? She was delighted to see them. She'd go down and join them, say goodbye one more time.

Lucy lowered the purring, black Persian to its feet and murmuring 'come on, Precious,' eagerly headed for the wooden beach stairs. She stopped there, hesitated, then took off her shoes and stockings and left them on the bottom step.

Her smile growing wider, she yanked her skirts up and started to run toward the trio.

***

Cort saw her first.

He looked up when Lucy was still a couple of hundred yards away. His worried frown alerted Lady Strange. She turned her head and saw Lucy in the distance, running eagerly toward them.

Smiling nervously, she leaned down and said to Lochlin, "Dearest, that sweet Lucy Hart has spotted us from the Boardwalk. She's come down to the beach and is heading in our direction." Lochlin could no longer even blink his eyes to object, but Cort Mitchell was a perceptive, sensitive man.

He knew.

Cort said, "Lochlin, I imagine you'd rather Lucy not see you like this. I'll go stop her."

The Colonel walked fast across the sand. He intercepted the running Lucy when she was still more than fifty yards away.

Gently clasping her upper arms, he said, "Child, Lochlin's...he...well, he isn't feeling his best this morning." He smiled down at her. "He told me he'd skin me alive if I allowed any pretty young ladies to see him looking anything less than his handsome best."

Lucy looked into the Colonel's calm, gray eyes, then past him to the others. "But I...I'm leaving at noon and I just wanted to say one last goodbye." Her eyes returned to Cort's face. And she knew. Somehow she knew. Had known all along. "Colonel, he's...Lochlin is dying, isn't he? I mean right now, this morning?"

"Yes, Lucy, he is." She saw his Adams apple move slowly up and down in his throat. He continued calmly, "He won't live out the hour. Bless his heart, he's such a proud man; he wants to go with as much dignity as possible."

Tears again stinging her eyes, Lucy nodded. "I understand. "I knew you would." He saw the tears brightening her green eyes, lifted a hand and gently cupped the back of her head. "Don't be sad, child. Don't grieve for Lochlin. It's a merciful God that's freeing him this morning from the prison of his useless body." He kissed her cheek, then hugged her. "Go now, and take with you only the good memories of your visit. Will you do that?"

"Yes, Sir, I will," she said, the words muffled against his shirtfront.

"Have a safe journey home, Lucy."

He released her. She turned away. He stood there and watched as she ran bare-footed across the sand, skirts and chestnut hair flying in the rising winds.

Cort took a deep, spine-stiffening breath and started back. When he was still a few steps away, he called, "She didn't suspect a thing, Lochlin, she said...she..."

He caught sight of Lady Strange's tear-wet face and stopped speaking. Silently he moved around in front of the wheel chair and looked down at the man seated there. The lone tear that had formed in Lochlin's left eye was still there. It had never fallen down his pallid cheek.

Cort Mitchell took a freshly laundered, linen handkerchief from his pocket and gently blotted the tear from the corner of Lochlin's eye. He put the handkerchief away.

With his right hand he gently closed the dead man's sightless eyes and said, "Good-bye, old friend. May the wind be at your back throughout all eternity."

Then Colonel Cort Mitchell turned and took the weeping Lady Strange into his comforting arms.

CHAPTER THIRTY THREE

A chill, wind-driven rain greeted Lucy when she stepped down from the train at the Colonias station. Other than a few scattered sprinkles, it was the first real rain the community had seen for more than three weeks. The hard driving rain peppered Lucy's face and the winds pressed her beige traveling suit against her slender body as she dashed into the shelter of the depot's small waiting room.

That same wind and rain was lashing Lucy's quiet white house a few blocks away, banging the screen door back and forth incessantly. The telegram left inside the screen by young Bobby Flatt on the morning Lucy left for Atlantic City had remained there while she was gone.

But it blew away in this afternoon's late summer rainstorm. The yellow envelope skittered across the front yard and sailed into the street. It stayed there for a time, snagged on a brittle limb that had broken off the apple tree in Lucy Hart's front yard.

The telegram lay there as Lucy, parasol unfurled, stepped down from the carriage before her front gate. Lucy was preoccupied with seeing to the unloading of her luggage, paying the hired cab driver, and getting in out of the blinding rain. She never glanced at the street.

As she hurried up the walk to her front door the soggy yellow envelope came loose from the broken tree limb and was carried swiftly down the gutter by the surging, muddy rainwater.

The telegram, informing Lucy that Mr. Theodore Mooney would not be coming to Atlantic City to meet her due to his sister's sudden serious illness, would never be seen by her.

Lucy had barely gotten inside and changed into dry clothes before she heard the loud knocking on the back door. She smiled and hurried through the house. Her neighbor Kitty Widner and the adorable golden curled four-year old Annie stood on the back porch. Mother and child each held a covered dish in their hands.

"I was beginning to think you were never coming back," said Kitty, hurrying inside, pressing her rain-wet cheek to Lucy's.

"I considered it," said Lucy, beaming down at the big-eyed Annie. "Is that for me?" she asked the beautiful little girl.

Nodding so vigorously she set her golden curls to dancing, Annie smiled shyly and held the cloth-covered plate out to Lucy. Lucy took it, lifted the dishtowel, looked at the fancy sandwiches, and said, "Mmmm, they look delicious. Thank you, Annie."

"Did you bring me a present?" Annie asked.

"Annie Widner!" her mother scolded as she crossed the spotless kitchen to deposit the freshly baked pineapple upside down cake on the table.

"I sure did, Annie," Lucy told the little girl. "Wait right here."

She set the sandwiches on the cabinet, dashed into the other room, came back and plucked the little girl up into her arms.

Annie's enormous blue eyes lighted happily when Lucy presented her with the pink seashell she'd bought on the Boardwalk.

Annie's observant mother, noting the lettering on the souvenir, clapped her hands and said, "Atlantic City! So that's where you've been all this time! You went to Atlantic City!"

"Yes."

"You know something? You look different! I noticed it the minute I walked in this house. Something about you has changed," Kitty smiled cat-like and shook a finger at Lucy, "I'll bet I know what it is. You met somebody in Atlantic City! A man!"

Lucy felt her face flush with warmth, wondered if had turned scarlet. "Yes," she said, attempting to sound blasé, "I did. I met a rather nice gentleman and we...we spent a good deal of time together."

"I knew it!" squealed Kitty Widner. "Oh, I knew it! Is he a postmaster? Or a college professor perhaps? An accountant or bookkeeper with some reputable firm? How did you meet him? What did the two of you do when you were together? Will you be corresponding with him? Will he be coming to Colonias? Promise you'll tell me everything, Miss Lucy!"

Lucy inwardly recoiled. She was jarringly reminded that here in her hometown she was still very much *Miss* Lucy. Even to her closest friend. She had almost forgotten that she was Miss Lucy. Had been Miss Lucy for years. Would always be Miss Lucy. Amazingly, in just two short weeks she'd grown used to being simply Lucy.

"There's really not much to tell," Lucy lowered the golden-curled Annie to her feet. "Why don't we sit down," she inclined her head toward the kitchen table.

Kitty eagerly took a seat, her expectant eyes never leaving Lucy's face. Lucy knew Kitty was waiting to hear about some shy, stuffy school teacher or accountant that her prim, spinster friend, Miss Lucy Hart, had met on holiday in Atlantic City.

Lucy was half a mind to set her straight. Imagine Kitty's shock if she'd known the truth. Lucy was tempted to tell the other woman that she had spent all her time with a worldly New York playboy who had become her passionate lover!

But, of course, she couldn't do that. Miss Lucy Hart would never have behaved so shamefully, much less have spoken about it later. Had she still been the carefree, madcap Lucy of Atlantic City, perhaps she *would* have told her friend something of the libertine lifestyle she had embraced on her long seaside holiday.

She found herself longing to brag to Kitty about the handsome, worldly Blackie. To boast that the most eligible bachelor in Atlantic City had chosen *her*, and that he was wonderful and romantic and exciting and sophisticated and sexy and funny and...

Lucy didn't dare tell Kitty--or anyone--about her summertime love affair with a dark, handsome stranger. Kitty would have been horrified. So Lucy said only that her gentleman friend was a thirty-three year old bachelor from an eastern real estate family. Which was true. Never mind that Blackie was anything but a gentleman and his family had ostracized him years ago.

Referring to him as Robert LaDuke, Lucy told of their excursions along the busy Boardwalk and of the afternoon band concerts, and the frightening rides at the amusement piers. She spoke at length of the thrilling sights and sounds of the City by the Sea. No, she answered when Kitty repeated the question. She wouldn't be corresponding with Mr. LaDuke. Nor would he becoming to Colonias. It was, she said, just one of those meaningless summertime romances,

Nothing more. And changing the subject, she told Kitty of the other friends she had made, a southern Colonel, a titled noblewoman, a crippled seaman.

The rain and the wind continued to lash the house as the three of them sat at Lucy's kitchen table. While Annie pressed her ear to her pink sea shell attempting to hear the ocean's roar, the two women talked until Kitty, hearing the grandfather clock in the hallway chime the hour of six, leapt up out of her chair.

"Good Lord, Bruce will be home from the lumber yard any minute and I haven't even started supper."

Lucy pushed back her chair and rose. "Thank you both for coming and for bringing the sandwiches and cake."

Kitty, her hand atop her daughter's blond head, was pointing Annie toward the door. "You're very welcome," she said, then paused at the back door and added, "I'm happy you enjoyed yourself, Miss Lucy. But I'm glad to have you back home where you belong."

Kitty picked up Annie, stepped out onto the back porch, and skipped down the steps. She darted across the yard in the rain, slipped through the back gate, and disappeared into her own big back yard.

***

The house seemed usually quiet and lonely after her two exciting weeks in Atlantic City. Lucy ate a solitary supper of sandwiches and pineapple upside down cake as darkness fell with the rain. She wasn't really hungry. Her appetite had left her.

She cleared the table, washed the dishes, tidied the kitchen, and went into the bedroom to tackle the chore of unpacking.

The first thing she took out of her luggage was the treasured oyster shell music box Blackie had given her for her birthday. She placed the exquisite box on the night table beside her bed. Her fingers caressed the ivory porcelain gardenia on the lid before she slowly opened the music box.

The tiny, golden couple popped up and began spinning about on their mirrored dance floor as music began to play. Lucy looked at the golden couple and saw Blackie and herself whirling about on the parquet floor of the Atlantic Grand's Blue Room.

Lucy turned back to the open valise. She unwrapped her white tulle evening gown from its protective tissue paper, lifted the dress, and saw a few loose grains of sand against the white of the paper. She smiled and a sweet rush of warmth swept through her. For a moment Blackie was again kissing her in the moonlight on the beach.

The wave of warmth quickly passed and was replaced by a surge of intense loneliness. A loneliness far greater than any she'd ever known. She shivered and hugged herself. The poet had said 'Tis better to have loved and lost than never to have loved at all' but she wondered if that was actually true.

Before Blackie, she had been lonely at times, bored now and then, had daydreamed and longed for a kind of excitement she never expected to find. Nonetheless, for the most part she'd been comfortable and fairly satisfied with her well-ordered life.

Now she would never be content again. Before Blackie, she could only imagine what falling deeply in love would be like. Could only speculate and guess and wonder exactly what it was about love and intimacy that was powerful enough to make fools of wise men.

Now she knew.

She loved Blackie with all her heart and making love with him had been the most beautiful, pleasurable experience of her life. Nothing else could compare. A patient, caring lover, he had taught her the sweet mysteries of his body and her own. They had been as intimate as two people could be and it was far more wonderful than she had ever dreamed. Every look, every touch, every kiss would live on in her heart.

She had lived--really lived--and nobody could ever take that away from her.

Yes, she decided, the poet was right. It *was* better to have loved and lost than never to have loved at all.

Lucy finished with the unpacking. Everything was back in its place. Just as it should be. Including her.

The rain had finally stopped when Lucy got into bed that night. Tired though she was, she lay there wide awake in the quiet stillness of her house. Funny she'd never noticed before how deafening was the silence. And had the clock on the night table always ticked so loudly?

Lucy slowly turned onto her side and looked at the window beside her bed. The curtains were open, but the bedroom was dark. It was dark outside as well. The world was dark. Pitch black.

A new moon was just starting to rise. A puny sliver of a moon that would shed none of the silvery radiance that had spilled across the bed in Blackie's penthouse suite.

And bathed two naked, entwined lovers in its heavenly light.

"Blackie, Blackie," Lucy said aloud, "Not only did you take the sun with you, you took the moon as well."

CHAPTER THIRTY FOUR

The 7:10 from Rochester was right on time, and so was Post Office Champ.

The minute the heavy mail pouch was tossed from the moving freight train, Champ pounced on it. Snarling, he clamped the bag firmly in his teeth, yanked it up, and wheeled about. He leapt down off the platform, rounded the tiny depot, and raced away, heading directly for Colonias' white-fronted post office two blocks away.

Lucy had reached the post office at straight up seven. She immediately brought the folded American flag outside, unfurled it, clipped it to the grommets, and raised it up the steel flagpole.

When she finished, she didn't go back inside. She lifted the gold cased brooch/watch penned to her starched shirtwaist and looked at it. 7:04. She heard the blast of a whistle in the distance as the morning freight train roared nearer to the Colonias station. Only a few minutes now.

"Why, good morning, Miss Lucy!"

She looked up, smiled. "Good morning, Judge Fite."

A minute passed.

"Mornin', Miss Lucy," Matthew J. Henderson, president of the Colonias bank, tipped his hat. "You've been away a long time. Glad to have you home."

"Thank you, Mr. Henderson. It's good to be back."

A dozen gentlemen came up or went down the sidewalk outside the post office in the six minutes Lucy waited there. They were all cordial, friendly, happy to see her.

Every one of them addressed as 'Miss Lucy'.

Inwardly sighing, Lucy looked at her brooch/watch again, then expectantly up the street. Sure enough, Champ was sprinting toward her, his long, full tail curled up over his back, the mailbag clenched in his teeth. Lucy's face broke into a wide smile and went to meet him.

The huge, silver Siberian was so excited to see her, he dropped the mail while he was still several feet away and barked a loud greeting. Lucy went down on her heels on the sidewalk to affectionately pet him. Champ jumped up on her and licked her face before she could turn away.

But she laughed and hugged his big, warm body, saying, "I'm glad to see you too, Boy."

Champ barked wildly and wagged his tail.

Lucy gathered his great jaws in her hands, looked into the big eyes, which were startlingly blue in the intelligent silver face, and said, "Since it's a special occasion, I brought bacon for your breakfast."

As if he understood exactly what she said, the husky pulled anxiously away, spun out of her grasp, and made a beeline for the post office door. Amused, Lucy laughed, rose to her feet, and followed.

By ten minutes of eight the usual crowd was gathering in the small front lobby of the post office, visiting, chattering, hoping for a letter or postal card or the latest copy of the *Ladies Home Journal*. Several of the ladies who waited just beyond the closed caged window whispered about Lucy, as if because she couldn't see them, she couldn't hear them either.

"...and thought she might have gone to Saratoga but Leslie Bennett said that was out of the question. Ruthie Douglas figures she went down to Texas to her brother's," said Fredda Barnes.

"I imagine Ruthie's right." It was Myrtle Poyner. "Most likely they invited her to come so she could take care of their children while they went on vacation."

Lucy, standing behind the closed window unhurriedly turning the tiny rotors on the cancellation stamp, smiled to herself. They felt sorry for her, but they wasted their pity.

If you only knew, she thought with relish.

But they didn't. And they never would. It was her lovely secret and hers alone. Actually *she* felt sorry for *them*. None had ever met--much less been made love to--by a man half so exciting or handsome as Blackie LaDuke. Not the prettiest woman in town, or the richest. None had ever known a single hour of joy that could compare with the lovely two week interlude she, Miss Lucy Hart, old maid postmistress of Colonias for whom they felt sorry, had spent with the marvelous man of her dreams in the romantic City by the Sea.

Lucy drew a deep breath, glanced at the sleeping silver Siberian, smiled, turned back and raised the caged window.

It was after six p.m. when Lucy lowered the flag, folded and boxed it, closed the grilled window, locked up, and left. That night after supper, she walked the four blocks to the Harrisons for the weekly card game. The next day, the first of her handful of piano students came for her regular evening lesson. Sunday were church

273

services and afterward the usual chicken dinner at Bruce and Kitty Widner's.

Everything was the same. Yet nothing was the same.

And Lucy, knowing it was foolish, began looking anxiously forward to Champ's morning mail delivery. She'd been back home only ten days when a nice, long letter came from Lady Strange. A week later she heard from Colonel Mitchell; he sent her a postal card from London, England.

From Blackie she heard nothing at all.

***

Autumn came early to Colonias.

The muggy heat of summer gave way to a precious few cool, crisp days of extraordinary beauty. A bright sun shone down from a cloudless blue sky and the faintest hint of a chill made the clean air bracing, invigorating. The leaves were beginning to change to their vibrant autumn shades of red and rust and gold. Exhilarated citizens of Colonias went about their varied tasks with renewed vigor, remarking to one another as they did every season that upstate New York in the fall was surely the prettiest spot on God's own earth.

Lucy wholeheartedly agreed. Autumn in her hometown was beautiful every year. This year it was almost too beautiful, achingly beautiful to her. More than one cool, quiet evening she sat alone on the steps of her front porch, arms wrapped around her knees, watching the harvest moon rise over the peaceful town. And seeing Blackie's handsome face there instead of the man in the moon.

As the end of September approached, the sun was less in evidence. The cool, bracing air had changed to a biting chill that seeped right through light clothing. The trees' colorful leaves began to turn brown, curl up, and flutter listlessly to the dying grass below. The dwindling days of September saw the skies turn gray and cloudy.

Lucy was lonely. Painfully lonely. She missed Blackie so much it was like a physical suffering. She thought about him at least a thousand times a day, wondered where he was, and how he was, and if he ever thought about her.

But she didn't feel sorry for herself. Not in the least. The Colonel had been absolutely right about memories. She could remember no bad ones. Only the happy ones came back with vivid clarity.

Amazing. Truly amazing.

Routine had returned. Life had become a slow, uneventful, normal existence again and Lucy had smoothly adjusted, just as she had adjusted to every change that had ever occurred. She did so now with the customary ease and reminded herself to count her many blessings.

She had her position at the post office, the safe haven of her home, the respect of her friends and acquaintances.

She had no regrets. No complaints. No worries.

Or so she thought.

Until a cold, drizzling rain began late Sunday afternoon, the very last day of September. It continued throughout the night and into Monday morning. Lucy awoke to the rain peppering the window beside her bed. And to a dreadful, devastating feeling of nausea.

Like a bolt out of the blue, Lady's Strange's prophecy came back to her as if the royal reader of tealeaves was shouting in her ear, 'When you leave this place you will be very different. You will be a changed woman. When you have been back home for several weeks you will learn of yet another change that occurred while you were here. And this change will forever alter your life.'

Lucy trembled with fear and rising nausea.

She'd pushed the nagging uneasiness to the back of her mind each time it had surfaced, refusing even to consider such an improbable catastrophe. Now she could no longer fool herself. She'd had no monthly since the week before leaving for Atlantic City. Her cycle had always been as regular as clockwork.

The missed period, the awful nausea. It could only mean one thing.

Lucy was almost certain she was pregnant.

CHAPTER THIRTY FIVE

There were no secrets in Colonias, so Lucy didn't dare visit the trusted town physician who had tended her since birth. Not that dear old Doc Spencer would have revealed anything about one of his patients. But if a single woman who had neither a cold nor a fever visited the good doctor, people might wonder. Especially when the woman in question had been away on a two-week holiday.

Lucy made the necessary arrangements and at the end of the week took the train up to Rochester to see a doctor. After the mortifying physical examination finally ended, she quickly dressed and waited in his private corner office for the physician's verdict.

The white coated Doctor Abel Ferrer came in, smiled, circled his cluttered mahogany desk, and took a seat across from her. He leaned back in his swivel chair and began absently patting his breast pocket, searching for something.

Lucy inhaled with difficulty and squirmed in her own straight-backed chair.

"Ahhh," he said, spotting a pair of spectacles resting atop a stack of unfiled patient charts.

He picked up his glasses, unfolded them, raised them to his ruddy face, carefully fitted the wire earpieces over his ears and adjusted them on the bridge of his nose. Then he frowned. So did Lucy.

The doctor took off the glasses. He hunched up sideways onto his left hip and thigh, reached down into his right trouser pocket, drew out a clean white handkerchief, and carefully began wiping the spotted lens of his eyeglasses. First one. Then the other.

Hours, years, centuries passed as Lucy sat there waiting, so tense she wanted to scream, while the doctor calmly cleaned his spectacles.

Finally he put the glasses back on, looked over them at her, and said, "Well, congratulations, Mrs. Jones. You are going to have a baby." He smiled then as if he'd just given her great news and said, "You and the lucky Mr. Jones can expect your child around the first of June."

"That's...wonderful," Lucy heard herself say and the only thing that went through her mind was whether her weak legs would support her if she attempted to stand. "Wonderful."

Dr. Abel Ferrer told her what to expect at each stage of her pregnancy, giving advice on how she should take care of herself, and offering suggestions as to what she should and should not do in her delicate condition. Lucy paid no attention to his instructions. She didn't really hear him. She saw his mouth moving, but his words didn't penetrate the loud roaring in her ears.

All at once it was so stuffy in Dr. Ferrer's office Lucy could think of nothing but getting outside and taking long gulps of fresh air. She was dizzy, terribly dizzy. She felt as if she were going to be sick. A hand at her temple, Lucy rose unsteadily to her feet. The room around her swam out of focus and darkness closed in.

"Mrs. Jones, wake up, wake up." An unfamiliar voice pierced the fog. "Mrs. Jones, are you alright?"

Lucy's eyes opened on the ruddy face of Doctor Ferrer directly above her own. Full consciousness gradually returned. She realized she was lying on the floor and the doctor was leaning over her, his plump nurse standing behind him with the smelling salts.

Both were solicitous and caring. The thoughtful nurse asked if Lucy would like them to get in touch with her husband. Have him come down and pick her up.

Lucy anxiously sat up. "No. No, I'm fine. Really I am."

"Are you sure? How far away is it to your home, Mrs. Jones?" the worried physician inquired, helping her to her feet.

Lucy waved a dismissive hand and lied, "Not far. Thank you both, you've been most kind." She gave them a weak smile. "Please don't worry about me, I can manage."

Lucy did manage.

In one of those strange interludes of calm, which sometimes come in even the worst despair, she left the doctor's and serenely walked the six blocks to the depot.

The weather was sunny and warm, a perfect fall day, Lucy noted. Yet by the time she reached the train station, a forbidding coldness had penetrated her very bones. She had to keep her jaws tightly clenched so her teeth wouldn't chatter. Even then her chin quivered and Lucy knew it was from fear. Gripped by stark terror, she was at a complete loss. For the first time ever, she didn't know what to do.

Heartsick, Lucy had never felt so alone and afraid in her life. She had nowhere to turn. If she was to give birth to the baby, she would be an outcast, ostracized by everyone who knew her. Worse, by far, than her own shame would be that of the innocent child. Her baby would be labeled a bastard and carry the terrible stigma for life. If that was not enough she would lose her position at the post office and how could she possibly feed and clothe a child if she was unemployed?

These frightening thoughts tortured Lucy as the train carried her homeward, but as worried and miserable as she was, she didn't cry. Didn't shed a tear. She had far too much pride to allow the other passengers to see her weep. Weeping was to be done in private.

Worrying that night, walking the floor and wondering what was to become of her, Lucy did cry. She cried until her eyes were red and puffy, and her head ached violently. She sank to her knees on the parlor floor and sobbed uncontrollably. She fell over, put her head on her folded arms, and cried her heart out, her slender body jerking spasmodically. She cried so long and so hard she finally exhausted herself and cried no more.

But she never once considered trying to contact Blackie. The blame was not Blackie's, nor was the problem. Both were hers. It was she who must deal with the predicament, she who must pay the price.

She and no other.

***

Lucy kept her dilemma to herself. She told no one. Not even her good friend, Kitty Widner. Kitty and Annie were in and out of Lucy's house at least once a day, but Lucy never let on that anything was wrong. At least she hoped she revealed nothing.

The closest she came to giving anything away was one evening later that same week. The golden-curled Annie popped in unexpectedly. The little girl caught Lucy lying on her stomach before the fire, chin in her hands, a shimmer of tears blurring her vision.

The treasured oyster shell music box was on the floor in front of Lucy, the lid open, the music playing, the tiny, golden couple dancing on their miniature mirrored dance floor.

The four-year old Annie never noticed Lucy's tears. Her own wide blue eyes were riveted to the beautiful oyster shell box. "Pretty!" Annie said, pointing, and fell to her knees before the box as Lucy rose up to her own.

"Yes, isn't it?" said Lucy, anxiously blinking.

A small, short-fingered hand reaching out to touch the magical box, Annie asked, "Who gived it to you?"

Lucy swallowed hard. Her voice was soft but firm when she said, "Someone who means a great deal to me."

The little girl looked up, studied Lucy's face with the frank curiosity only allowed children, and in her innocence sensed what adults overlooked. Wordlessly, Annie rose to her feet, carefully circled the playing music box, threw her short arms around Lucy's neck, and squeezed with all her might. Lucy hugged Annie back while hot tears again stung her eyes and she fought to gain control of her emotions.

"Don't cry," Annie said, a small hand patting Lucy.

Lucy's eyes filled. Her throat aching, she couldn't answer. Could only nod and hug Annie tighter.

***

Lucy put up a good front for her friends and acquaintances. When she was outside her home, she was very careful to appear cheerful and at ease, to act as if nothing whatever was bothering her.

She continued to arrive, as she always had, at seven sharp each morning at the post office. And no one, save her sympathetic canine friend Post Office Champ, knew she suffered such terrible bouts of nausea that, at times, she barely made it to the small bathroom in back before retching.

Just as little Annie had seemed to know she was sad, Champ seemed to know she was sick. The big silver Siberian stopped falling asleep the minute he'd finished his treats. He never even stretched out and dozed; he stayed wide-awake and alert, his baleful blue eyes following her as she moved about the small office. It was as if, without being asked, he had taken on a new duty, watching after her through the worst parts of her day.

Lucy inwardly cringed when anyone pointed out that she was looking a little peaked of late. Was she alright? Wasn't she feeling well? Perfect, she quickly assured them, hoping they would hurry up and get out the post office door before she had to regurgitate again.

She would have to, she decided, keep up her regular activities as long as possible. She was determined to behave as if nothing was wrong. She would continue giving piano lessons to her pupils. And going to the weekly card game at the Harrisons. And she would never miss church or the big dinner at Kitty Widner's after the Sunday services.

***

Then came that sunny, Saturday morning in mid October.

A listless Lucy moved about her house, cleaning and dusting as if by rote. It had been little more than a week since she'd learned she was pregnant; it seemed like a year. A year of agony in which she could think of no suitable solution to her problem.

She could not stay in Colonias and give birth to this child. The shame would be too great to bear. Abruptly, Lucy smiled. She could see Blackie's flashing dark eyes, could hear him saying, as he had repeatedly in Atlantic City, 'Ah, come on, Lucy. Let the gossips sizzle in hell'.

That's what she would like to do. But she didn't have the courage. Nor the means. The only possible resolution to her problem was one she couldn't bear even to consider.

She'd heard the unkind stories whispered by the town's married gossips. She realized that throughout America there were other cases exactly like her own. Unfortunate, single women who became pregnant without hope of marrying the child's father. Those women were left with no choice but to give their babies up.

"No," Lucy murmured a tortured denial, a protective hand going to her flat stomach. "Dear God, no, I can't...I can't let..."

A loud knock caused Lucy to jump, startled. She was immediately puzzled. Who would be calling on a Saturday morning? Kitty and Annie never came to the front of the house. She had no piano lessons scheduled.

Lucy opened the door to see Bobby Flatt, the telegrapher's young son, standing on the porch, the collar of his colorful plaid jacket turned up around his ears.

"Why, Bobby," Lucy said, "Good morning to you. And you, too, Champ." Champ barked loudly, wagged his tail.

"Mornin', Miss Lucy," Bobby said, patting Champ's head to quiet him.

"Come in out of the cold. Both of you."

Boy and dog came into the spotless parlor. Lucy invited Bobby to take off his jacket and sit down but he shook his head.

He said excitedly, "Miss Lucy, I came to tell you there's a stranger up town asking about you."

"A stranger asking about me?"

Bobby nodded and Champ shook his great silver head. "Yes, ma'am. He's wanting to know where you live and..."

"The stranger is a gentleman?"

"Uh-huh and he wanted Papa to tell him where you live and all, but Papa said before he could be giving out any information like that he'd have to send me over here to find out if you wanted your whereabouts known. The gentleman said he understood and he'd be happy to wait. So me and Champ came straight on over here and..."

Lucy's heartbeat quickened. Anxiously she interrupted, "Bobby, describe the gentleman. What did he look like?"

"Oh, I don't know what he looked like. Just a man."

"Bobby, you do know. You saw him," Lucy said almost sharply. "Now you think real hard and describe him as best you can."

"Well..." the boy said, shrugging his narrow shoulders and screwing up his face, "he's...he's tall and slim and...and he's dressed real fancy for a Saturday morning." Bobby scratched his head. "Oh, yeah, he's got dark hair and his eyes are dark, too and he..."

"Go!" Lucy said and anxiously shoved him toward the front door. "Go straight back and tell the dark stranger exactly how to get to my house. Hurry!"

"Sure. Okay," Bobby said, as Lucy closed the door on him and the barking, jumping Champ.

Trembling with hope and excitement, Lucy rushed into her bedroom to get ready. She chose one of her prettiest dresses, a soft, merino wool the exact shade of her emerald green eyes. When she had the dress buttoned, she brushed her curly, chestnut hair down around her shoulders the way Blackie liked it best. She pulled one side back off her face and secured it with the hair clasp Lochlin MacDonald had given her. She pinched her pale, hollow cheeks, bit her lips, and dabbed some of her treasured *Bal Versailles* perfume behind her ears and inside her wrists.

Lucy flew about the spotless house, plumping up cushions on the sofa and straightening family photographs atop the square rosewood piano. She picked up the poker and stabbed at the logs smoldering in the fireplace. Flames burst from the glowing sparks and shot up the chimney.

Lucy replaced the poker and turned away from the fire. Her eyes made a quick, appraising sweep of the parlor. It was clean and cozy and cheerful.

The doorbell rang.

Lucy lost her breath. Her hand went to her fluttering heart. She hurried to the front door. Her green eyes aglow, a wide smile on her flushed face, Lucy, murmuring soundlessly, *'Blackie, Blackie'* yanked the door open, and saw a stranger standing on the porch before her.

The smile left her face. She shook her head as if to clear it and said, "Yes?"

The tall, spare man said, "Lucy? Lucy Hart?"

Speechless, she nodded.

He smiled shyly. "Lucy, I'm Theodore Mooney from Cooperstown. May I come in?"

CHAPTER THIRTY SIX

"Theodore Mooney?" Lucy managed weakly, staring open-mouthed at the tall, slender man. Her disappointment was so acute she was sure it showed on her face. She had forgotten there was such a person as Theodore Mooney. "Yes, yes, of course," she said finally, her innate good manners slowly emerging, "please do come in."

"Thank you," Theodore Mooney said with relief, stepped inside, and timidly thrust out to Lucy a white box tied with pink ribbon.

She automatically took the gift, and then gesturing with it, directed him into the parlor. "If you'd like to sit down, Mr. Mooney, I'll fix some hot tea."

"That would be nice," said Theodore, his pale face turning beet red, his nervousness apparent in his every awkward movement. Lucy laid the box on the low table before the sofa. She left him and, shaking her head in mild annoyance at the intrusion, went into the kitchen to put on the kettle. Theodore J. Mooney was the last person she had expected or wanted to see. She couldn't imagine why he'd come to Colonias. Furthermore, she didn't care; her only thought to get rid of him as quickly as possible.

Theodore rose to his feet when Lucy returned with the hot tea and shortbread cookies. She placed the tray on the low table and motioned for him to sit back down. He took the cup of tea she poured for him, and Lucy noticed that his hand shook slightly. She poured a cup for herself and started to sit down in an armchair near the couch.

"No, please, Lucy," Theodore entreated, sounding anxious, yet determined. "Won't you come sit here by me? I've traveled all this way just for the opportunity to speak with you in person."

Lucy sighed and took a seat on the sofa, leaving plenty of space between them. "Mr. Mooney, I don't mean to sound impolite, but I..."

"Theodore," he gently corrected, tugging nervously at his too tight, white shirt collar. "Don't you remember? You were to call me Theodore and I was to call you Lucy." He attempted a disarming smile, managed only to look incredibly uncomfortable.

"Yes, well, that was before...before..." She shrugged slender shoulders. "I'm sorry, but I really can't see that we have anything to talk about."

"Please, don't say that," Theodore Mooney pleaded, his voice, so soft and strained, conveyed a deep timidity. "Surely after all our letters and...and..." He swallowed convulsively, "I was hoping you might be able to forgive me, Lucy. I realize I spoiled your holiday, but mine was spoiled as well. You shall never know how badly I hated having to cancel our plans, and I can well understand your disappointment. But I can't understand your lingering anger." He drew a labored breath as if he had been rehearsing just such a speech for a long time.

Truthfully Lucy said, "Mr. Mooney, I'm not angry with you. Believe me I'm not."

"Then you'll give me another chance? You'll listen to what I have come here to say?" His soft brown eyes held such a hopeful expression Lucy's heart went out to him.

"I'll listen," she said, her tone more kindly. "You've come all this way. Let's talk. Get acquainted." She finally smiled at him.

Theodore Mooney blushed and stammered that he would like nothing better; that he had come to Colonias solely for that purpose. Then he grinned like a bashful boy and looked down at his carefully buffed brown shoes.

Lucy was immediately afraid she had offered him false encouragement. So she quickly spoke up, "I'll listen to what you came to say, but I'm afraid you'll have to be brief. I have an engagement within the hour." She hoped the implication was there that she was expecting a gentleman caller.

Theodore's disappointment was immediate and evident. But he nodded and said, "I shan't detain you, I promise."

He sat there at a proper distance from her, mild and gentle, and clearing his throat nervously, he began to talk. To clear up the mystery of why he hadn't met her in Atlantic City.

Over hot tea and shortbread cookies in Lucy's cozy parlor, the quiet bachelor postmaster from Cooperstown lost some of his reticence in an eagerness to make amends. Listening courteously, Lucy was genuinely surprised to learn of the telegram he had sent. A telegram she never received.

He was so sober, so serious, she believed him when he said he had sent the telegram the moment he knew he couldn't meet her in Atlantic City. He swore on all that was sacred that the wire explaining how his sister had suddenly fallen ill should have arrived in Colonias that Saturday morning in August well before her departure time.

Lucy studied his face as he spoke. He was not a handsome man, but he was nice looking in a staid, rather stuffy way. He dark hair, which was deep, deep brown as opposed to black, was parted down the middle and neatly clipped and combed. His brown eyes were honest and kind. His nose was straight, but a trifle to thin and too long. His complexion was pale, but clear and his hands with their clean, square cut nails were nice hands, gentle looking hands.

His mouth was by far his best feature. It so was full and pleasingly wide; it appeared out of place in his long, thin face. His lips looked as if they'd be very smooth and warm.

Lucy wondered idly what might have happened if his sister hadn't fallen ill. If he had arrived in Atlantic City right on schedule and the two of them--she carrying her ivory gardenia and he wearing a matching one in his lapel--had met at nine that Sunday evening in the lobby of the Atlantic Grand.

Just as planned.

Had that happened, she would never have met Blackie LaDuke. And if she had never met Blackie--if she had no idea that such an unforgettable man existed-- she might have been content with Theodore J. Mooney.

When finally Theodore concluded with his soft-spoken explanations and heartfelt apologies, Lucy set her teacup on the low table beside the pink ribboned, unopened box.

"As I said, I never received the telegram, Theodore. And that's too bad really. Things might have been very different if...if..." Her words trailed away. She paused a moment, then told him, "I'm afraid it's too late now."

"Lucy, don't say that," Theodore, looking stricken, gently pleaded. "It isn't too late at all. You see, I've come here to make it up to you and..."

"You don't understand," Lucy interrupted. "You don't really know me, Theodore. There are..."

"Yes, I do," he broke in, desperate to press his case, "we've corresponded for three years; we know each other well from..."

"I'm not the same Lucy who wrote to you," Lucy frankly admitted. "I can't explain, but things are very different now. *I'm* very different now. I'm...I'm not even someone you'd like to know better."

"But you are," he said, unconvinced. "Listen to me, Lucy, your letters revealed a great deal about you. I feel as if we've known one another for years. Whatever it is that is different, whatever may have happened...whatever way you may have changed, it doesn't matter. Not to me. I don't care. You're the woman whose letters have made my life worth living."

"Oh, Theodore." She felt terrible. "You simply don't understand."

"Then tell me so I *will* understand. You can tell me anything and it will change nothing. I'll feel the same way about you. Or, if you don't wish to tell me, that's fine too. I'll never ask you, never pry. Never. Won't you at least extend the same opportunity you offered when we were to meet in Atlantic City? That's all I'm asking you for, Lucy. Just for the two weeks I missed. We missed."

Before she could reply, he told her clumsily, yet sincerely that he still had his two weeks vacation time coming and he wanted to spend it in Colonias. With her. He would check into the hotel and come to call on her as often as she would allow. They could make it their long planned holiday together right here in Colonias.

"Won't you say yes, Lucy," he concluded, so nervous he was perspiring; tiny beads of moisture dotted his hairline. "Won't you give me that one chance?"

For a long minute, Lucy didn't reply. Touched by the speech she knew had been so hard for him to make, Lucy's soft heart again went out to him.

"You're free to stay in Colonias, if you choose, Theodore. I can't promise I'll spend much time with you," she said, but her words lacked a ring of conviction.

She felt herself engulfed in a wave of pity for this lonely, sensitive man who had come all the way from Cooperstown to see her. There was a time, not so long ago, when she would have been flattered by Theodore J. Mooney's attention. Now she felt that he was pathetic. She almost wanted to weep for him. Or was it for herself? Or maybe for them both.

Lucy suddenly realized that Theodore had risen to his feet. She stood up to face him as he said, "My hour is up so I'll be going now."

"Your hour?" she gave him a puzzled look as they crossed the parlor.

"Your prior engagement," he reminded her. "When I first got here you said you had an engagement within the hour."

"I've decided to cancel it," Lucy said, surprising herself almost as much as Theodore. They had reached the front door. She smiled up at him. "Why don't you come back around noon. I'll fix us some lunch."

Theodore Mooney lit up like a Christmas tree. "I'll be here."

"So will I."

Lucy closed the door behind him, sighed, and returned to the parlor to clear away the tea service. Her eyes fell on the box Theodore had brought. She picked it up. She slipped the small card from underneath the pink ribbon and read it.

I attempted to find the real thing and failed.

This is supposed to carry the exact same scent.

Theodore

Lucy frowned, puzzled, and laid the card on the table. She untied the pink ribbon, took the lid from the box, and pushed aside the pink tissue paper. Packed neatly in a row were three bars of fancily carved bath soap. Lucy lifted the box and inhaled. The faint scent of gardenias made her suddenly sad. Tears welled up in her eyes and dropped to the starched shirtwaist of her dress.

***

Theodore J. Mooney checked into the Colonias Hotel for a two-week stay. He was back at Lucy's front door at straight up twelve noon. He returned again that evening to take her out for a fine dinner at the hotel dining room. And he came back again Sunday morning to escort her to church services.

Theodore was clearly intent on wooing her, and by the time the weekend was over, Lucy didn't like herself for what she was beginning to consider as a way out of her terrible trouble. Theodore Mooney, while not handsome and charming like Blackie, was a kind, soft-spoken, respectable man.

Lucy had learned a great deal about being a woman from Blackie. If she set her mind to it, she might be able to persuade Theodore to marry her. If she hurried, if she managed to make him fall in love during the two weeks he was in Colonias, neither he nor the world need ever know that she was pregnant with another man's child.

***

Despising herself for her intended duplicity, Lucy spent every free hour with the bashful, pleased Theodore. It was she who took the initiative, she who speeded things along when the backward bachelor seemed perfectly content with nothing more passionate than hand holding and an occasional embrace.

Fighting her irritation that she practically had to draw him a map of where her mouth was, Lucy managed, one Wednesday evening as they sat together on her sofa, to turn her head just at the right moment so that their lips collided.

The kiss lasted only a few seconds.

Theodore immediately fell to apologizing. "Lucy, forgive me. I never meant to be so...so forward and loose with you. If I've offended you, I'm dreadfully sorry."

"You haven't offended me, Theodore." Lucy raised a hand to his face, touched his jaw with her fingertips. "I wanted you to kiss me."

"You did?" His brown eyes widened and his Adams apple moved up and down.

She nodded, smiled. "Mmmm. And you know what else?"

"What?"

"I want you to kiss me again." Her lashes fluttered and lowered as her gaze dropped to his mouth.

"Oh, my dear," he said excitedly, his hands trembling as he reached out and clasped her shoulders.

Theodore drew her to him and kissed her. And Lucy wanted to weep. His lips--although they were the wrong lips--were well shaped, full and smooth and warm. His appealing male mouth was almost as sensual looking as Blackie's.

But there all similarity ended. Her heart didn't pound from Theodore's kiss. Her toes didn't curl. Her bones didn't melt.

It made no difference, Lucy firmly told herself. You don't judge a man by his kiss.

Or you shouldn't.

"Lucy, Lucy," Theodore whispered, so shaken he was obviously far more affected by the caress than she was. His trembling arms went around her and he drew her closer. His smooth cheek pressed to hers, he buried his face in her fragrant, chestnut hair and asked, his voice rough with emotion, "May I...kiss you...again?"

CHAPTER THIRTY SEVEN

If Lucy's beloved Blackie LaDuke was everything Theodore J. Mooney was not, the same could be said of Theodore. He was everything Blackie wasn't.

The charming Blackie was a self-proclaimed ne'er-do-well, who had--and always would--lived his life recklessly, with a shameful disregard for security or honor. Theodore, on the other hand, was a dependable, hard-working man who had--all his life--unfailingly adhered to the dictates of decency and decorum.

To Blackie everything was a nonsensical joke, something to poke fun at and laugh about. He looked at life with an amused indifference; a mischievous twinkle in his beautiful, black eyes and a charming smile, which showed his white teeth in the almost Latin darkness of his handsome olive face.

Theodore had a woefully underdeveloped sense of humor; he never saw the ridiculous in anything; never teased anyone and couldn't abide being teased himself. He was a serious minded man who had spent his youth, as well as his adult years, accepting responsibility, behaving modestly, offending no one. He was a bit of a stuffy purist, but underneath his prudishness lay a character nice enough and strong.

Blackie was the embodiment of an exciting, romantic figure who could sweep a woman off her feet. And had. Theodore was the epitome of the timid, cautious suitor who could never make a woman lose her head.

Blackie was the reckless rogue who made a good lover.

Theodore was the thoughtful gentleman who would make a good husband.

Lucy had had the thrilling, irresponsible lover.

She needed a stalwart, trustworthy husband.

While loving him was out of the question, Lucy did admire and respect Theodore Mooney. In her growing guilt, she promised herself she would be a good wife to him, would spend the rest of her days making up for her unforgivable deception.

***

The budding romance between the bashful bachelor from Cooperstown and their own spinster postmistress was the talk of Colonias. Lucy introduced her quiet companion to the curious townsfolk and the gentry was quick to accept the mannerly, soft spoken Theodore Mooney.

Over back fences and across dinner tables, their liaison was discussed and those who knew Miss Lucy best thought her Mr. Mooney a perfect match for her. Kitty Widner let no moss grow under her feet. She gave a get-acquainted party for the welcome out-of-town visitor, and invitations to the gathering were coveted and R.S.V.P'd immediately.

Theodore Mooney was unquestionably beguiled and didn't care who knew it. He spent every moment with Lucy that she would allow, even whiling away the cool, autumn afternoons with her at the post office. If he'd had his way, he would have been there all morning as well, but Lucy forbade it.

She pointed out that--as he well knew--mornings at a post office were so busy and hectic she'd have no time to visit with him. Longing to be near her, he reminded her that he was, after all, a postmaster. He could sort the mail and put it up. Lucy stubbornly declined his offer of help and Theodore reluctantly bowed to her wishes.

The real reason Lucy kept him away was that she still suffered from bouts of morning sickness.

Mornings were the only part of the day that the two were not together. They were seen out in the evenings, dining in Colonias' only fine restaurant and strolling down Main Street holding hands. They would wind up at Lucy's white frame house and it was there, in Lucy's warm, cozy parlor that the timid Theodore was most content.

While darkness deepened outside and the temperature dropped rapidly, they read poetry together by firelight and discussed the works of their favorite authors and artists. Lucy would play the square cherry wood piano in the corner for the appreciative Theodore.

Literature and music were passions they shared and Lucy quickly learned that when she played Chopin or a bit of Beethoven or some hauntingly beautiful piece, it stirred something in Theodore's gentle heart. Touched some inner emotion, leaving him vulnerable and more receptive to her feminine charms.

He would sit on the sofa and watch her with dreamy, brown eyes as if the sight of her seated there and the sweet sounds she coaxed from the aging piano were a soothing balm which relaxed him totally, yet at same time filled him with an inexplicable yearning.

And it was then, when he was in a warm, pliant state of mind, that Lucy would stop playing and come to him. Shocking him, pleasing him, she would sit down on his lap, put her arms around his neck, and lower her lips to his.

Theodore's less-than-heartstopping kisses began to improve after a few such nights on the sofa with Lucy. Recalling with vivid clarity Blackie's dazzling, breath-snatching kisses, she tried to kiss Theodore the way Blackie had kissed her.

Her hands in his dark brown hair, she provocatively brushed her mouth back and forth over his, tempting him, toying with him until she drew the proper response.

Quickly warming to the titillating exercise, instinctively protesting the lovely torture of her mouth as it refused to linger on his, Theodore's lips began to heat and cling, forcing hers to stay where they belonged-- pressed squarely against his own. His hand curled around the back of her neck, he exerted a gentle pressure, drawing her face down to his, even as his lifted to meet hers.

And Lucy experienced a surge of triumph.

She put out the tip of her tongue and ran it slowly along the seam in his lips. Theodore shuddered against her and his lips parted. Lucy's tongue didn't penetrate. Not yet. First she scattered little plucking kisses along his top lip and to the corners of his mouth. With sharp, white teeth she nipped harmlessly, playfully at his full bottom lip. She drove him half crazy before she finally put her tongue into his mouth. He groaned with building pleasure. Lucy continued to kiss him and stroke his hair and press her breasts against his chest. To sensually torment him until his pale face was flushed and his heart was pounding and he was eagerly, anxiously--if inexpertly--kissing her.

As Theodore's two-week visit moved rapidly toward its final days, the same scene was played out nightly on Lucy's sofa until the smitten Theodore did what Lucy wanted him to do.

He proposed.

Tie askew, hair ruffled, brown eyes glazed with passion, the enchanted Theodore slid dazedly off the sofa onto his knees, took her hand in both of his, and said anxiously, "Lucy, I know it's much too soon for me to be asking you this, but...would you consider...marrying me?"

"I would," she said without hesitation. "I will."

***

He could learn, Lucy told herself, be taught how to make love, just as she had been taught. Everything else about Theodore was fine, good. He would be an excellent husband. And father. He was kind, patient, dependable, and trustworthy.

And she couldn't do such a despicable thing to such a good man.

She had to tell him the truth.

The next evening they went straight to Lucy's house after an early dinner at the hotel. No sooner were they off with their coats then Theodore was anxiously urging Lucy into the parlor. He dropped down onto the sofa and patted his knee, ready to start the kissing.

He looked so happy, so delighted and eager, that Lucy was overcome with a deep, kindly pity for him that was akin to love. Suddenly she hated Blackie for giving her a glimpse into another world, a world so exciting and far removed from the one in which she and Theodore Mooney belonged.

Filled with self-loathing, she sat down beside Theodore. He immediately turned and reached for her, but she stopped him, throwing up her hands, and saying, "No, Theodore. Please don't."

His brown eyes clouded quickly and he frowned. "My dear, have I done something wrong?"

She smiled sickly. "No, I have."

She took his hand in hers, looked directly into his questioning eyes, and said, "I'm not the kind of woman you think I am."

He squeezed her hand reassuringly and said, "Lucy, if you're worried that our lovemaking has given me the wrong impression, let me put your mind at ease. I don't think any less of..."

"Dear, dear Theodore," Lucy sadly interrupted, "that isn't it at all."

"Then what is it? Tell me, dearest, please. Don't you remember what I told you the first day I came here? You can tell me anything and it won't change the way I feel about you."

"If only that were true," she said, half hoping that it was, yet knowing better.

"It is, Lucy. Now tell me what's bothering you, let's talk it out and put it behind us."

Lucy nodded, drew a deep breath. "It all started with a misunderstanding. As you recall I was supposed to meet you in the lobby of the Atlantic Grand on the Sunday night we arrived at the resort."

"Yes." Theodore shook his head. "Yes, I remember."

"Well, I...I didn't know about the telegram, didn't know you weren't coming. So I waited in the lobby looking for a tall, dark-haired, dark-eyed man with a gardenia in his lapel. Finally I saw one and naturally I thought he was you."

"Naturally," he echoed her.

She paused, rubbed her hand over her eyes, and sighed. "The gentleman in question had been drinking, so when I called him by your name, he didn't bother correcting me."

"Good Heavens! When did you learn of your error?" Theodore was beginning to scowl.

"Oh, after only a few minutes. I realized that..."

"So that was the end of it? You excused yourself and..."

"It wasn't the end. It was only the beginning."

Lucy swore she had gotten away from the impertinent imposter as quickly as possible. And she would have come straight home, but for the next three days she kept expecting Theodore to show up. He never did and she had no idea why. She was hurt and disappointed and the man she'd mistaken him for wouldn't leave her alone.

Lucy talked and talked, telling a stunned, disbelieving Theodore the whole story of how she had foolishly fallen for the other man and had given herself to him.

"Theodore, I'm going to have his child," she said flatly. "I am pregnant."

The straight-laced bachelor was horrified. Theodore jerked his hand free of Lucy's as if it was dirty.

Censure and disgust in both his voice and his eyes, he said indignantly, "My sister warned me about you, but I wouldn't listen. She said that only a loose woman would agree to meet a stranger of the opposite sex at a fancy Atlantic City resort."

His face scarlet, he leapt to his feet.

Lucy rose to face him.

"Your sister was probably right," she said in a low, level voice. "Lord knows I did behave wantonly with a stranger of the opposite sex at a fancy Atlantic City resort or I wouldn't be in the fix I'm in." She managed to smile then and said, "But you tell your sister for me that if I had it to do over again, I'd do the very same thing."

Lucy calmly ushered him to the front door.

They stood there in silence for a time, Theodore looking at her, hurt and crestfallen, attempting to comprehend and digest all she had revealed.

Then softening--for he was a decent man--he finally asked, "What...what are you going to do?"

"I honestly don't know," she admitted.

He sighed heavily and said, "I'm sorry I sounded so judgmental and unforgiving. I don't care what my sister thinks." He swallowed hard, lifted a hand and touched Lucy's cheek. "We could...I could still marry you, Lucy. Give your child a name."

Lucy smiled and patted his chest. "You're a good man, Theodore Mooney. Too good to marry a woman like me."

CHAPTER THIRTY EIGHT

Dead leaves covered the winter-brown lawn as October waned away. The trees stood black and naked in the cold wind, their stark branches rising to meet gray-laden skies. The days were chilly. The nights freezing cold.

The golden warmth of summer was totally gone from the land and from Lucy.

Alone again, she bundled up one evening to sit on the front porch steps as the scarlet-streaked, winter dusk descended. The street was quiet at that time of day, the silence broken only by the distant shouts of children playing in someone's back yard.

But the stillness brought no peace to Lucy.

A suffocating dread never left her, a paralyzing fear unlike anything she'd ever experienced was always there. Her tortured thoughts went in a continuous circle, always coming back to the same, miserable starting point. The same unanswerable question.

What was she going to do?

For weeks she had debated whether or not to call on one of her brothers for help. She'd written at least a dozen letters to both of them, but had never mailed a one. She couldn't bear the thought of either knowing that their old maid sister had brought shame on the proud Hart name.

Her tarnished reputation, her unspeakable disgrace, would surely reflect on them and on their families.

Would they ever be able to forgive her for ruining their lives?

Lucy swallowed, tasting the familiar acid in the back of her throat. Her eyes filled. She blinked away the unwelcome tears. More came. Too many to blink away. The hot tears poured down her chilled cheeks. Lucy sighed wearily, leaned over, put her forehead on her knees, and cried.

After a few moments she became aware that her own choked sobs were not the only ones she heard. Someone else was weeping. Whimpering faintly.

Lucy's head shot up. She blinked rapidly to clear her blurred vision and then squinted, peering into the thickening twilight. Then she sighed with genuine relief.

Post Office Champ, the silver Siberian, stood there on the front walk a few feet from her, wailing sorrowfully. In a flash he was right there, beside her, pressing his big, warm body as close to hers as possible and moaning plaintively.

"Oh...Ch...Champ," Lucy hiccoughed, wiping her eyes on the back of her hand and coughing, "what am I going to do?"

The Siberian bayed softly and licked her tear-wet cheek. Then he looked at her with those big, baleful blue eyes, tilting his great head to one side, his ears standing up in a questioning attitude, as though asking if there was anything he could do for her. The canine's kindness brought on a fresh flood of tears and Lucy threw her arms around Champ's powerful body, sagged against him, and wept once more.

Champ stood very still and whimpered plaintively while she cried.

***

Thanksgiving was gray and gloomy.

It was a raw, bitter cold day. The wind howled wildly, moaning around the eves of the house and banging the screen door. Bare tree limbs scratched at the roof and by late afternoon sleet tapped at the frozen windowpanes.

Inside Lucy sat cross-legged on the floor directly in front of the fireplace. She stared fixedly into the dancing flames. A shawl pulled tight around her slender shoulders, her green eyes glazed in thought, she deliberated on paying a visit to the Colonias State Bank come Monday to see about a loan. If she put her home up as collateral, the bank president, Matthew Henderson, would surely allow her to borrow a substantial sum of money. With the loan and the small savings she had managed to put away since her mother's death, she could go away.

Far away.

December, that cruelest month, was ushered in with a bone-chilling winter snowstorm.

And the disappointing news that Lucy would not be allowed to borrow on her house. Not without the consent and co-signatures of both her brothers.

"You see, Miss Lucy," Matthew Henderson patiently explained, "the Hart house is owned equally by the three of you."

"It's my home, Mr. Henderson. My brothers wouldn't care if I took out a loan."

He smiled indulgently and laced his chunky fingers together atop his desk. "I'm sure they wouldn't. But they'll have to sign the note. Banking regulations. You understand."

"Yes, I understand," Lucy said and rose.

Matthew Henderson came to his feet. "What you needin' such a large sum for anyhow, Miss Lucy?"

"Good day, Mr. Henderson."

***

The last Christmas season of the century came to Colonias.

The time for Peace on Earth, good will toward men found Lucy Hart still desperate and alone. She continued to keep her own counsel and the face she showed the world betrayed none of the hopelessness she felt. But then that was nothing new for Lucy. For the past decade she'd had plenty of practice at hiding her feelings and frustrations.

The weather was uncharitable. One blizzard after another roared across the Genesee Valley that cold December, blanketing the rich farmlands and wide meadows with deep swirling snow. There *was* one advantage to the cold weather; it required the wearing of warm, bulky clothing. Lucy's heavy, winter clothes concealed a waist that was rapidly thickening.

Soon she would no longer be able to keep her condition a secret. Then what would she do?

On a frigid, snowy Sunday afternoon a few days before Christmas, the doorbell rang at Lucy's white frame house.

Lucy made a face. Already it was starting. From now until after New Years she'd be forced to endure a steady stream of holiday callers stopping by with cookies and fruit and good tidings.

Sighing, Lucy smoothed her chestnut hair, touched the knot at the back of her head, and looked worriedly at her stomach. She hastily rearranged the gathers of her full-skirted woolen dress and drew in her breath.

Lucy put a placid smile on her face and opened the door. Her smile froze in place and she winced audibly, her green eyes widening in disbelief.

Blackie LaDuke stood there on her frozen front porch, his arms loaded with brightly wrapped gifts. Snowflakes sprinkling his dark head, clinging to his long, sooty eyelashes, and dusting the shoulders of his black cashmere jacket, he was grinning like a kindly imp out of hell.

Lucy's eyes met his and there was a long pause that stretched between them. A silence that spoke volumes.

"Does Lucy Hart live here?" Blackie asked at last.

"No," Lucy calmly replied.

"No?" His impish smile fled and his black eyes clouded.

"No," Lucy shook her head. "Lucy Hart went to Atlantic City last summer and never came back."

"Then I've traveled a great distance for nothing," he said, smiling again. "All the way from London, England."

Blackie swept into the house on whoosh of cold air, dropped the wrapped packages to the floor, reached out, and took the startled Lucy in his arms.

"I tried," he said, his chilled lips brushing her hot cheek, "but I can't get you out of my mind. Kiss me, Lucy."

"No, please, I..."

"I've come for you, darlin'. Now kiss me."

Blackie's lips silenced any further half-hearted protests. He kissed Lucy with all the power and passion she remembered so well and she felt her knees buckle beneath her. But it didn't matter. She felt the strength of Blackie's arms around her and knew he wouldn't let her fall. Her hands glided over the snow-dampened cashmere of his black overcoat and slid around his neck.

Lucy held nothing back. Logical thought took wing as she sucked at Blackie's lips in a wet, urgent kiss and eagerly touched her tongue to his. Melting against him, she felt his hands slip from her waist, move down over her hips. She moaned softly when his tanned fingers spread and filled themselves with the twin cheeks of her buttocks.

The door was still wide open as the pair stood there eagerly embracing in Lucy's chilled parlor. The cold, howling winds blew in swirling snow and frigid air, but neither noticed. Kissing greedily, anxiously, they were warm. Plenty warm.

They kissed and kept on kissing, over and over again, their lips separating only long enough to gasp for air and murmur endearments. They kissed until Blackie's long legs grew almost as weak Lucy's.

Together they sagged to their knees and continued to kiss. It was Lucy who finally tore her burning lips from Blackie's, leaned her forehead on his firm chin, and panting breathlessly, murmured, "You've come for me, Blackie? What are you going to do with me?" She raised her head, looked into his obsidian eyes.

"Do with you?" Blackie paused one beat. "Why marry you, of course. Say you'll marry me, Lucy Hart."

"I'll marry you, Blackie LaDuke."

"Well, not so fast," he teased, grinning again, "I'm supposed to spend a lot of time persuading you to go through life with the likes of me."

Lucy laughed, squeezed him, and said, "That would be nice, but I don't have the time." She pulled back, cupped his handsome face in both her hands, and said, "Blackie, there is something you must know. I am pregnant. I'm going to have your--our baby in June." Lucy stopped speaking, held her breath.

The wide smile left Blackie's face and Lucy's expanding belly did a nervous flip-flop.

"And you weren't going to tell me?" Blackie was incensed.

Lucy shook her head. "No. I didn't want you to feel obligated and I..."

"God, Lucy girl, you are incredible," he was smiling again. "How did I ever get lucky enough to find you?"

"Then you're not unhappy about the baby?"

"I'm delighted about the baby, sweetheart," he said, his eyes twinkling merrily. "And you can believe it or not, I'll be a good father."

"I believe it," she said as he placed gentle hands on her slightly rounded stomach. "Blackie, you're not just being noble are you? You do love me, don't' you?"

His hands lifted; he clasped her upper arms. He said in a low caressive voice, "I love you, Lucy, with all my heart. Do you love me?"

"Oh, yes, darling," she whispered, her hands clutching the collars of his cashmere coat, "I've always loved you. I mean, I've never loved anyone but you."

"I know that," he said with a touch of his old arrogance. But he immediately made amends by saying, "It's the same with me, Lucy. I never loved anyone else and you won't be sorry you married me."

"I know that," she said, smiling happily.

"There is something you *don't* know," he told her proudly.

"There is?"

He looked smug. "I now have gainful employment."

"You're teasing me."

"I'm not. Colonel Mitchell hired me the week I left Atlantic City. I've been in England ever since. Sweetheart, I'm the sole London agent for the Colonel's

309

prosperous cotton brokering firm. I've worked really hard and I'll keep on working hard. I swear I will. I've come to take you back with me. If you'll go."

"I'll go," she said, deliriously happy.

"We'll get married in New York and sail to England on our honeymoon. We'll buy a small London townhouse with a nursery and...and...Lucy, sweet Lucy, I do love you...*so* much."

"You love me now, but for how long?" Lucy asked, her tone serious. "How long will you love me?"

Blackie kissed her temple and said with solemn sincerity, "Until the last day God has for me."